The Boy Who Loved Death

and other stories

Hal Duncan

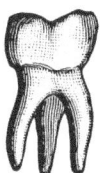

Bizarro Pulp Press
an imprint of JournalStone Publishing

Bizarro Pulp Press books may be ordered through booksellers or by contacting:

Bizarro Pulp Press, a JournalStone imprint
  www.BizarroPulpPress.com

  ISBN: 978-1-942712-61-9

Printed in the United States of America
JournalStone rev. date: October 21, 2015

  Cover Art: Matthew Revert
    www.matthewrevert.com
  Interior Formatting: Lori Michelle
    www.theauthorsalley.com

The Chiaroscurist

The First Day of Creation

In the nook of the tavern, the old man's face—or part of it—catches the fireglow slanting through the frame of oak door left ajar as he leans forward across the table, elbows on the wood, a glinting silver mechanism in one hand going *clunk, chik* with the flicking of a thumb, while, with his other hand, he holds a cigarette up to his mouth to draw a breath in—*foosh*. He holds it for a perfect moment of satiation, head raised now so that his bliss-closed eyes come out from under the shadow of his hat's wide brim, as if basking in the warmth of sunlight blood-red through their lids; and even beneath the bush of drooping grey moustache that his fingers seem half-buried in, there is a hint of smile on the lips pursed round the roll-up. *Let there be light*, I think, and then he leans back, disappearing into the leather shadow of the nook to blow out billows of blue-grey that curl and unfurl in the air like offerings of incense rising. An invocation in volutions, the breath of smoke immediately conjures up, in my mind's eye, an image that I seize—that old man's face half-lit as now in sharp chiaroscuro, shrouded in the swirling nebulae of chaos, of the first day of creation.

I must have him for my God.

—Maester, your stout.

The barkeep blocks my vision for a second as he lays the tumbler of black liquid on the table, and it brings me sharp out of the reverie.

—Grazzis, I say out of habit. Thank you. How much?

He waves a hand as I reach into my longcoat's inner pocket.

—Full board and beer, he says. It's all on the Monadery . . . Fader

Pitro's orders. He hopes—*we* hope—to make your stay here as pleasant as possible.

With a tilt of my glass to him I take a sip and smile at the busy tavern of sandminers and craftsmen, quarriers and traders, farmers in for a few quick jars before Evenfall; it's not the sort of place you'd find in the Merchant Quarters of Vrienze or Nephale where I so often have to smooth my way from one commission to the next with smiles as painted as the courtesans . . . but it's not so different from the harbour inns or carter's lodges that I spent much of my apprenticeship in with my own Maester. Less knife-fights, I suspect, though.

—I'm sorry that we didn't have your room ready, he says.

—No problem, I say. A well-poured stout is all it takes to keep me happy.

—I've sent word to the Monadery that you've arrived.

—Maya grazzis. Thank you. Thank you.

The bells of the Monadery di Sanze Manitae toll Evenfall, audible even over the tavern din of lewd jokes and earnest discussions, which changes tone in response to the knell as arguments find quick, laughing resolutions; chairs scrape back; friends say goodbyes, off home down the cobble-street slopes before darkness descends. The door opens and closes, opens and closes, until there are only a dozen or so customers left, drinkers more devoted or, perhaps, who live in the safety of the lamplit squares and strazzas of the market area, close enough to scorn superstition for the short walk home. The atmosphere becomes more homely with just these groups of three or four here and there, without the escalating racket of voices raised over voices raised.

Relaxing with a second pint, I watch the swirling settle of foamy stout, the silken eddies of shades of brown separating gradually into tar-black body and a white head thick enough to sculpt; and my mind drifts back to my commission, the vague images and ideas for it that rise into momentary resolution only to sink back into the darkness. There are only so many scenes to choose from, of course, the conventional tableaux of Invocations and Pronunciations, the Exile From the Garden, Orphean's Journey, and so on—and I have hardly even discussed with my patrons the layout of the antesanctum to be painted, let alone laid eyes on it—but if I have one fault it is my enthusiasm over grand schemes. This will be my first work on such a scale—not just one little frescoed wall or altarpiece, but a full antesanctum—and I feel . . . the anticipation of a young lad sitting in a brothel for the first time as his Maester, hand on his shoulder, says, *Tomorrow you will be a man, eh?*

A *tump* from the nook—feet dropping onto floor—turns my head and I see that the old man's face is visible again—is he still sitting down?—and then the door opens fully as he comes out into the tavern proper and I realise his height. He's gnomish, or *hobben*, as they call them in these parts, and I find myself caught in a fleeting sense of shock and shame, staring at him as if he has no business to be here and then looking away quickly because *I* have no business even thinking such thoughts; it's not so much disgust as it's the fear of disgust, the knee-jerk reaction of a tolerant and open-minded man, suddenly panicking at the challenge of reality. *Are you? Are you sure? Did the word* grotesque *not whisper through your head for a fraction of a second when you saw the stump of him?*

He asks the barkeep for another and the man pours him a draft of what looks like a wheat beer, golden but cloudy. I only realise I am staring when he notices and raises his glass to me. I salute him with my own, my momentary angst dissolved in the return of that aesthetic impulse. His stunted body is of as little interest now as when it was hidden in the shadows of the nook. His deep-lined face, as robust as it is wrecked, is all I see. The face of God.

He turns to go back to the nook and I wonder if it is his exile or simply his privacy; there are many taverns that would not serve his kind at all and I imagine that even if the hospitaliter himself is friend to all, some of his customers may be less inclusive.

—Sir, I say. A moment. A word.

—Yes? he says.

—I have a . . . request, I say.

Hal Duncan

The Measuring

—It is the perfect blank page, is it not? says Fader Pitro.

In a way he is right; the antesanctum of the Monadery de Sanze Manitae, skinned in its fleshtone of plaster, with its floor of mottled concrete, is an almost empty space, only the unvarnished oak intricacies of the dais with its pulpit, altar and chorum pews creating any sort of complexity—that and the ribbing of columns and windows that break up the side walls into architectured rhythm. Then there are the doors of the entranceway behind me and the two doors at the back, to either side of the dais, leading into the forbidden sanctum. On the whole it is, to the layman, a plain and perfect ground waiting humbly for its frescos, murals or mosaics. But I am a chiaroscurist. Even the simplest of spaces may contain the subtlest tricks of light latent in the slant of sunbeams through windows sidling round from dusk till dawn.

—There's no such thing as a blank page, Fader, I say.

I work by eye and foot at first; before the measurements and calculations begin, I scout the vacant hall in an intuitive way, pacing its length and breadth, circling and crouching. I note the south-westerly aspect that will send a shaft of late-afternoon light through the circular window high above the entrance to the wall over the altar—slightly right of centre and down. I observe the rhomboid slices of long morning produced by the windows in the south-east wall, geometric projections on the facing plaster, the shadow of the Monadery Tower outside that will rupture this pattern between dawn and noon. As much as I appreciate the work of the masons who have built this spare but sublime little chapel for the brooders of the Manitaen Order, it is the architecture of light that I revere, as mutable as it is stable, cycling with the days and seasons, changing its very substance from granite grey to marble white with the gathering and scattering of cumuli and stratocirrus across the sky. The antesanctum—any building—is only a shell in which the light builds its own structures, not a blank page but a blueprint which a chiaroscurist like myself seeks to give form.

When I'm finally satisfied that I have the key points and the general flux of light fleshed out in my mind into a rough terrain of potential drama—highlights and low points—I turn back to the doorway and notice Fader Pitro still standing there, picking at a loose thread on the hem of his cassock's drooping sleeve.

—You don't have to stay, I say to the Fader. I'll be here for a while and I'm afraid it won't be very interesting to an observer.

He gathers his long hair into a ponytail and brings it over one shoulder, twirls a finger round a curly white lock; the Manitaens wear unusual tonsures I have noticed, shaved at the sides like a horse's mane. The Fader plays with his when he's thinking.

—I do have business to attend to, he says. Dukes and books, he sighs. But I'll send Brooder Matheus to keep you company, in case you need anything.

I tell him there's no need to bore the poor brooder with such duties, but he shushes me with a waggling finger.

—Brooder Matheus will find it a relief, I'm sure, he says. And it will stop him ruining any more vellum with his godless scrawl. A hand too used to the hawk's hood, he mutters, and none too delicate with its feather. Honestly . . .

He wanders off, muttering to himself about spoiled second sons and the quality of tutoring amongst nobility these days.

I pick my carpetbag up from the doorway where I left it on entering the antesanctum and open it on the altar to take out my instruments, the sextantine and the compass, chalks and slates, coalsticks and notepads, measuring tape and, most important of all, my photometer. It is the most expensive item I possess, a delicate precision instrument that I keep in its own wooden case, padded with cotton wool and fretted over on each trundling cart journey from town to town, from commission to commission. When my Maester first gave it to me, indeed, I often irritated the poor carters with constant guidance over how to take the bumps in the road less jarringly or sat with the case in my lap for the whole journey, unsnicking the latch every ten miles or so to check that it was still intact.

I lay all these instruments on the altar like a surgeon's tools, and am unlatching the photometer's case when voice and footsteps echo behind me.

—How does it look?

Brooder Matheus, I assume—the same elven lad who came to fetch me from the tavern this morning to meet with Fader Pitro—gestures to encompass the antesanctum. He nods at the photometer in my hand.

—Is that for measuring the light?

He seems genuinely interested, the look on his face of a child who wants so much to play with an adult's toy but knows it would be wrong to ask; so I show him the way the hood widens and tightens to set the aperture, the glass bulb inside with its incredibly fragile vanes and tiny metal sails to catch the light as a windmill catches air, how one holds it up and looks through the eyepiece at the back to see the flickering rhythm, the earpiece for listening to the tone of whirr.

—Is there no needle, no gauge, he says.

I shake my head.

—It takes a while but you learn to . . . *hear* the speed, to *see* the force of light, I say. Now. I'll have to ask you to be quiet for a bit, if you don't mind. I want to start my measurements.

—Of course, he says. Of course.

The Separation of Light And Dark

I close the shutters on the window a little more and come down from the stepladders to check the effect, step back up to adjust the mirrors and, finally satisfied, take my place at the easels. The tavern's attic is one of the most effective studio spaces I have ever had, with its four small windows—embedded two on either side of the sloping roof—solid fits for my rigging of adjustable-angled reflectors and screens clamped into place on the window-frame and swivelled, tilted, until the daylight that pierces the room does so exactly where and how I want it to. My Maester would have been horrified at this, working as he did in sun-drenched spaces of whitewashed walls and floors, seeking to suffuse his work with that airy quality so bold and innovative in his day, the thin washes of colour in his tempera frescoes painting religious mystery in pastel tones lit up by the white of plaster glowing like moonlight underneath. Gauche and opalescent, his works still shimmer like the air on a hot summer day. *God is light*, he used to say. *And that is what we paint, what we are paid to paint.* A traditionalist, he did not approve of the chiaroscurists' innovations.

—I am not sure I approve of this, grumps Iosef.

The old hobben sits on a child's schoolchair, elbow on the desk-arm, fist under his chin, brows furrowed in a glower that's more uncertain than unhappy. As a hobben, I know, his religion stands against the graven images that are my livelihood. Idolatry, he calls it, and if it were just the money involved—no matter what others might say about 'gold-grubbing gnomes'—I do not think he would sit for me at all; but over these last few weeks of nights of drunken blather in the tavern's candle-lit warmth, we have come to respect each other's utterly opposed opinions, enjoying the sheer intransigence of each other's attitude. He was a rephai—before the pogrom that burnt him from his home and drove him through fields of horror to eventual sanctuary here under Fader Pitro's sackcloth wings—and the tradition of argument runs in his blood. For the hobben, God is not reached through images but through words, through the text and the exegesis of the text, debate, discussion. So he sits for me as a favour to a new friend, I like to think—but probably also as a favour to an old friend, Fader Pitro. And then also, there may be just a little of that secret thrill so many humble men have when you ask them to sit for you.

—Admit it, I say. You're flattered by the thought of being the face of God.

—I am *not*, he says. It's a blasphemy. Pride and arrogance, that's what it is, he says, to think that you can give a face to God.

He digs into a pocket for his tobacco and cigarette papers, starts to roll a cigarette. I study the changed position for a second then lay down the coalstick with which I have been sketching on the right-hand easel, shuffle over to my left and pick up the chalk sitting on the left-hand easel's lower clamp. I have worked this way ever since I struck out on my own, leaving my Maester to his dreamy pastel tones; I use two easels, one with white paper clipped to it to sketch in charcoal-black, the other with the blue-black paper of a draughtsman, on which I sketch in chalk. If God is light, as my Maester insisted, well, the world we live in is filled with the shadows cast by His material creation, by these forms of flesh absorbing so much on the side that faces Him that on the other He is utterly absent. I find that to capture this effectively, to grasp the form of the subject, I have to sketch my studies in dual media, layering charcoal shadows on a ground of light, chalk highlights over midnight blue. In the actual work, of course, these dual perspectives should be fused.

—But what is so blasphemous, I say innocently, about letting our imagination give a human face to that which we don't understand?

He lights up his cigarette, puffs on it and coughs, then points it at me as he lectures. If I were one of those artists who must have their subjects sit like silent statues while I sketch, I think Iosef would drive me mad. He cannot sit without talking, cannot talk without gesticulating—though he tried, bless him, stiff as a board the very first time he sat for me, like a youth being interviewed for membership in the highest merchant's guild, until I told him that he wasn't a king sitting for his portrait, that I *wanted* to see the varied attitudes and angles of his self, to just *relax*, man. So now he leans forward to make a point, sits back in satisfaction afterwards, crosses his arms or waves them in the air. He jabs the air with his rollup.

—The Absolute doesn't have a face, he is saying now. God is infinite, transcendent, and you limit him when you try to define *that which cannot be defined.*

I trace the jut of solemnity in his jaw, the old man's outrage in his bottom lip, almost petted as he blows smoke out and up.

—But I only try to define his face, I say. Where the presters and the rephais and the imams, why, you try to define his *mind.* Wisdom, justice and mercy, no?

The Boy Who Loved Death

I switch back to the easel of white paper, carving a curve of black upon it with the coalstick, the furrow of a knitted brow.

—Is it not pride and arrogance, I say, to think that you can give a *mind* to God?

—You . . . he says, shaking his head. Heresy like that will get you into trouble.

His voice goes quieter, softer.

—You should be careful, Maester.

The Protection of The Innocents

—Iosef, I think you should go inside.

Fader Pitro worries a rosary between his fingers as he gazes out over the Monadery's low dry stone wall, over the red-tiled roofs of the town, the jumble of houses that slope down the hill and scatter out into the patchwork farms of the surrounding countryside. He stands, unsteady in the middle of the rockery in the western corner of the gardens, screwing his eyes to watch the road from the north, from Nixemburg and Murchen. I know what he is looking at. A cloud of dust. The flash of armour. The flutter of a banner. There are peregrins coming.

I hold the door of the antesanctum open for the carter who brought the news along with my latest supply of paints and primers, feeling helpless as he carries each barrel past me, lays it down carefully in the centre of the concrete floor. Brooder Matheus, my unofficial apprentice these days, helps him, humping the crates of coalsticks and chalk that I will need before I even pick up palette and brush; I have the preliminary design now for the interior, but it will take me months just to transfer the sketches from paper to plaster; the scaffolding has not even been erected yet.

The carter lays another barrel on the ground, a blond rock of a man, unconcerned by our atmosphere of agitation. Brooder Matheus keeps glancing at Iosef and the Fader. Iosef has a look set on his face.

—The Fader is right, Iosef, I say. Now's not the time for stubbornness.

Iosef crouches down to clip a twig off a shrub with his secateurs. Ignoring me completely, he stomps over to a bench set against the wall, puts the secateurs down and picks up a fork and trowel. He puts them down again and turns to me.

—Am I to spend my life cowering in the shadows? he says angrily. Is that what I am? A half-thing of the darkness? Half the height so half the man? *Hide in the shadows, Iosef*?

He points past me.

—Maybe I can crawl under the altar and hide there, eh?

I think of the stories he has told me of his old town, of hobben boarded up inside their burning homes, the elders of his little community dragged out into the streets to have their beards hacked off with razors as trophies for the mob, gnomes who had harmed no-one moaning out of broken, skinned jaws. Choking in a smoke-filled hiding-hole.

He strides past me, past the carter and into the antesanctum.

—Perhaps you should spend the night here as well, Maester, says Fader Pitro.

—No, I say. I'll be alright.

—And how she *squealed* for her mother!

I gaze at the flame of the candle, the flicker so vibrant, so alive, and without pattern. How can something so chaotic be so beautiful? The candle is low, most of its wax now dribbled and solidified as white trails layering the dark-green glass of the bottle that serves as candlestick. A molten lump like some limestone grotto's creation, slick and glistening in the dark. A drip of wax splashes on the table and I dip a finger into it before it cools, smooth it over the fingertip with my thumb.

—Some more of this fine cat's piss here, man.

The peregrin officers fill the tavern though there's only half a dozen of them; they fill it with their boorish brags, their swaggering contempt that shoves its way through crowds with elbows in the side or hands flat in the face, and with the ugly stares of men hungry for violence. Brooder Matheus and I sit at a corner table, safe with the carter sat across from us, as calm, he is, as if the peregrins were simply nuisance children running wild in the absence of authority. Everyone knows the reputation of the carter's guild, men who are trained to see a cargo safely through the wildest regions of the hinter, whatever bandits or demons might lie in their path. Everyone knows the legends.

—I hear . . . says one of the peregrins, I hear there's a filthy hobben in this town.

The carter slugs his beer back and stands up. His voice when he speaks is quiet, loaded.

—Brooder. Maester, he says. Do you have a message for the Fader?

He has no reason to return to the Monadery, of course, but . . .

—If you're going that way, I say, I think we both might join you, eh Brooder?

Brooder Matheus nods and downs the last of his beer for courage, coughs.

—You are mistaken, m'sire, says Fader Pitro.

His voice, outside, is loud and clear but there's a waver in it—audible fear. The peregrins are gathered outside the very doors of the antesanctum, the officers and their whole band. They announced themselves on the staggering march up from the tavern with a pounding drum of swords on shields, a chorus of ape-calls. There are curses and laughter now.

—Bring him out and we'll cut him down to size! shouts someone.

More laughter.

Brooder Matheus sits on a crate, looking nervous, and I wonder if there's anyone out there he would recognise, some second cousin twice removed perhaps. Elven nobility, I think. Iosef stands on the dais itself, a hand touching the altar. They would not kill him in a house of God, would they? I stand at the door, listening.

—There are no hobben here, says Fader Pitro and I hear the sound of someone spitting in reply.

The carter moves me aside with one hand. The other holds his spike, the seven foot steel bladed lance that can be used as sword or staff or spear. There is one story that the guild was formed from an order of knights sworn to protect the early peregrins on their way to the Holy Lands, before these sons of the grey erles twisted the pilgrimages into a crusade. Even if there is no truth to it, I have seen for myself the brutal skill with which a carter wields his spike. He takes the brass handle of one of the doors and swings it full open, suddenly, smoothly.

The hellish orange of torchlight pierces the antesanctum, picking out Brooder Matheus as he stands up from the crate, a palette knife in his hand of all things. Iosef at the altar. The peregrins cannot fail to see him there, surely. But they cannot fail to see the carter either, the way his eyes and spike capture the flame of their torches and reflect it back at them, so bright that the antesanctum behind must be darkness in comparison.

He simply stands there, silent, until they leave.

The Temptation of the Faithful

—I have to go, I say. Brooder Matheus will be waiting for me eager as a pup. I lay the first stroke today.

—Brooder Matheus can wait till you've had breakfast, says Rosah.

She kicks down the bedsheet and pulls herself up onto her elbow. I admire her as I pull on my linen trousers and shirt, all crisp and freshly laundered, perfumed by the petals left in the bottom of the basket by Maria, Hier Nerjea's wife, who rules the tavern's lodging rooms with the same ironclad sense of hospitality as her husband rules the public house below. Rosah is beautiful and she lies there on the bed, my angel whore, knowing it. Her skin is pale as porcelain, paler than it should be with such amber hair and eyes of flashing green; when I undressed her that first night I expected freckles, copper skin, the feel of powder on my fingers as I caressed her face, but there was only the silk of skin, as soft and clean as if it was just out of the bath and toweled dry. It is I who am usually masked in powder, charcoal and chalkdust griming my face and fingers when I come back to the tavern late to take my supper and drink with her, and later as the night goes on, slip my arm around her waist and pull her, laughing with lust the both of us, up to my room. Rosah's beauty is unsoiled by rouge or eyeshadow, her only concession to vanity the vermilion lipstick with which she paints my chest with a kiss each night over my heart. I feel my cock stirring as I look at her coquettish contrapposto pose, the locket that hangs between her breasts, the trim of her fuzz; I am remembering her salty taste. I leave the shirt untucked as cover, shaking my head.

—You will spoil me for other women, I say.

—Then you must marry me, she says. Take me away from all this and make an honest woman of me.

I sit on the bed to kiss her. It is a little joke that has developed between us these last few months, but like all such jokes it has just the tiniest sting of truth behind it and we are both sometimes, I think, a little sad, thinking it might be nice and knowing it will never happen.

—Me? I say. I am as much a whore as you. More so, mi caria, since I have slutted myself in more cities than you could probably imagine.

—Ah, but if you took me with you when you go, I could give you some competition, I am sure.

I laugh. I love Rosah, as a friend and as a sensual delight, as a favourite whore and as a trusted confidante; and her fondness for me runs deep enough for her to declare now and then, on some night when perhaps she feels a little lonely, *tonight there is no money and no clock, mister painter, no limits, only you and I, and we will explore each other's body as if we had never even touched before.* We are both whores, yes, but I think we are both whores by vocation, willing to give more of ourselves in our work than most.

But neither of us will ever lose ourselves in the other, I know. Even in the nights when we make love rather than merely fuck, we are never truly *lovers*.

—I have to go, I say.

—Artists, she says. You're no whore. You're more married than the Nerjeas.

—Tonight? I say and kiss her on the forehead.

—Eat something, she calls out the door after me as I go down the stairs. Maria! Make him have some breakfast.

—Breakfast? I say.

I throw the apple across the antesanctum to Brooder Matheus, who catches it in one hand. I polish another on my shirt and take a crunching bite.

—Fader Pitro was asking how things were going again, he says. I told him you're two months behind and that yesterday you completely wiped the first four panels of the south-east wall.

He takes a bite out of the apple, a mischievous gleam in his eye.

—I am a bad influence on you, I say.

—It's the truth.

I am behind schedule admittedly, but what the brooder didn't tell the old monk is that the cleaning of the panels is the next stage of the process. I look around at the surfaces of the antesanctum—what you can see behind the scaffolding—ceiling and walls all but covered in the chalk and charcoal sketches copied from the papers that now carpet the concrete floor. The panels above the door and behind the altar are the only ones that have still to be filled; I have not made my final decision on the latter yet, and the former, well, the idea I have in mind I would rather keep from the Fader's prying eyes right now.

As for the four panels that I 'wiped' yesterday, though, the ones around the far-left window—Brooder Matheus may be amused at the thought of the Fader in a flap but yesterday it was himself looking on in horror as I went at them with my rags and fluids. I gave him a few minutes of panic before explaining that charcoal and chalk make a less than effective surface for my technique and, you see, I have the images that belong there imprinted in my mind now so I only have to close my eyes to visualise them. The cleaning was only preparation for the real work to begin.

The outlines of the four panels bordering the window are the only charcoal marks left from the previous months of work on this area. Offset and defined by one line running out from each corner of the window, the panels should produce a sort of elliptical structure on the whole, moving the eye around from this one to the next. I decide to start with the panel on the lower-left.

The brooder has already prepared the buckets of water and the basins we will need, so I crack open the barrel of plaster mix and set him to work while I wind the clockwork pick then start to vandalise the smooth pink skin of the first panel. The little steel point of it whirrs as it hammers, chipping away at the surface, roughing it up so that the plaster I apply will bond. There should be no danger of my work crumbling off the wall three years after completion in the middle of some funeral . . . as happened with di Vineggio's *Nocturna d'il Houri*.

I finish preparing the first panel and take the first two basins of plaster from Brooder Matheus, handing him the pick to wind. It is the same sculpting plaster in each bowl—thicker than normal plaster, softer than clay—but where one basin is white the other is tinted dark with the same black ink the monks use in their Velllumary. The two will mix a little as I apply them, but that is to be expected. I will be painting over them anyway; all I am doing now is building up the undercoat of light and shadow, the white that will shine through from beneath a cerulean sky, the darkness that will lurk behind a devil's eyes, building it up gradually, with a finger and thumb of slick plaster here or there, a thick wet lump smoothed into shape with a knife, another lump on top of it.

Slowly the form of a face starts to take solid shape, as if emerging from the very wall. After a while, I stand back to uncrick my shoulders.

—It catches the light, says Brooder Matheus. Where you've put the white plaster, it catches the light coming in the window. Just so, just . . .

—Just right? I say. That's the general idea.

The Seeding of the Earth

—And, generally speaking, do you have an idea when it will be finished?

It has taken me two years just to do the ceiling and the Fader manages to sound casual in his enquiry, but I can hear the note of worry in his voice. The costs are escalating now that the paint is flowing and the wagon rolling constantly between here and Murchen, bringing the pigments and media I require from the great Artist's Market of the Strazza d'il Tintorum, powders made from rock and plant: sulphuric yellow from the Salt Sea or green-gold sapphiron from the distant Aurient; porphyr made from mollusc's shells in the Phonaesthian city-states or the iridescent verdan of Aegys's crushed scarab wings. Elysse, north and south, is full of natural hues, nut-browns and ochres, umbers and siennas, and I make full use of these, but the pigments most saturated with yellow, red and blue must be imported from their more exotic origins, so these materials are expensive; and although the brooders' benefactor, the Duke Irae, is rich with the plunder of the Holy Lands even he may balk at paying such a ransom for escape from Hell.

So the Fader sees the antesanctum only a fraction complete and, thinking of how much money it has cost already and how far it has to go, has visions of catastrophe.

—It will probably be finished, I say, the day after you give yourself a heart attack, Fader . . . at this rate. Or if you want I could paint the rest all white and you could tell the Duke it symbolises God's eternal radiance. That way it would be finished within the week.

He twirls a lock of hair between his fingers, brushes his lips with the end of it.

—It's not *my* heart giving out that I'm worried about, he says. The Duke has expressed his desire to have . . . given all the honour that he can to God while still on this earth.

I grab a bar of scaffolding, swing from my crouch up on the plank down to the platform beneath. Holding onto a ladder that rises up past me, I lean out into the fifteen foot of air that separates me from the Fader and Brooder Matheus standing behind him.

—Tell him he could die tomorrow, I say, so he should swear his sons to carry on his patronage. Or tell him that the Butcher of Instantinople shouldn't be such an old maid.

I wrap paint-rags round my hands and slide down the ladder.

—Tell him, I say, that God will not *let* him die until his purpose is fulfilled and he stands here, where you and I are standing, looking up into His face; that if he dies before the antesanctum is complete it will be the greatest sin he's ever committed.

Brooder Matheus points at my forehead and I touch the wetness, wipe the paint off with the back of my hand. Alizarin crimson. Fader Pitro looks unusually stern, but he seems a little distracted, as if there's something less tangible than money and time worrying him. Brooder Matheus puts a hand on the Fader's arm.

—Tell him it will be worth it when the chapel is finished, he says. Look. Is it not true?

A mix of indigo and porphyr, the night sky painted on the ceiling of the antesanctum is not black but blue, the purplish hue so deep that, in contrast with the crescent moon of Iosef's raptured face and the plumes and strands of clouds he breathes into existence, it recedes as into an eternal darkness; but it is a poor chiaroscurist who does not understand that there is colour even in the deepest shadows; so, although I work in light and dark, there is no black upon my palette, no black in the night sky. I keep a watch on the Fader's tilted, swivelling chin of pointed beard as his eyes follow the path mapped out for them. On the barrel ceiling, the low relief of Iosef's face sits off-centre and down so as to catch the eye first by catching the diffuse sun coming in the windows of the south-east wall. The subtler forms of streams of smoke modelled around the image of the Creator lead Fader Pitro round and out; smoke becomes scatterling clouds in a night sky, spatterings of stars. At the edges of the ceiling, as if the viewer is looking up from the middle of a forest clearing, thick plaster foliage of branches and leaves is painted in the olive drab of night and edged in bone-white. An owl rises from a branch but otherwise it is a quiet sky, the first few days of Creation. Mankind is yet to appear; the unborn animals are only suggestions in the insubstantial swirls, seeds waiting to be sung and sprung into existence under Orphean's feet.

—We can't all create a world in six days, I say.

Fader Pitro's eye travels the scene, his body turning, stepping back and round to the side every so often to accommodate his angle. I watch with pleasure as he is brought back to the face of Iosef, the beginning and the end.

—I'm just hoping that it's not six years, he says.

But he nods. He looks around at the sculptures pressing out from the walls all round, shapes emerging from the plaster as if they too are part of the moment above, emerging into existence from the clay of the earth beneath the sky, and he nods, mutters some vague encouragement and leaves.

—Iosef is ill, says Brooder Matheus after he has gone.

—Schitze! says Iosef. I'll be tending their garden and their graveyard long after the Fader is fertilising my plants. Pitro's a worrier.

—I've noticed, I say. I sometimes think he only took his vows to give his fingers rosaries to play with.

But twice tonight Iosef has been racked by coughing fits that halted conversation as he creased with the effort of containing them, the table shuddering under the weight of his hand. He will not see a doctor and he will not give up his rituals of tobacco, however much his lungs and throat protest with rasping hacks and muffled judders; that much became obvious when I joined him in his nook, taking the chair diagonally across from his customary cushion-raised booth seat, and tried to broach the subject—and the air turned blue with curses and with smoke blown in my face. I'm not sure which of them made my eyes sting more, the invective or the noxious weed, but I thought better of continuing the role of nag. It doesn't suit me anyway.

Of course, I can remind him of how others worry for his health. *Absurdly*, I say. *But they do worry.*

—Let's talk of something else, he says. Have you decided on the designs for the end walls yet?

He takes a drag on his roll-up and I wince as he explodes into another fit, spluttering into a white-knuckled fist. He thumps the table in frustration and I ignore it. The hobben have a phrase—*ch'yem*—which roughly translates as *may it be*. The will of God is inevitable, they mean, as I understand it. I think it is a phrase very close to Iosef's heart these days.

—The end walls? I say. I do have some ideas.

The Exile from the Garden

—And whatever will they say at the sight of a whore painted as blessed Queen Titania?

Rosah looks over her shoulder at me with an arched eyebrow; she finds the whole idea both wicked and delicious, but rather than being in conflict over what I've asked of her she has thrown herself into it with delight. It is strange, but having heard her say her prayers at night—more open and relaxed with me as she has been in this last year or so—I have discovered a quite pious side to my Rosah, with the little saint statues on the shelf in her room, the single candle that always has a flower at its side, and her tiny bowl of honey and coins. I think now if I'd asked her to be my Titania two years ago she would have refused, saying it was sacrilege, and I would have . . . laughed probably, in shock. Now I'm not sure why she agreed at all; perhaps the deeper the belief in sin, the greater the thrill of courting it.

—They'll say you are the very image of her, says Brooder Matheus.

She blows a kiss at him and he mimes a catch, grinning, but blushing at his own boldness. At least it brings some colour to his cheeks; the two of us got roaring drunk in the tavern last night, after visiting Iosef up at the grounds house, and if I woke up with a hangover, the poor brooder, by the look of him, was at death's door. The original grey erle.

Matheus and myself now pace about the studio, setting up the easels and the paper, arranging the mirrors and shades on the windows. Rosah sits on a bench before us, leaning over an open chest of props, holding necklaces of coloured glass jewels up to her throat, throwing feathered boas and fur stoles over her shoulders, trying on a stuffed snake, a tiara—and all the while glancing at herself in the mirror like a child playing dress-up. Every so often, these last few months in particular, I find myself glancing at her when she is not looking and I feel this joy I can hardly explain. It is in moments like this. I try to put my finger on it. She is not performing—no—she is not performing for *me*, or for the brooder, not seeking our attention, but simply, happily, lavishing it upon herself.

I think that is it. She is no longer *my* Rosah. Now she is simply Rosah.

When Brooder Matheus and I have everything set up to my satisfaction, she drops the centaurian's helmet that she's holding back into the box and stands, walks into the centre of the room.

—You're ready, yes? Where do you want me? How do you want me?

—In white silk, I say. Just a moment.

I dig the dress I want out of the box, not so much a dress as a drapery of veils and ribbons, and while I untangle it, tease out the folds and complexities, she slips off her shoes, hikes up her skirt to peel down her stockings.

—Brooder Matheus, she says, will you help me with this?

Her hands reaching behind, she turns her back to him and the brooder looks hesitant and shy for a second before taking those steps across the room. His fingers fumble with her buttons but after the first couple, the rest come loose easily. I notice the delicate confidence with which he slips the straps off her shoulders, the way he can't help but smooth the palms of his hands over her skin. Last night, in drunken camaraderie, he confessed to me how unsuited he feels to his vows. He had little choice in the matter; as a second son, the law of primogeniture leaves him no estate, no path to follow but war or religion. And while he has no great urge to go and slaughter, with his noble elven brethren, the demon races that now rule the Holy Lands, he said, chastity was never his strong point.

It's funny, I suppose; in all the years we've known each other now, watching him grow from adolescent to adult, I had always pegged him as, at heart, an innocent naïf. As it turns out our naive brooder lost his virginity two years before I did and spent most of his youth from that point on tupping any girl who batted her eyelashes at him.

Rosah's dress slips off her shoulders and crumples on the ground at her feet. She steps out of it and takes the white silk costume from my hands, begins to wrap herself in it. It adorns without hiding, veils without disguising. Every curve of her, every sacred secret place of her is somehow more revealed with it on than in her nakedness, and I'm more sure than ever that this is the Titania of the Exile from the Garden that will go on the wall above the antesanctum's entrance. This is the faery queen, the virgin whore, the spirit of lush forests, of morning dew like the sweat on a lover's body, of oceans salty as blood and semen, who runs her fingers over the vine-grown trunks of trees, the green-veined cocks of men, through grass and hair, as the ruler of them all, the mother of all living things, mother of Orphean who died for our sins.

I dip into the box again and pull out the velvet robe, dark purple, long and soft as fur. Brooder Matheus reaches out a hand for it but his eyes are on Rosah, transfixed; it takes him a few seconds of grasping in the air to realise there's no point in me giving him the robe quite yet, and then he turns to me with a wry, sheepish smile on his face, red with a blush or with the flush of sexual tension. Finally he pulls the cassock over his head and stands there, cockish and puffed with an uncertain audacity. He runs his fingers through the dark-red hair that silks over his shoulders, brushing it back, half nervousness, half pride. I hand him the robe and he pulls it on, leaves it hanging open. Slender and straight beside her curves, he is the dark to her light, the auburn to her titanium white. The Oberon to her Titania.

As they turn to each other, their hands, their bodies, beginning that exploration of the world outside innocence, discovered in an age long before our own, I walk to my easels and look from chalk to charcoal and back again, trying to decide which to begin with.

The Last Days

I am on the last panel now. It has taken me four—no, nearly five—years to paint the antesanctum of the Monadery d'il Sanze Manitae and at last it is almost complete. I sketch directly onto the wall now, working as fast as I can and keeping a rag at hand to correct my errors and insincerities. Insincerities? In any painting such as this, in any work of a chiaroscurist such as myself, it is easy to become too bold in the drama, too theatrical, too focused on the power that light and dark have to evoke a profound sense of mystery. Subtlety is lost when the artist blusters his own ideas in forms too overblown, brushstrokes too broad. Of all the panels of the antesanctum, I cannot allow this one to lose its import in mere impact. I will not.

So I draw with chalk and coalstick onto the pink plaster and, again and again, I find myself cursing and taking the rag to the wall in bitter frustration because this structure is too crude, that contrast too bold. Too clichéd. Too unusual. Too trite. Too grandiose. It should be the simplest panel of them all, in some ways, for its subject is the most universal. It is one of the most traditional of scenes, though it is usually placed in some dark area, as a hidden mystery.

I am drawing the body of Iosef, which lies upon the altar now. I am drawing death.

I work non-stop for two days finding a form that does not really satisfy me but is, at least, not an insult to his memory, not the self-important sweeping statement of a young chiaroscurist more concerned with the glory of his work than with who and what it is meant to represent. Even as I begin the modelling work, layering on the black and white plasters, building up the relief sculpture of Iosef's ruined body, I do not know if I can do him justice. Will this reduce his life to no more than an empty symbol, only resonating for the viewer because it is so hollow without the totality of his life to fill it? How can I show in the cracks of his knuckles and the stumps of his fingers, the way those hands worked so delicately with the flowers and herbs of the Monadery garden, or rolled his cigarettes with such unconscious ease and precision that half the time his eyes would be on something else, on myself or Matheus, as he lectured us on our many follies? How can I show in the still barrel of his chest, the wheezing up-and-down of it as he lay in his sick bed for that last year and a half, fighting to keep the last breath in his body? How can I show that the smoke that ruined him was not just the smoke of his own creation but the smoke of his destruction, of the temple with his congregation gathered in it on their holy day to sing the word of God, and the mob outside with fire?

I only knew him for four years and there is so much that I did not know.

All I can show are these last days of him, of his remains.

The decay of the body is quick in the heat of summer. Skin of Payne's-grey blotches phthalo blue and viridian in the shadows; it dulls with the yellow ochre, burnt umber, burnt sienna of rot. Maggots wriggle, iridescent and ivory white in the slick of him. The surface of the altar is stained with the blood pooled and coagulated in the lowest areas of his body in the early stages of decay, now transformed by the process into some thicker, darker fluid. I see haematic red in it, alizarin crimson. It glistens aemberic orange in the candlelight. Every colour in my palette is mixed in the putrefaction of the corpse and I paint them on the wall in layer upon layer. I mix paint with plaster and sculpt with my fingers until my nails are filthy and broken by the scratching.

Fader Pitro sits vigil over Iosef's body while I work, because this is the tradition of the hobben and there are no others in the town to perform the rites. I think that Iosef would have wanted the Fader at his side anyway, but this is cold comfort to the monk; he frets that he is failing, that he cannot do it *properly*, that it should be done *properly*. The brooders recite verses from the Old Book in Litan but they do not know the hobben words or the soaring wavering tunes this poetry should be sung to, so as I work their choral chants echo in the antesanctum, giving the same sentiments in the words and song they know.

We have sent word to Matheus and Rosah but I do not think they will arrive before the burial.

I am laying a stone on his grave when I feel the hand on my shoulder. Rosah. Matheus stands behind her. I embrace my Titania, kiss her on the forehead. Matheus and I shake hands, both of us two-handed, clasping each other's grip firm and tight as if anchoring each other. We talk for a while, words that we forget as soon as they have been spoken. Sometimes there is laughter, sometimes tears. Matheus is still not sure of what he will do now he has left the Order, but the two of them seem, even in sorrow, to have found their true vocations in each other. Have I really finished now? they ask. Yes. And did I really paint the Death of God as the very focus of the whole chapel, the work you see first as you enter through the doors? Yes. They will see how the structure of light and shadow in the antesanctum demanded it. When they see it they will understand, I hope.

After a while I leave them to have some time alone at the grave and return to the antesanctum.

The walls are filled with the townsfolk and the brooders, every character based on one local or another—the Nerjeas, Rosah and Matheus, even Fader Pitro as a saint in one high corner—but it is Iosef whose face holds you as you walk in, not in the moment of creation on the ceiling but on the wall behind the altar, on a dead body, lying on its back but with its head turned towards you so that face stares out with hollow eyes, eaten away to bone here and there, a white skull cloaked in the shadows of flesh and night. I do not know if I am satisfied with it. I could not hope to paint, in his death, the whole reality of his life; all I can show are his remains, on the painted artifice of an altar on the wall behind the real thing as if it were a dark mirror still reflecting what is no longer there.

Maybe those few precious glimpses that I had, in the years of moments that I knew him . . . maybe these are enough to know the form of someone, even if the rest is darkness.

The Last Shift

8:30

own the steps and out of the airtram station, showing his ticket to the guard at the door, Billy strides along the paving stones of Coats Street, sticks his morning roll-up in his mouth and stops to light it at the corner of Dyers Wynd, glancing up at the War Memorial for a second before—with a puff of smoke and steam in the cold winter air—he walks on. He fumbles the woolen glove back onto his left hand, right hand cupping the fag for warmth. The wind blows the hood of his parka down and he curses, shivers as a drip of rainwater blown from a roof somewhere above hits the back of his neck and dribbles down between his shoulderblades. He flips the hood back up over his horns, spine rippling involuntarily with the tickle of water. Bastard. He hates the winter, hates this weather, hates having to wear umpteen layers of clothing all the endless months from autumn to spring. You can't even fly in this weather.

The bell of the town hall clock across the river chimes half-past and he quickens his pace to a jog over the pedestrian crossing with the red man showing. Back to a stride on the other side. He nods a wee joke of a forelock-tugging *good morning, guvnor . . . and good morning to you, sir*, to the greened gray bronzes of the Gilmour Brothers as he walks between them—Thomas with his thumbs tucked under his frockcoat's lapels, Peter with his top hat nooked in a crook of elbow, both of them every inch the solemn Empire-builder, dark wings spread out wide behind them. Aye, but they look like sentinels surveying the very furthest dominions of Albion, gazing out over Afrita and Nagastan, the Aerient and the New World. Even their horns are solemn and patriarchal, curving ram's horns thick and heavy as their mutton-chop sideburns. Oh aye. Albion's finest.

Down the steps Billy goes, and into the little ornamental garden with its statue of Queen Titania, bulky in her widow's black bustle, out onto the cobbles slick with rain (being not quite cold enough for ice last night) where Thread Lane cuts a narrow path between a row of old sandstone offices and the rail of the wall that drops down to the river below. Swans nesting in the weeds and litter sail slow on the murk of the Black Cart, beneath the bunting of Christmas lights all strung from side to side across the river, dull baubles without the power on at this grey time of the morning. He follows the lane along till it hits Needle Road and crosses the river. Cars thrum past him in a stream of dopplering noise.

Upriver from the bridge and squat beside a natural weir of white foam crashing over hidden rock, the old Anchor Mill is a hulk of red-brick, rowed and columned with windows, square tower perching at one corner. Billy flicks his dead fag out over the river towards it as he crosses the bridge. The building's under renovation just now, being turned into luxury apartments. Scaffolding almost swallows it, adding to its ugly bulk. Under the mill, like some long lump of worn, cracked granite swallowed by surf at the bottom of a seaside cliff, an outcrop of stone—gray and green with damp and moss—juts out into the water. The old mill used to belong to Gilmour; the whole town of Fergusley in a way used to belong to Gilmour—a centuries-old family company of dyers, weavers, threadmakers and more. Benefactors of their home town, the Gilmours and their business gave half of the streets their names. There's a Gilmour Church, Gilmour House, Mill Road, Carpet Wynd . . . and it goes on.

Times change though, of course.

The Boy Who Loved Death

8:45

Billy tilts his head like he used to do when he was younger. If you look at it the right way in the right light, the rock in the river seems to have the shape of a man embedded in it—there's the face and the horns, and there's the right hand and the pinion of his left wing pressing out, as if, long ago, some poor soul fell into the molten rock of an unformed earth, to be trapped as an insect in amber, or as a fossil, flesh itself transformed to stone, lost and then uncovered by millenia of riverine erosion. It used to fascinate Billy as a wee boy— still does—this form of a man that's trying to free itself through time's slow action from the stone, and the mill, the dark shadow of industry that lowers over it. As a kid, he was always being told off by his ma for playing on the rock, him and his mates daring each other to walk out onto the slimy surface of it, jump, wings batting the air, across the whitewater where it broke through. *William David Hunter, if ah hear you've been near that river ah'll shoot the boots off ye.* How many times did he hear the story of the MacKay boy who fell in and drowned before anyone could get to him?

He follows Needle Road along, gagging as he hits the rotten egg and rancid milk stench of the tannery, trying to breath through his mouth so the smell isn't quite so bad. He still can't understand how anyone in their right mind could think of turning the Anchor Mill into apartments with this stink on the doorstep. All it'll take is for the wind to be blowing in the wrong direction and, Tamuz Christ, the yuppies'll be boaking on their cornflakes. But on the other side of the tannery as well there's a housing development, one of those red and brown brick mini-estates that looks like it belongs out in the suburbs rather than here, all car parks and tarmac paths and grass verges, flats with tiny windows looking out of tiny rooms. Billy was brought up in one of those estates, but he's lived in an old-style sandstone tenement flat ever since he flew the coop, moved into Kentigern for uni, can't imagine staying in anything as poky as this now. Especially with the reek from the tannery next door.

Cutting through the estate takes a good ten seconds off his journey, so he strides through the car park between the brick blocks, comes out on the road that leads into the Mile Bank Factory. Another red-brick monster, this is the younger sibling of the Anchor Mill, and its all that's left now of T & P Gilmour in the town of their birth. Inside the factory there's a model of how it used to be—the Anchor Mill over here, the Mile Bank Factory over there and the whole area between them with no tannery, no estate, just huge red warehouse buildings, workers' houses, a hostel for the winding women. All of it Gilmour. All of it gone. Back in the day Gilmour didn't just make the thread for magic carpets but the rugs themself; Christ, they were the ones brought the patterns back to Albion in the first place. The town's name is synonymous with the swirls and whirls of multicoloured mystery, of Fergusley Pattern.

The Mile Bank Factory is a later building than the Anchor Mill, more ornate in its brickwork, reminiscent of some strange Titianian idea of a castle, with a patterning like buttressed battlements where the walls meet the roof, a bell tower like a turret high above the entrance. Tall, thin windows like the slits in fortress walls, scaled-up for giants to fire tree-trunk arrows through. A huge, octagonal chimney rises to one side and back, twice the height of the five-storey factory building Even now, you can smell the chemical smoke that used to come spewing from that chimney, even now when it hasn't been active for the last three months at least. Billy darts across the road between the cars turning in through the iron gates of the factory, the last stragglers arriving. The factory bell is clanging out the start of the day shift now, quarter to nine, time to clock in. Billy flicks the hood of his parka down and strolls in through the front doors.

The Boy Who Loved Death

10:30

Fred sits alone in his room in the turret, counting the seconds as they tick on the clock. Forty-one years, he thinks. Forty-one years. They gave him a gold watch last summer, to mark his anniversary, an old-fashioned pocket watch but with this newfangled alarm built in to ting out chimes at preset times. He hasn't had the alarm set for a month though, hardly seemed worth it now.

Forty-one years. He's been working at Gilmour since he was a lad, since he left school at fourteen to take his apprenticeship. Working the warehouse first, lugging great barrels off carts onto trolleys and wheeling them down the long hallways of shelves. Nipping into the dark corners at the back with the other lads for a fly smoke and a game of cards when there wasn't a delivery due. Aye, but they put a stop to that, they did; Health and Safety, dangerous chemicals and open flames; ach, but they didnae think about that in his day.

Then there was—what was it?—ten years on the dyehouse floor, at the weigh station, getting the druglines from the office and searching out the right dyes, spooning out powder of all colours onto bowls on scales small as a jeweller's, or pouring great scoops into buckets, scales that ye could weigh a man on. He always thought he'd be put onto the machines at some point, get to do something that took a bit of skill, like. But instead they made him a foreman—for his timekeeping, because he was always there bang on time. Clockwork Fred, they called him. You could set your watch by him pushing the front door open with a *mornin all*, and a *how's yersels thiday?* And that would be when Old Huntley's bell would go off—*clang, clang, clang*—ringing in the start of the shift.

Breathless arrivals flapping rain off their wings, peeling caps from their heads, unwinding scarfs. *Is Fred in yet?* they'd ask. Not *am I late?*

So they made him foreman and he'd walk around in the background with his clipboard and timesheets, and his job it became all about listening to piss-poor excuses from boys who should know better, and giving out written warnings when he really had to. He was proud of his lads though, for the most part, only had to dock a man's pay— what?—four, five times in all the years he's worked at Gilmour. Well. Ye have to give them a wee bit of leeway when they're coming in the morning after their sister's wedding or their old man's funeral, two hours late and pale-green wi their wings dragging in the dust behind them, running off to the bog to throw up. Or back before the factory closed down over Christmas and ye'd get them all in on the 27th at all sorts of times. Why, there was one year the boss himself didn't show up till half ten and Fred just kept popping down to the door to reset the timeclock for each straggler's arrival. *Right then, get yer coat off and get to work and if anyone asks ye've been here since quarter to, right?* They'd smile weakly. *Aw, Fred, yer a fuckin star.*

It was always on the cards, he supposes, that when Old Huntley retired, well, who is it that takes over the job of bell ringer but Clockwork Fred? His heart trouble had started by then and the boss—well, as he said, it wasnae good for him to be on his feet all day. *Yer looking awfy grey these days, Fred. And really, yer the perfect man for the job. Yer own wee office wi a desk and a windae.*

Aye, there's a part of him that didnae want to go upstairs and leave the lads on the floor. But, of course, by then the lads on the floor weren't the *same* lads on the floor. Big Tam had emigrated, Shuggy, he'd gone off and joined the polis, and now there was a new generation of *lads on the floor*. Boys wi hair like bloody lassies, and carvings on their horns of all things, and feathers all the colours under the sun. They didn't call him Clockwork Fred anymore; they called him Old Fred.

So he'd moved upstairs, as far upstairs as anyone could go.

He watches the clock now, watches the seconds ticking by until its time, and when the seconds hand reaches twelve, he gets up off his chair and ambles up the spiral staircase, through the trapdoor, into the bell room to clang out the start and end of this shift or that. He has a wee look at his golden pocketwatch, set to the exact same time as the clock in his office. It's 10:31 now. Ach, with all his daydreams he's bloody late.

He takes hold of the old iron bell's clanger and rings out morning break for the day shift.

10:40

—So how's things in the warehouse? asks Alice.

—Ach, it's fuckin deid noo, says Tam. Ah tell ye, ye walk roon there and there's no a soul in sight.

—A'right, says Billy as he closes the door behind him.

—Hey up, says Alice.

Tam gives him a nod.

Billy walks across the room and takes his usual seat. They all have their usual seats in the smoking room—Alice in her labcoat at the wee table just beside the door, Tam in his boiler suit in the corner beside her, sitting up on one of the high stools at the counter that runs round three walls. A window set in the wall beside Tam looks out into the canteen, twenty-odd tables and only one of them with folk sat at it. Billy slides up onto a stool at the wall facing Alice's table, where another window looks out onto grass and bushes, an iron fence and a wee shop on the other side of the road outside the factory. A couple of suited greywings from Sales sit at the other wall, talking quietly between themselves in a language of unknown reports and foreign countries. That's what it all comes down to— Albion can't compete with the booming Ashen economy, the cheaper wages of kobold workers.

—So have they told ye where yer going yet? asks Alice.

Billy shakes his head.

—They're talking about moving us into the Kentigern office, but . . . He shrugs.

—Typical fuckin Gilmour, eh? says Tam.

Billy gives a wry smile, brings out his rolling tobacco, papers and lighter, dumps them on the counter. Alice has her pack of Mayfair sitting on the table beside her mug of tea. Tam's Golden Virginia tin sits on the counter. Billy in his suit-jacket, tee-shirt and jeans, smokes Drum Mild, a toker's tobacco, sold in every corner shop in the student-filled, bohemian area of Kentigern where he lives. There's a silence as he rolls up, an unspoken discomfort—on his part, at least—with the knowledge that Alice and Tam are being laid off while he's . . . one of the lucky few. The whole factory is closing down production, even the Technology Centre that services sites around the world is mostly being shipped off abroad. It's only Billy and the Colour Systems team he's part of that are keeping their jobs.

The smoking room is a democratic zone where everyone is equal in their pariah status, but he can't help being aware of certain things. That a degree and a programming job cuts him off from his roots, from the factory town he was born in, and the working class folks he used to be one of. That his horns are carved with the names of punk bands, his wings the iridescent blues and greens of a rebellious teenager. Billy, he's not blue collar or white collar, but no collar at all. He'll go home at the end of the day, maybe do a bit of painting, maybe head up to the Art School, see if he can score some sweeties. No worries about job interviews, or Christmas. It's alright for him. A factory having its plug pulled and all he has to worry about is fucking survivor's guilt and where exactly his new office will be opening in the New Year.

—Aye, that's Gilmour through and through, says Tam. Cannae even get their arses in gear tae tell ye where yer goin.

Us and them, thinks Billy. It's Tam's way, he thinks, of saying yer one of *us*, not one of *them*. He appreciates that.

In a way, it's true. Last Christmas it was his job on the line, with talk of offshoring the development work to contractors in Nagastan—just like the manufacturing is shifting year by year to the vast Sinese 'economic zones' or the ex-Soviet republics of Eastern Elysse. In the end, it was only a change of management that saved him, a new MD with a new attitude, a new plan, another new initiative. In the end, white collar or blue collar or no collar at all, it doesn't really matter; industry—manufacturing or services—it's all moving out East to where the workers and the governments are cheap. That's where all the magic carpets are made these days, so that's where the thread has to be dyed. Alice, Tam or Billy, no-one has a job for life these days.

He's only really got to know them in the last six months or so, as well. Used to just nip outside for his fags rather than go all the way from the Technology Centre to the canteen. It was only since the bosses decided that the whole site, outside as well as in, was No Smoking (cheaper to insure that way) that he's come here, rather than walk even further just to stand outside in the freezing rain at the factory gates. He doesn't have to take his breaks when the bell rings for the factory workers but somehow even when he doesn't hear it ringing as he sits at his PC, coding away and listening to music on his headphones, he still ends up in the smoking room around the same time as the others.

—Did ye hear back from Wilsons? says Tam to Alice.

—No yit. Ah wouldnae think ah'll hear tae after Christmas noo.

—Naw. Ah wouldnae think so.

Billy sparks his lighter, brings it up to the fag now hanging from his lips.

12:15

Fred looks up at the clock on the wall, then at his watch, then at the clock again. The clock says 11:43, but his long service watch and his own internal clockwork tells him that it's lunchtime, quarter past twelve, so he climbs up the staircase, rings the bell with a tired *clang-clang clang-clang*, and climbs back down. He stretches his wings—the left one's giving him a fair bit of gyp these days—then furls them in behind him as he sits back down in his chair. He opens the drawer of his desk, takes out his paper and the tupperware box with his sandwiches inside. He peels the lid off and lays it in the drawer, takes out the apple and the yogurt and sits them at the back of the desk, one to the right, the other to the left. He opens up the foil wrapping on the sandwiches and sits them between the apple and the yogurt, spreads the paper out in front of him. Only once he's scanned the headlines on the front page does he reach out, pick up the first neatly cut, white bread sandwich, and take a bite.

—Is that not yer problem there? says Billy.

He leans in to click a fingernail on a line of code on Dave's monitor, but even before he starts with the explanation, Dave is clenching a fist at the PC.

—Fucking bastard! Duh.

Billy laughs, kicking his chair off on its wheels and swivelling round back to his own desk. He grabs the mouse, sails the pointer across the screen and clicks to bring the Media Player to the front. He's got about five or six windows open already, Visual Studio, Query Analyser, Enterprise Manager, a remote connection by Terminal Services to the server in Odorhei . . . and Firefox, of course. He slips his headphones on, restarts the track and brings up the Firefox window, a Google search on "graey folk". One of the links takes him to an e-text graey story about a man who fell in love with a graey and followed her to the magic land; how after a hundred years, an old man now, he returned to find only a year had passed in his own world, time running faster in the magic land of Grae.

Fred stands at the window, sandwich in hand, looking out across the houses and the tannery and the river. God, how it's all changed in the years that he's been working here.

He remembers the long, hot summer of '76, when the lads on the dyehouse floor, or in the warehouse, or in Finishing—Sales, Orders, almost everyone—they would all come to work in shirts with the sleeves rolled-up, jackets slung over their shoulders, horns poking out from under their flat caps.

And when the bell rang for the end of the shift, with no bulky coats to bind their wings beneath, and so eager to be out in the late afternoon sun, down the park or the pub, they'd all pile out through the front doors but instead of jumping into cars or heading off to the bus stop or whatever, they'd simply run towards the factory fence, not giving a damn about the gates but scattering in every direction, wings unfurling, spreading wide, and flapping, fluttering, like a flock of birds bursting into the sky from some city square. A flock of workers in the air, wheeling and darting together like starlings.

~~~

—What's that?

Billy pulls the headphones off his ears, lets them hang around his neck. Dave is pushing back from his desk.

—It's lunchtime. Didn't you hear the bell? Anybody want anything from the shop?

Billy looks at the clock in the bottom-left corner of the screen; it says 11:47, but then it's been resetting itself from the server every time he reboots, and the server does run slow sometimes. He thought they had that fixed. The clock on the wall says 12:19 but then *that's* running fast. Doesn't really matter; he's not sure if he's hungry right now or not.

He grimaces in a conflict of laziness and indecision. If he says no, then he'll have to go out himself, what with the canteen closed now. But he has no idea what he wants and the shop across the road has such a shit selection.

Ah, bollocks.

02:45

The bell above the fishmonger's shop door tings again as it closes behind Agnes. It's Friday, so it's fish for tea tonight of course; her man Fred's a good Catholic and he wouldnae have it any other way. Sometimes they get special fish suppers from Da Vinci's just round the corner from the house—if she's got the wee yins too look after, like—oh, but they're right spoilt, so they are, but is that no what yer gran and granda are for? Anyway, the weans are staying at their mum's tonight, so it's just her and Fred. But maybe that's for the best; Fred's been awfy quiet these last few days, as his last shift at Gilmour got closer. Quiet and grey, his wings no longer the brilliant blue they were, so bold and dashing when they first met at the dancing all those years ago.

O, how he swept her off her feet, he did, waltzing her up into the air, those wings beating so strong in time with the swing of big band jazz, up and down and round and round till she was giddy. That was proper dancing, not like nowadays when ye go to a do, for a wedding or an anniversary, and the young ones have only gone and hired some DJ to play an awful racket far too loud; the young ones seem to like it, bopping through the air this way and that, but in her day the dances had moves. The hall would be filled with couples swirling through the air in waltzes and foxtrots and what-not, and even though nobody really watched out above or below or around, somehow they never collided, moving as they were in the same patterns of grace.

—Three cod fillets please, Jimmy.

—Two IPA and a lager tops, Dan, cheers.

Dan picks up a glass in either hand and swivels them upright, puts the first one under the tap and the second to one side—on the black plastic tray under the Guinness—heaves the handle of the Deuchars IPA pump down towards him slow and steady.

—Starting early thiday, lads, are yez no?

—Ah, fuck it, says Malkie and leaves his jaw gaping open afterwards, realising.

—Come on there, Malkie, says Dan. There's ladies present.

He nods towards the couple in the corner-booth, both OAP's but dolled up to the nineties like they're off to the dancing. The man smooths the white duck's-arse of his hair down nervously, a widower courting maybe. It was him who put Bobby Darrin on the juke-box. *Somewhere Beyond the Sea.*

—Sorry Dan, says Malkie quickly. Sorry. Ah wisnae thinking.

—Just . . . mind yer language.

A foul mouth is one thing Dan'll no have in *The Wee Hauf*, and they all know that. Malkie should know that by noo. But Dan lets him off with a warning look; the wee man's been right scunnert since he got laid off from Gilmour in the summer, after all. Ye've got tae make allowances.

—There ye go.

The Boy Who Loved Death

—There ye go, Mrs Jones. Is there anything else yer after?

—No thanks. That's all.

She counts out the coins from her purse to pay him, puts the parcel in her shopping trolley and says goodbye. She doesn't have time for a blether, has to get home to put the washing on. And she's some ironing to do before she puts the tea on. Fred'll expect it ready for him when he gets in, five past five on the dot, as always. How Sadie and the others used to pull her leg about the way she'll stand at the kitchen window, cleaning the counter or just footering really, until she hears the end of shift bell off in the distance. Then she knows it's time, ye see, so over she goes to the gas cooker—cause she could never be doin wi those electric ring things, ye can never tell if they're still on—and lights the match, and turns the knob until the fire flares up yellow. Then she'll put the pot of oil on for the chips, turning the knob to get just the right colour and size and quiet roar of yellow-tipped blue flame under it. *Honestly, Agnes,* Sadie would say, *ye keep yer time by the Gilmour clock as much as yer fella.* Agnes would prim her lips. *Well it's better than putting yer man's tea on when the bell rings for last orders*, she'd say.

The truth is, she's no the only one knows just when their husbands, or their sons or daughters, will be home by the sound of a bell that rings out over a town that's woven through with Gilmour thread.

The bell above the fishmonger's shop door tings again as she swings the door open to leave, waving a goodbye.

Malkie takes a Regal from his pack and slides the ashtray towards him over the low, tiled table. The clock behind the bar, being set to pub time, is a little fast, but he reckons Big Tam'll probably be in the smoke room right this very minute, wi his own copy of thiday's Sun open at thiday's page three. Tam's copy sits folded on the table in front of him. What was her name thiday? Melissa or Melanie or Melody, he thinks. Smiling wide but with a hint of a pout to her lips, head tilted, wings as white as a swan's, furled round to wrap her shyly in her feathers, just one nipple showing the way she's half turned away, wingtips meeting to cover her privates in front but still show off the curve of waist becoming hip becoming buttock. A right stunner.

Tam and the rest'll be here at the usual time, of course, still going for the Friday drink straight after work in a way that their old men probably did too, only in those days the kitty would be coming out of brown paper packets instead of wallets with cashline cards in them. It's funny. In the last three months, being here before the others, he's just now noticed the way Dan starts to gather stacks of glasses to clean at just the right time, preparing for their arrival.

04:30

—I'm sorry, Mr Jones, he says. It's time.

He stands there in silence for a second, and Fred says nothing himself. There's nothing more to say really, is there? All the *end of an era* platitudes have been exhausted over the last three months, in the canteen, in the smoke room, in the office, in the warehouse, on the dyehouse floor. All the might-have-been's and the could-have-done's. What's past is past. Time marches on.

Fred nods and his boss, Bob, nods back at him, as if to acknowledge that it's better not to try and put into words what can, in words, only sound trite and inadequate. Oh, there's been many a time that Bob has done just that, in all the meetings where the cutbacks and redundancies were announced, trying to bolster the spirit of the survivors with talk of initiatives and pulling together, metaphors of ship's crews, jokes about the Spirit of the Blitz. Not now. Now he just nods and turns away, closes the door behind him, leaving Fred alone.

The clock on the wall says twenty-five to three now, even further off than before. He bought new batteries for it last week, but never got round to putting them in; it hardly seemed worth it. The second hand ticks sluggishly past twelve and the minute hand jerks forward a distance so small it seems completely inconsequential.

The Boy Who Loved Death

Billy closes down all the abandoned windows on his PC and dances the mouse across the screen with a click here and . . . here . . . to tell it to shut down. He picks up the plastic tumbler of red wine from his desk and drains it, realises he's a wee bit drunk, not having any lunch and all. He's gasping for a fag now as well; that's the thing with drinking in the office. But it's Christmas and this is the nearest thing they're having to a do. It just didn't seem right having a night out under the circumstances, so the boss just brought in a whole load of beer and wine, vodka and gin, and come three o'clock, they all downed tools, so to speak, and headed to the break area for a strange mix of muted conversations and loud laughter.

—Right. Ah'm off.

Billy grabs his parka from the coat-hook and starts doing the rounds, wishing everyone a happy Christmas and a good New Year when it comes.

—Are ye not going to the pub? says Dave.

—Ah cannae, he says. Got to get home for the dog.

Billy gives a wry shrug. He was well up for it as well, but she's overdue her booster shots and this is the last chance he'll get at a vet's appointment for a while, he reckons. It's a right fucker, though.

—Ah'll see yez in the New Year, he says. Somewhere.

—Aye, Dave laughs. If they just fuckin tell us where to go.

Billy brings his wings in, folding them low and tight to his back, and swings his parka round and over—arms in the sleeves—and on. He gives a shake to settle himself snug in the fur lining.

—Right then.

Fred stands teetering unsteady on the chair, wings out to balance him as he takes the clock down from the wall. He bends to hold the back of the chair as he steps carefully down from it. He can just imagine the horror on Agnes's face if she saw him doing this, like when he insisted on papering the living room himself. *Will you get down from there, for the love of God? O, Myrrh, Mother of Tamuz, ye'll kill yerself one of these days, so you will. Ah, shusht, woman. It'll be fine.*

He sits back at his desk, a little out of breath from his adventure, wing sore and chest strained from the stretching. He's not as young as he used to be, that's true.

The second hand still ticks round—he can hear it—as he turns the clock over and finds the black plastic knob for setting it. Fingers on the low, notched disc, he turns the clock face-front and starts to twiddle. The minute hand swings by half-past and quarter to, through the hour and round. The movement of the hour hand is so slow, so slight it's only just perceptible.

The second hand ticks of its own accord. It ticks. It ticks.

He swivels the time through all the minutes between three and four, and on.

The second hand ticks.

He stops to take his watch out of his pocket, laying the clock down on his desk. He's got the watch out and in his grasp before the second hand ticks again. The tick of the clock, the tick of the watch felt in his palm, the beat of his heart, all move at separate rhythms, different speeds. With the watch in his hand, he sets the clock to 4:29, as if . . . as if he just wants to hear it from the clock, for the clock to, one last time, tell him that it's time to ring the bell.

The second hand . . . ticks.

He rubs his chest, wondering if he strained a muscle trying to balance himself with his wings like that.

The second hand sits only two ticks from twelve. It sits there. It ticks.

The watch in his hand keeps a steady rythm, far steadier than his heart, but he ignores them both, only watching the clock.

The second hand sits one tick from twelve.

And Agnes stands at the kitchen window, a cloth wet with water and Dettol in her hand, poised on the counter-top as she looks out, listening for a bell that will never come. And Dan holds a glass upside down over the bristles of the brush in the sink, the bristles that should be turning, churning up water to wash it, but which are frozen in this moment, as caught in this single moment as the water, frozen and yet warm, still and yet churning, as a photograph of bubbling foam. And Malkie holds the cigarette to his lips, head tilted down to read the sports results in the paper open in front of him, smoke from his fag forming an upwards trail of curlicues, a weaving thread of involutions through the more dissipated billows of his breath and a single smoke ring that floats still in the air in front of and above his lowered horns. And Fred sits alone at his desk in his office, smiling sadly at the clock stopped at the wrong time, one hand reached up to his chest, a finger gently probing the so-slight pain in his chest, the other hand closed around the fob watch.

But Billy walks through the factory gates, flicking the hood of his parka up over his head, sort of hooking it on his horns so the December wind won't catch it, blow it down. Huddled into himself from the cold, his wings cramped under the bulk of his coat, he hurries along past cars moving as slow as if the road were black ice, slower, slower. Eyes on the ground in front of him, his mind on other things, he hurries on towards the station and the airtram that will fly him home from Fergusley to Kentigern.

The Tale of the Six Monkeys' Tails

In the Valley of the Rift

Once far ago and long away, in the Valley of the Rift there were six monkeys who each thought himself the best. Each struggled to be better than his brothers, to gather more fruit and nuts, to catch more insects and spiders, to win more attention from the females so that, in the end, they'd have more children as proof that they were best. Each day, in trying to outdo each other, they'd travel far and wide across the land, exploring every inch of it, as far even as the mountains that bounded their territory, each brother seeking to be the first to find whatever tasty prize might be out there, waiting to be found. Each night, when they returned, they'd argue loudly amongst themselves over who had done the best. One brought back fruit and nuts, while another brought back insects and spiders. One brought back fruit and spiders, while another brought back insects and nuts. One brought back nuts and spiders, while another brought back insects and fruit. And each one howled and shrieked and gibbered that he had done by far the best.

The noise of their argument grew louder every night until eventually it became so loud the other animals could not sleep. They clawed at the earth and heaped it over their heads to muffle the intolerable sound. Still they could hear it; they just couldn't escape it. All that they could do was complain: Somebody shut those bloody monkeys up! We cannot sleep!

The complaints of all the animals were carried into the rock by the soil, and it woke the earth god up. He began to grumble: Somebody shut those bloody animals up! I cannot sleep!

The Boy Who Loved Death

The grumbling of the earth god was carried into the ocean by the rivers, and it woke the water goddess up. She began to roar: Somebody shut the bloody earth god up! I cannot sleep!

The roaring of the water goddess was carried into the sky by the waterfalls, and it woke the air god up. He began to moan: Somebody shut the bloody water goddess up! I cannot sleep!

The moaning of the air god was carried up to the stars by the winds, and it woke the fire goddess up. And the fire goddess came down, in the cloak of flickering stars that are her sparks.

—What is going on here? she demanded. Why are you bloody monkeys keeping everyone awake?

The monkeys fell silent for a moment then began to blame each other; quickly, the blame became an argument over who made the most noise, which became an argument over who had the right to make most noise, which became an argument over who was best.

—Enough! cried the fire goddess, flashing with a fury that scorched the fur from each of the six monkeys' bodies, leaving only a little on the top of their heads. It is clear to me that you are each no better than your brothers, and have no basis for your foolish pride. Each day you travel far and wide, as far even as the mountains that bound your territory, in search of whatever tasty prize might be out there, waiting to be found. But each of you is as likely as the other to win that prize. You're all equally rubbish!

The monkeys fell silent again as they all thought about this, then all at the same time, as they all had the same thought, they all began howling and shrieking and gibbering.

—Then make me the best, great fire goddess. Grant me a boon that I may be the best of all! Grant me a boon, great fire goddess! Please! Please!

—Silence! said the fire goddess. If I give one of you a boon, I must give you all a boon. And I must have something in exchange, the most precious thing that you possess—your tails. Give me your tails and I will grant you each one wish.

The six monkeys considered this for a good long time, none of them wanting to give up their tails. But each of them knew that if they did not do so, well, one of their brothers might and, with his wish, become the best. As they all decided that they couldn't let this be, and opened their mouth to make their wish, the fire goddess silenced them with a blast of flames from her open palm.

—Wait, she said. One at a time. And remember that you only have one tail, so you will never gain a wish from me again. You'd best make this wish count, monkeys. You'd best think big.

And she looked at the first monkey,

The First Monkey

The first monkey thought: Each day we travel far and wide, as far even as the mountains that bound our territory. And the words of the fire goddess came back to him: think big. Surely, he thought, if I can travel farther I can find the greater prize beyond that territory. So he said:

—I want to be the greatest, to stride over the mountains in my path, to blow away the clouds around me with my breath.

—Very well then, said the fire goddess.

And she picked him up by the tail and flew off into the air. She took him out of the Valley of the Rift, over the mountains that bounded it, and over a sea to the East. When they were over land again she turned North, and carried on until they were at the Veil of Clouds, where the highest mountain in the world is. There she snipped off his tail so that he fell to the snowy ground. As he lay there she gathered the clouds, and drew from them the water and the air. She blew the air into his body to stretch him, poured water into the hollows of his bones and froze it, did this again and again until he was as tall as a tree and broad in limbs, his skin silvery-white as the moon.

—Now you may stride over the mountains in your path, she said. And now you have the secrets of water and air within you, so the clouds are yours to command. Learn how a butterfly's wing can cause a storm and you will blow them away with your breath. You are no monkey now, but a jötunn, first of the jötnar.

And she flew off into the air, returning to the Valley of the Rift, where she looked at the second monkey.

The Second Monkey

The second monkey thought: To stride over the mountains is to go up and along and down again, three journeys in place of one. And the words of the fire goddess came back to him: think big. Surely, he thought, if I can go straight to the prize no matter what, then I can beat my brother to it. And so he said:

—I want to be the strongest, to smash through the mountains in my path, to bend the rocks around me with my hands.

—Very well then, said the fire goddess.

And she picked him up by the tail and flew off into the air. She took him out of the Valley of the Rift, over the mountains that bounded it, and along a river to the North. When they were out over the sea she turned West, and carried on until they were at the Island of Smoke, where the hottest volcano in the world is. There she snipped off his tail so that he fell to the smouldering stone. As he lay there she gathered the lava, and drew from it the earth and fire. She ripped the bones out of him and set them on fire, made a crucible of the earth and scorched him in it so he shrivelled and shrunk. Then she poured lava in where his bones had been, and let it set, and then filled his veins with fire. When she had finished he was half the size he had been, but a hundred times as strong, his skin blue-gray as ash, granite or iron.

—Now you may smash through the mountains in your path, she said. And now you have the secrets of earth and fire within you, so the rocks are yours to command. Learn how to draw on the power in their veins and you will bend them with your hands. You are no monkey now, but a kobald, first of the kobalds.

And she flew off into the air, returning to the Valley of the Rift, where she looked at the third monkey.

Hal Duncan

The Third Monkey

The third monkey thought: To smash through the mountains is to toil against the rock, work that can only be as slow as wading. And the words of the fire goddess came back to him: think big. Surely, he thought, if I need not toil but am simply free to pass, then I can beat my brothers to the prize. And so he said:

—I want to be the fiercest, to scour all obstacles in my path, to make the world itself shrink from my gaze.

—Very well then, said the fire goddess.

And she picked him up by the tail and flew off into the air. She took him out of the Valley of the Rift, over the mountains that bounded it, and over a jungle to the West. When they reached the coast she turned North, and carried on until they were at the Sands of the Sun, where the most scorched waste in the world is. There she snipped off his tail so that he fell to the desert dunes. As he lay there she gathered the siroc, and drew from it the fire and air. She poured fire in his mouth and fed it with air until it burned away all fat in his flesh, all marrow in his bones. She ripped out his heart and put a flame in its place, so that his breath was scorching hot. She put flames into his eyes so that his gaze was terrible to behold. When she was finished he seemed to float in the air, as if the earth itself feared the touch of his skin, flashing gold as sunlight or flame on sand scorched to glass.

—Now you may scour all obstacles in your path, she said. Now you have the secrets of fire and air within you, so the world is yours to burn. Learn how to unlock the energy in those atoms of matter smaller even than a grain of sand, and it will shrink from your gaze. You are no monkey now, but an afrit, first of the afritim.

And she flew off into the air, returning to the Valley of the Rift, where she looked at the fourth monkey.

The Fourth Monkey

The fourth monkey thought: To make the world shrink from you is to make an enemy, an enemy who may work against you in ways you cannot know. And the words of the fire goddess came back to him: think big. Surely, he thought, if the world is my friend, a longer route may be made much easier, and I can beat my brothers to the prize. And so he said:

—I want to be the fastest, to reach the prize before all others, to find the secret paths of the world.

—Very well then, said the fire goddess.

And she picked him up by the tail and flew off into the air. She took him out of the Valley of the Rift, over the mountains that bounded it, over a strait, a desert and a gulf to the North. When they reached land again she turned East, and carried on until they were at the Tree of Life, where the banyan whose roots run round the world is. There she snipped off his tail so that he fell into its wild branches. As he lay there she gathered leaves and branches, and drew from them the earth and water. She flensed him of his flesh, packed earth around his bones and watered it till vines sprouted and grew in place of muscle and sinew, thinner and tighter as they wove themselves together, until his form was smooth as green wood stripped of its bark, leaking sap that she smoothed into his body like linseed oil. When she was finished he was lithe as a cat, so light he could perch on the weakest branch, and yet so sleek the strongest wind could not get a grip on him, his skin the golden green of an apple.

—Now you may reach the prize before all others, she said. And now you have the secrets of earth and water within you, you may know them as you know yourself. Learn how to sense the streams of life running through you, and you will know all secret paths. You are no monkey now, but an aelver, first of the aelven.

And she flew off into the air, returning to the Valley of the Rift, where she looked at the fifth monkey.

Hal Duncan

The Fifth Monkey

The fifth monkey thought: To reach the prize is not to win it, not if one who arrives late can take it from you. And the words of the fire goddess came back to him: think big. Surely, he thought, if I cannot beat my brothers to the prize, I can still cheat them of it after, take it from them. And so he said:

—I want to be the craftiest, to outwit all opponents, to win all challenges.

—Very well then, said the fire goddess.

And she picked him up by the tail and flew off into the air. She took him out of the Valley of the Rift, over the mountains that bounded it, along a river to the North and out over the sea. When they reached land again she turned West, crossed a sea littered with islands, and swooped down into a forest, down into a cave, down and down, until she came to the deep cavern of the great stalagmite which is the Pillar of Time, its mountainous height built up over eons counted in an echoing drip . . . drip . . . drip . . . drip. There she snipped off his tail so that he fell into the cold darkness. This time she did not separate the elements, for it is the cavern itself that is the mixture, a hollow of air within the earth, a form in space and time defined in the meeting of the two. Instead she gathered the dust of dead eons that filled the cave and the echoes of lives that danced them as motes, the earth and the air already separate. The first she mixed with his blood and, using it as ink, wrote the words of his desires into his heart. The second she mixed with his breath to make a song that whispered the words of his thoughts into his head. When she was finished he stood there, a bald monkey without a tail, his ochre-hued skin patched pink and brown in the flicker of firelight.

—Now you may outwit all opponents, she said. And now you have the secrets of earth and air within you, you have the secrets of all forms in space and time. Learn how to describe the space and time that fits each form and you have the answer that fits each challenge. You are no monkey now, but a human, first of the humans.

And she flew off into the air, returning to the Valley of the Rift, where she looked at the sixth monkey.

The Sixth Monkey

The sixth monkey thought: To win the prize is to win the prize. How can I best my brother who has wished to always win by craft? I cannot take it from him as the great take from the small. I cannot take it from him as the strong take from the weak. I cannot take it from him as the fierce take from the timid. I cannot take it from him as the fast take from the slow. I cannot take it from him as the crafty take from the dim. If ever I take it from him, it will be his prize to win back, and by his craft he will. What else is left for me?

But then he thought: To win the prize is nothing if the prize is but a bauble. And so he said:

—I want to be the most persuasive, to charm my opponents, to convince them what is prized and what is not.

—Very well then, said the fire goddess.

And she picked him up by the tail and flew off into the air. She took him out of the Valley of the Rift, over the mountains that bounded it, to a place that no one knows now how to reach, to the Serpent Isle, which may be in a lake or river, sea or ocean, where the coils of the sleeping dragon that exists beneath all things break the surface of reality. There she snipped off his tail so that he fell, landing on one of its great scales. This time she did not separate the elements but joined them. She squeezed fire from her hands into the six monkeys' tails and threw them down into the water where, when the fire and the water mixed, they were transformed to snakes. The snakes swam up onto the dragon's back, to where the sixth monkey lay. They coiled round him, tighter and tighter, shedding their skin as they did so until their skin was his. They bit him, again and again, pumping their venom into his veins until it filled his blood, the burning fluid, fire and water coursing through his body, filling his head with the delirium of a poisoned man, visions and voices. When they had finished there was no more of them, for they had used themselves up in remaking him. When they had finished he stood there, a bald monkey without a tail, his form patterned in snakeskin, red and green. Before the fire goddess's eyes he shed that skin for one coloured like ochre, then for one like apple, then for one like flame, then for one like granite, then for one like whitest silver. And with each shedding of the skin his form changed too, growing larger or smaller, more squat or more lithe. And with each transformation he spoke quietly, as if practising:

—Trust me. We are the craftiest, are we not? Then this is what we're meant to do.

—Trust me. We are the fastest, are we not? Then this is what we're meant to do.

—Trust me. We are the fiercest, are we not? Then this is what we're meant to do.

—Trust me. We are the strongest, are we not? Then this is what we're meant to do.

—Trust me. We are the greatest, are we not? Then this is what we're meant to do.

The fire goddes waited till he had shed a final time so that his form was once again patterned in snakeskin.

—Now you may charm any opponent, she said. Now you have the secrets of fire and water within you, so all their powers of illusion are yours. Learn how the water twists the light and fools the eye, and you may fool all of your brothers into thinking that the prize is there instead of here. You are no monkey now, but a naga, first of the naga.

And she flew off into the air, returning to her home among the stars.

And To This Day

And that, little one, is how the Six Peoples came to be, from the six monkeys that lost their tails. It is why, to this day, the jötnar live in the mountains and control the skies from their vast airships. It is why the kobalds live in their mine-warren manufactories building trinkets and technologies. It is why the afritim come howling from the deserts, razing any settlements on their domain down to scorched earth. It is why the aelven know the jungles and the forests they live in so well that they can trade their medicines for oil one day and trade that oil for silk halfway across the world the next. It is why the humans, through the steady drip-drip-drip of centuries, of millennia, have slowly built their villages into towns, towns into cities, cities into kingdoms, kingdoms into empires.

And it is why we, little one, the naga, live among them—all of them—quietly making sure, with a suggestion here, a question there, for their own good, that they do all of this exactly as we want them to. It's what my father did before me, and what I did when I was young. It's what your father does right now, and what you, little one, will do when you're grown up. It's what we're meant to do.

The Face of the Divine

On the Banks of the Adji Chay

I found Enoch in a small village in Azerbaijan, on the banks of the Adji Chay river which runs east from Lake Urmia, through a fertile valley walled in by the Savalan and Sahand mountains. The Tigris and the Eupharates rivers rise in that region. The Araxes has its source somewhere to the north, in a region once known as Cush, while to the south the Uizhun flows through the land of Havilah, rich in gold, obsidian, onyx, lapis lazuli and other gemstones.

We sat on a rug in his one room hut, drinking coffee, tar-black but sweet with rosewater.

The Hushed Breath of the World

He took a sip of the dark liquid.

—Once, he began, to the west of this valley lay the meidan of a powerful adonai, a man of fabulous wealth and power that stretched out all across this land. In his domain no-one could hunt or fish, harvest wild grain or gather forest fruit without his word. It was said that in his realm the rain itself would not fall without his permission, that when the morning mist rose, forming dew upon the grass, this was the moisture in the hushed breath of the world as it waited for his command.

Gods of the Rains

—As if the water answers to anyone, he smiled, man or god. All rains fall from the sky and soak into the ground, or flow in rivers, streaming down into a lake, a sea, an ocean. Springs rise from the abzu underneath the land. We dig our wells down into it. Yet we mumble tales of this god of summer rains or that god of the storm, a god for each river, and then gods for all the seas. Surely we should have gods for every shower, every rainfall, every drop of water, every bead of dew . . . or for none.

Stories Are Like Trees

—But no. They say the adonai's word held such command that on his death the shabti shaped from clay to serve him in the netherworld echoed his last word. As they laid it in the grave beside him, it still whispered, so they said, as if his breath still moved in it, his will within the breath.

He smiled wryly, mischievously.

—But stories are like trees, growing into vast canopies from a single seed or from a broken branch that takes root in the right soil. They grow wild and proud, but sometimes, sometimes, they should be pruned back, no?

The Darting Silver of a Fish

—I remember my father walking with me beside Lake Urmia once, pointing to the reflections on the water. The sudden splash of it torn by movement underneath, the darting silver of a fish, a surface rippled by the wind . . . and yet a mirror of this solid world surrounding it. He used to say that we were also mirrors. He would tap the side of his head, and the side of my head, then point down at our images in the water. And as he blew on it, the image rippled.

—*That* is the face of the divine, he would say.

The Garden of My Birth

—The adonai had a walled garden filled with every tree of fruit and flower, every bush and herb of the known world, sight and scents and tastes more exquisite than any artisan of paint, perfume or pot could ever hope to imitate. A freshwater spring rose from deep within the heights of Mount Sahand off to the south, babbling down through the foothills clear and cool, to the edin, the valley floor, to feed the garden of my birth.

—My memory of this is . . . mist though. I had not reached my first year when my family left that place forever.

Signs in Rocks

—My father loved learning with a passion equaled only by his love for my mother, and he used this knowledge in the service of the adonai, keeper of his gardens, managing the meidan with care. This was no simple work of gardening, for within those grounds the adonai had specimens of even the very rarest plants and trees, prized for their aphrodisiac or medicinal, perhaps *magical* properties. My father prized only knowledge.

—He was a curious man, my father, a teacher and a thinker. He looked at rocks and read signs in them that the earth had once been liquid.

The Two Trees

—In the centre of the garden, by the stream, there stood two trees. One bore a fruit that gave wisdom to those who ate it, while the other bore a fruit that gave eternal life itself. So it was said; a lie can hardly be shown-up until it's tested.

—But you must know this story of the adonai's wayward son, the baal, and how he led my mother astray. I imagine you know as much as I; neither my mother nor my father ever talked of the great shame that sent us out from there into the land of Nuadh.

Marks in Red Clay

—I told you that my name is Enoch; that is not quite true. My father had a way of naming things with marks, you see. Each animal, each plant, he made a sign for in the red clay that was such a part of him he is forever known by it; and in these marks he wrote my name in two parts, En and Ki. As I travelled down into the land between the rivers Tigris and Euphrates, where I built a city, a whole civilisation, I taught those who asked me that those marks meant Enki, or Enoki . . . Enoch.

Eyah Asher Ea

—After Eridu in the marshlands of Iraq, I came to be called Ea. *Eyah asher Ea*, I said when they asked: *I am that which is called Ea.* But that is not the name I was given at birth either; I have not answered to the name my father gave me since the day I heard it as a curse.

Not En Ki, but Ki En. My true, my oldest name, is Kien, or *quayin*. It means craftsman in our tongue. It is a name I wear carved on me to this day.

—I understand you usually pronounce it *Cain*.

The Face of the Divine

Later, he was to tell me of the others, of Adad and Rapiu, of Shamash and Irra, and of those who would be known, in Torah and Koran and in the Bible, as the angels of fire and ice, destroyers of cities, Gabriel and Michael. We sat in his hut, drinking coffee and talking until, with the setting of the sun, he lit a fire. I listened to his voice, old and sad, and watched the golden glow of flame that flickered in his eyes, across his weathered, scarred face, branded, marked with its curse, the face of the divine.

The Wolf and the Three Wise Monkeys

Once upon a time, there was a Big Bad Wolf, a cultivated guy, top hat and tails, but a bit of a cad, a cur, a bounder, not a bad sort per se, but of dubious scruples and insatiable appetites, a propensity for exotic narcotics and avante garde Swedish art magazines featuring young male cyclists in sundry stages of undress. He came to me, he did, in the bathroom mirror one day, saying, Where the fuck's my fairy story, scribbler?

Snickety-sharp teeth aglint in his grin, eyes of steel, he was switchblade, poetry, fury. What was I to do?

So I began: Twice upon a time, I said—since we're starting again— there were three wise monkeys. Tom, Dick and Harry; Larry, Curly and Moe, what they were called . . . we dunno. Let's call them See-No, Hear-No and Speak-No, the Brothers Evil, Esquire. A fraternity of swine, they were, unholy trinity of primal primate power-mongering, living lavish on their spoils of class war. They'd left their mother long ago, gone out into the world to make their fortune and fame, make a name to be spoken with awe. They built houses in the forests of Fantasia.

The first wise monkey built his house out of money, a paper-mache palace of five pound notes, no windows, so that everywhere he looked he saw the wonders of his wealth, blue notes layered and lacquered smooth to a mockery of marbling, balustraded balconies, broad steps sweeping down from a mezzanine to a ballroom with a bar fully stocked, bottles of every beverage you might name, and then some. Blood of the indebted. Tears of the bereaved.

Alone in luxury, gaze caged in the grandeur of his greed, he drank.

It was beautiful. While he could still see it.

Enter the Big Bad Wolf.

—Let me in, let me in, he says. Or I'll huff and I'll puff and I'll blow your house down!

—Not by the hair on my chinny chin chin, says the monkey. Or chest and back, whole body really.

Couldn't shave, you see, that monkey, lost his eyes in a game of Texas Hold 'Em.

So the wolf he huffed and puffed, and that house of money caved, came crashing down on the sophisticated simian. The wolf hauled him from the ruins, ripped his throat out, tore open his soft underbelly, feasted on his innards.

Second wise monkey built his house out of bibles, thick leatherbound tomes of scripture inscribed on illuminated calf-skin. Closed and sealed, of course, the books mere building blocks of walls to muffle the sounds of the material world beyond. A vast cathedral of catechisms was mere vestibule to a mansion temple, a monastery tower of myth and morals.

—My father's house has many rooms, he'd say, when visitors questioned the sheer scale of this city of the soul, when he still heard the questions. My father's house has many rooms; I've got to measure up to him, you know.

Big Bad Wolf strides up, proud citizen of Sodom.

—Let me in, let me in, he says. Or I'll huff and I'll puff and I'll blow your house down!

—What? says the monkey.

—Fucking let me in, kiddy-fiddler, says the Big Bad Wolf. Or—

The Boy Who Loved Death

—I can't hear you, says the monkey, eardrums sealed with candlewax to mute all dissent.

So the wolf he huffed and puffed, and that house of bibles fell as Babel, down upon the pious primate. The wolf hauled him from the ruins, ripped his throat out, tore open his soft underbelly, feasted on his innards.

Third wise monkey built his house out of bones, skulls of civilians slaughtered in airstrikes on foreign soil, fibias dug from mass graves of genocide, femurs of cannon-fodder carnage and collateral damage, vertebrae and ribs cemented in human glue, a fortress ossiary.

Squat and circular, the bunker of bone sat as a crypt, ash grey as concrete, filmed with the dust of death, only a few dark slits to let the light in, and a chimney belching black smoke, filling the forest with a stench of rot and roast pork.

Many found it unspeakable. Not least the wise monkey.

Behold, the Big Bad Bhagavad Wolf, devourer of worlds.

—Let me in, let me in, he says. Or I'll huff and I'll puff and I'll blow your house down!

—Aaaa, says the monkey.

—What? says the wolf.

—Aaaa, says the monkey, his tongue hacked out so no tribunal could make him talk of terror and torture.

So the wolf he huffed and puffed, but that house of bones stood solid as a skull, the military monkey secure inside. He huffed and he puffed but that house stood steadfast and silent—monolith, mausoleum, monument.

—Fuck this, said the Big Bad Wolf.

So the Big Bad Wolf climbed onto the roof, to the chimney. Inside, the monkey was shoveling filleted flesh into the furnace, when a stream of piss drenched the flames. And the wolf dropped down into sizzling, smoking embers.

Big Bad hauled that monkey from the ruins of flesh he hid in.

Throat, soft underbelly, innards, you know the score. Found the monkey's tongue, yanno, pickled in a jar on the mantelpiece, wears it round his neck to this day. Everywhere he goes it tells the atrocities it knows, to all who'll listen.

And they all live happily ever after.

What's the moral to this story? Is there a moral to this story? I don't know. I just made it up one day, when the Big Bad Wolf came knocking at my door.

—Let me in, let me in, he said.

—Sure, I said, and there he was in the bathroom mirror, snickety-sharp teeth and eyes of silver. Tongue round his neck.

—Where the fuck's my fairy story, scribbler?

So I gave him one.

—Cool yarn, said the wolf. Little preachy perhaps, but *I* liked it. Now . . . tell me the one about the Wolf and the Seven Little Archangels.

The Drifter Myth

Hey, **help me** out here, mate. You ever seen that show, you know, the one where there's this Chinese monk wandering round the Wild West, just drifting from town to town? He's, like, the stranger that comes into town and changes everything. *Ah, yes, grasshopper.*

That's it. *Kung Fu*, that's the one. Fuck, I haven't seen that show for fucking years. *Kung Fu*. You're a fucking star, mate.

Well, it's weird. See, I heard they were making this movie and the plot I heard, it was in the present day, but it was basically just *Kung Fu*. And I thought that's got to be an archetype, right? The Drifter Myth.

Yeah. Drifter Myth.

Well, it's like you've got this guy that wanders into town and . . . you know, like in that Western where Clint Eastwood rides into town and fucks the local whore and kills everything in sight.

High Plains Drifter. Abso-fucking-lutely.

Couldn't agree more. Fucking brilliant movie.

Well, see, it's the same idea underneath, I'd say. And it's all over the place. I mean, how many books or stories, how many movies or tv shows have you seen with that plot? It's an archetype.

Cliche smiche. Bollocks, mate. It's a fucking *myth* is what it is.

Well, he's the Drifter, right. He just drifts along, following the Tao and righting wrongs, doing his *Highway to Heaven* shit or painting the town red depending on his mood. But the thing you've got to know is, you never mess with the Drifter because he always wins. I mean, why is that? That's what I was thinking, you see. Why is that? And you know why it is? You know why it is?

It's because he's the fucking Devil, man. Or maybe he's God.

Like, in disguise, you know, incognito. That's, like, a town in New Mexico, is what it sounds like, eh? Where's God? He's in Cognito, mate. Is that Cognito, New Mexico or Cognito, Arizona? Is -

Ah, fuck 'em. Fucking redneck bible-bashers, eh?

Anyway, yeah, so the Drifter is the stranger, right? The Man With No Name. Nobody knows him. You could be sitting at a bar beside him and you wouldn't even know it. He could be me or you. You could be sitting at a bar with me and I wouldn't even know it. Wait, no, that's not right.

Huh? Well, he's not gonna look like Clint. I mean—I don't mean he's *literally* the Man With No Name, from the movies, like, just . . .

Oh, right. I get it.

Whatever. My point is, you should know, if you're the local big-shot, never fuck with the Drifter, right? But they always do, and it's always bad news.

Because the Drifter always fucking wins, mate. Always. And the thing is, when you think about it, when you think about it, every culture has the Drifter Myth. Like Dionysus, the Greek god. Sex and drugs and rock and roll, mate.

Bingo! That's what the Romans called him. Bacchus. Anyway, there's this story about Dionyus right, how he comes to this one town and sends all the woman crazy. So the king he gets real pissed and he tries to trap Dionysus, and Dionysus, well, he gets these crazy women to kill the king. See, he's really come to free the town. He has to drive it fucking crazy first but he's really here to save it. But think about it this way. If you're a tyrant, the moral of the story is pretty fucking simple.

Exactly. Don't fuck with the drifter. But there's all these other mythologies with drifter gods. Sometimes it's the main man, the big cheese, sometimes it's just some little god who likes humanity the most; anyway, he's the one who wanders around and sorts them out, righting wrongs but usually bringing a whole shitload of chaos as part of the deal. Odin does it in Norse mythology. He's like one of those medaeval kings disguised as a commoner so he can sneak about and see what things are really like in the kingdom, right, see what middle management are up to behind his back?

Exactly. It's like *The Quick And The Dead*.

Gnostic parable, mate.

No, really.

OK. You've got Gene Hackman ruling this town. He's the big boss, like the cattle baron in all the old school movies. He's the crooked judge. He rules the fucking place, thinks he's the fucking law. He has his right hand man who's turned against him, the devil. And his own son, who he kills. He's the Gnostic demiurge, man; he's fucking God. But Sharon Stone, see, she represents the higher power, the higher law, Sophia. Because she's got the marshall's badge.

Gnostic.

Well, see, the Gnostics thought this world was an illusion ruled over by an evil tyrant god, like the king in that Greek play. Basically they reckoned the god that you and I think of as God was a complete cunt, a total fucking -

Oh. Right. I do that sometimes. I'll try and keep my voice down.

OK, so one day, according to the Gnostics, the real god is going to return. He has to come as a stranger so nobody will recognise him, like Ulysses when he returns to Ithaca; he has to disguise himself as a beggar so he can get inside the palace. So he looks like a tramp. I suppose he's a bit of a trickster god, like Coyote, because if you're a god wandering about as a man you've got to be the god of disguise, right?

Both. There's no difference. That's the Drifter Myth at its ultimate. He's not just come to clean up the town or reclaim his kingdom. He's come to clean up reality itself. He's going to kick the fake god out of Heaven, and burn down Hell if he has to, whip the bad guys out of town. He's just waiting for the showdown. But he doesn't look like anything much because he's in disguise. In fact, he looks like a worthless scumbag, a nobody, a drifter.

The point is the Drifter Myth is everywhere. It's all over the fucking place. Every religion has its version.

Hindus? Fucking Krishna, mate. Dangerous little bastard, Krishna.

Buddhism? Who do you think? Then you've got Jesus throwing the moneylenders out of the temple, and—well, they're just all over the fucking place, these drifters, drifting all over the place.

But, I was thinking, see, where do all these stories come from? Why do all these different cultures have the same story? And I started thinking about Homer.

Donuts? Oh, right. I get it. Homer. That's funny, mate. That's funny. But you know I mean the poet, right?

OK. Well, there's all this mythology surrounding the historical guy, right, like he's a blind poet, he could never write, he just wandered around from town to town, telling the *Iliad* or the *Odyssey* in the marketplace. Another fucking drifter.

Sure. I know it's bullshit.

Oh, yeah, I know that. You can analyse the text and show how this part was written in this period, how this other part was written centuries later. Believe me, I know that. But. But, I say, suppose there *was* a Homer.

But suppose *that's* bullshit. Suppose it wasn't a whole load of different guys, just one guy who lived for a *really* long time. *Ah.* Never thought of that one, did they? And suppose that's where all those stories come from, all those stories where the guy wanders into town and does his stuff and then wanders out again. Maybe that's just the Drfter God wandering about our world, sitting in a bar in this town or that and waiting for the big finale. Maybe he just wanders from place to place telling his own story in one form or another, making it up like Homer, telling stories about all the things he's seen, but changing them a little bit with each telling because he has to, to suit each particular audience. And that's where all the Drifter Myths come from.

Yeah, but he's like Odin, you see. It's all riddles, all secret meanings. Only somewhere in these stories he drops in his own Drifter Myth just to spread a little truth. He just wanders about spreading the word that one day the tyrant is going to be overthrown.

Well, I guess it's Satan, if you look at it from a Gnostic viewpoint, wandering about the world, keeping his head down but undermining the Powers That Be whenever he can. Lucifer . . . spreading the light. Hallelujah fucking Lucifer.

I couldn't give a fuck if they're staring. Buncha godbothering shit-kickers *can suck my cock.*

Why, yeah, same again, cheers. Heh.

I don't know how far back. I'm trying to think if there's a Sumerian—

Ah . . . but, of course, you don't *have* to be convinced. You just have to hear the story and pass it on. That way it spreads, because the story *is* the Drifter.

Because gods are just root metaphors, right. You heard of memes?

Well, yeah, but the basic idea is just a metaphor for root metaphors, like, 'Time is Money', for instance. The basic idea spreads all through our language: you spend time; you waste time; time is precious. That's a root metaphor. And . . . but the point is, gods are symbols, archetypes, metaphors. They don't actually exist, but the idea of them is there in a story or a statue. So if you spread the story you spread the god.

Cheers.

Think about it. Right, you're a metaphor, an idea. If someone uses an idea all the time, you could say that it's alive. Not literally, but metaphorically. But if the idea stops being used, it's dead. If it gets passed on to someone else, that's like reproduction. You know the Gnostics talked about the Logos, like, the Word of God, as being a sort of living information. And Jesus is the embodiment of it.

But that's exactly my point. The story about the Drifter carries the idea of the Drifter, and the story *drifts*, so it carries this idea into every town it pops up in. It's like, all this argument over whether Christ was a historical person or not; it doesn't matter, because his story is the Drifter story, the stranger who wanders into town and sorts it out. And how is it passed on?

Fuck Sunday School, mate. That's fucking bullshit. No. I mean how was it passed on originally. Originally, it was just these wandering apostles, walking about, from one town to the next, and telling people about this guy they once knew. And what happens? We end up with Drifter stories about them, showing up in town, getting persecuted . . .

Well sure. But if the Drifter is the story itself, it *did* win. They spread the idea.

Well, mythologically speaking, The Devil and Jesus are basically the same. I mean, Jesus is a pretty transparent version of Dionysius, dead and resurrected, blood for wine, persecuted by the authorities. He's the lamb, the sacrificial animal, same way as Dionysius is the goat . . . the scapegoat.

Ah, fuck 'em. What are they going to do?

Anyway, Jesus is Dionysius, right, and Dionysius is the Devil, right—horns and hooves, and all that—so Jesus is the Devil. Light of the World, Bringer of Light—*Lucifer*. It's fucking obvious, mate. It's—

What? Mate, we're having a private conversation here. Do you mind?

Well, hey . . . *forgive me*. We're allowed to talk, right?

Well, this beer in my hand and this money on the fucking counter says otherwise, ya wank. What is this? The fucking Inquisition?

Nah, it's alright. I can handle myself against these inbred -

Ugh. Uh, what the fuck . . . shit . . . what the . . . shit, my fucking head. What happened?

Really? How long was I out?

Fuck me.

No, I'm fine. I'll be—fucking hell! What the fuck happened here?

No shit? Sorry about that. I can be a bit of a mouthy cunt when I get a drink in me. Thanks for . . . well . . .

No really, I owe you, mate . . . Lemme get you a drink . . . uh . . . ?

Fuck, I don't even know your name.

The Liberating of the Devil Boy

1

Now, you've all heard the fabble of Orphan, ain't yer? How's the Stamp were made in the days of yore, to Fix Orphan as the first ever Scruffian, so's he could go to Hell and back, rescue a princess from Death himself, without being washed away to a scrap of a shade. And you've heard the fabble of Scallywag Jack, the poor widow's son of Chapel Penniless, how's he rumbled them knights as begun the Institute, as started putting the Stamp on waifs took from Jews and Gypsies, for their Kiddies' Crusade, to send them imperishable infants against the Muslims.

You've heard all them fabbles of the ancient days, eh? Of how it were back in my day even, when's the Waiftaker General stalked the streets, and weren't none of the poor folks safe from having tykes scrobbled for the Institute, Stamped and sold for sweep's boys and millworkers; and how's the tinkers taught us to tweak our Stamps, tweak *how* we was Fixed, so's them what escaped could grow steel in their hearts and spikes on their knuckles; how's we lived wild in London's rookeries, fighting stickmen and scrufftraders, raiding and liberating, but ever in fear of a Scrubbing.

You've even heard the most important fabble of em all, ain't yer, the fabble of how's we stole the Stamp, and brung that bleeding Institute down round their ears, and did for the very Waiftaker General himself, lopped off his legs and bit off his bollocks, slit his throat and Stamped the fucker in his last gasp of breath, dumped him in chains in the shit of the Thames, where's he lies to this very day, Cock fuck his rotten soul—which is why we always spits in the water when we crosses Westminster Bridge, innit? You've heard all that.

Well, this here fabble is of the ancient days too, of the long-ago yonks-back misty days of yore what hardly no scamp or scrag would mind, what hardly a scallywag or scofflaw might *just* about recall if he *really* puts his noggin to the task and crunkles his brow to such a scowly frown of straining as he looks like Joey Picaroni there in his habitual sulk.

Why, like as not, ain't *none* of yer will recollect this fabble's twisty turns, on account of em happening in the far off forever ago of what we calls last Tuesday.

2

It were a dark night in the backstreet bivouacs as Joey Picaroni slunk through the shadows, streetlit and busy round Waterloo, but hushed where he were, in the little snick of Mepham Street tucked away twixt the station and the iMax, all bricked-up railway arches this side and that, all steel-shuttered loading bays, backdoors and wheelie-bins. He slunk past a poxy pub for the groanhuffs—filling an arch like the underpass beside it, beneath the railway lines what comes in off Hungerford Bridge—but that were shut now, in the hours before dawn, so all were still.

There was little brick hutchamacallits nooked to wall the corners of that underpass, little boxy buildings like some public loo Puckerscruff would cottage, or some suburban nob's backyard extension, scarce a scallywag's standing room between their flat roofs and the bridge above, and it were one of them roofs Joey scrambled up to, by way of a window ledge and door lintel, up onto a space as weren't much more'n three paces to the edge for a beansprout like him and an half a dozen in to where's the archway proper begun. A sneaky little snug it were. A hidey.

Weren't no broke glass cemented round the edges neither, nor wall spikes and barbed wire nor nothing—which is a bleeding miracle in this day and age when they's putting spikes on the ground in anything even half like a doorway what someone might doss in, Cock forbid. So it were a perfect spot for a scofflaw to kip, snuggled safe in their corner, among the scatter of Coke cans, newspapers, Tesco bags and such. A bona fide backstreet bivouac, it were, as are getting few and far between these days, with yer CCTV and the filth moving *undesireables* on.

Ain't all scofflaws as sociable as Moany Picaroni there, see? Moody cunts, Fixed as close to groanhuff as yer gets without being an actual Rake—and Rakes is generally twice as Scruffian, if yer asks me—they's all *Quit it!* and *Sod off!* and *Don't play frisbee with my vinyl!* and whatnot, so some of em fancies to fuck off from their cribs now and then, spend a night or two sleeping rough, like they did as strays, before they took the Stamp, somewheres quiet and peaceful. Safe. Except the backstreet bivouacs ain't safe these days. Them scofflaws been disappearing.

3

That were what Joey was about, yer see. Them scofflaws been Going Offsky, only they don't come back, and don't none of us know where they went. Not even Earwigger—and yer knows what they say: ain't a fart in the night in a bishop's cold bed, but if Earwigger ain't heard of it, it didn't never happen. Back in the old days, he had his bootblacks all over London, eyes and ears everywheres; and now we's in the Information Age . . . well, yer groanhuff surveillance state's our Earwigger's interweb blanket fort, nuff said. But even *he* don't what's going on.

Even a few *cribs* gone empty, so I hear. Back in my day, that weren't nuffink strange—cribs raided by the stickmen, scruffs took to be Scrubbed, and any scofflaw as went walkabout—or kipabout, really—they was tempting fate. Bonkers, they was, cause it's bully being Fixed so's yer always bounces back to *how* ye was Fixed, and it's fine and dandy to tweak yer Stamp—snip off the part of yer as was Fixed in mortal terror, say—but if they caught a Scruffian, it was a Scrubbing for yer, Stamp wiped like chalk off a slate. Oblivionated!

But them days are gone now. Shouldn't none of this be happening, not with the Institute brung down more'n a hundred years past, and the Waiftaker General at the bottom of the Thames. Them scofflaws shouldn't be vanishing. So Foxtrot, being the boss and all, he'd sent Joey out investigatering that night, sent him out for a nosey round the nooks and crannies where Katzenjammer Alleytat says she clocked some scruff or other huddling down to doss for the night, only they wasn't there come morning. Out playing snoop was Joey, and he weren't too chuffed about what he'd found.

That hidey were near empty, see, but not empty enough, cause there were a ratty old sleeping bag right back in the corner, but it weren't stretched for kip with a Scruffian snug inside, and it weren't even rolled to a sly stash for later. No, it were crunkled as a scallywag's blankie on an hot summer night—a scallywag with night terrors, moshpit dreams, or a pathological fear of the rat what just crawled over their tootsies. It were veritably *strewn*, that sleeping bag, and Joey Picaroni weren't in no doubt of the signs.

That scofflaw had been scrobbled.

The Boy Who Loved Death

4

At the sudden unmistakeable *clatterattle* of a can kicked in the street below, all echoey in the quiet hours, yer might expect Joey to be whirling where he hunkered over the scene of the crime, shiv out and peepers peeled. But, no. All's he done were *roll* his peepers, and then call back over his shoulder:

—Come out, for fuck's sake.

There was mumblings and whispers then, a muffle of flappy slappings and a *Shoosh!*

—I know yer there, says Joey.

And he walks to the outer edge of the roof to pop his head out, gander down the street.

—I can *see* you, says he. You can't hide for toffee, and when it comes to playing *Stalk the Nob*, you pair make Flashjack look fucking subtle. Just come out.

And down the street, where's he were gazing, there stood one of em chalkboard pub signs, chained to the wall by its legs so's it wouldn't walk offsky. And over the top of it now, a scrag's moppety bonce slowly rose to peep, like as that sign ought to read *Kilroy was here*. And behind, a scallywag's floppy-fluffed noggin rose too, to peek through the curls on that bonce.

Out they comes now, looking right sheepish. And why, if ain't our two freshest cribmates, the scrag with the cherub curls as makes him look all innocent-like—but in inversified proportions to the aktcherality—that scrag being none other than our very own Slickspit Hamshankery, and the scallywag at his back, natch, him of the emo bed hair what can't decide if it's hiding his eyes or reaching for the moon, him being none other than the very Quippersnap Rannigant what's sat right there cuddling his boyf even now. Yeah, Slick and Quip it were, our latest recruits.

Yeah, Slick, you's in this fabble. Ain't that what I just said?

Well, that's cause yer new, doofus. So yer bouncing back to how yer was Fixed, which is like to include yer memories untils you tweak yer Stamp to add a bit of RAM to the ROM, savvy—and we learns yer how to use it, like. Assuming the learning takes, that is. Foxtrot or Squirlet, they can mind back *centuries*, but most—

Me? Well, I carves the fabbles into me own Stamp. See? Lookit on me chest here. Yeah, that squiggle over me left nipple is Orphan, and . . .

5

Look, never mind. D'yer wants this fabble or not?

Well, shusht then. At this rate we won't get to the Myriad Carnival till *next* Tuesday.

Yeah, it should sound blooming familiar, Quip. You and Slick was the ones as went to snoop it out, on account of what yer found in that muss of bedding where the scofflaw'd been scrobbled, on account of when yer gave Slick a punty up, and scrambled after him, as the three of yer stood frowning at the ominous emptiness, why, what was it caught Slick's eye betwixt the porno mag and the poly bag . . . ?

—What's this? says Slick.

—It's called paper, says Quip. It was big in the 20th century, I hear.

—Smartarse, says Slick and flips him the finger as he grabs the paper and flapples it flat. It's a flier.

And that it is, scruffs. It's a flier what's fit to bursting with boasts, with big block titles and ickle elucidations, proclamations and promises of the *STUPENDOUS*, the *MAGNIFICENT*, the

SPLENDIFICENT and *MIRACULOUS*. A myriad wonders of a myriad extremities of the exotic, it trumpets in a style belonging more to Ripper Vicky's day than this.

—A fucking *circus* flier, growls Joey.

Now, Slick and Quip, they've heard the fabble of the taking of the Stamp, natch, on the night they took the Stamp themselves, become Scruffians by choice, so they knows how Joey run away from the circus to help the heroes, the first Scruffian to be Fixed of his own free will, no less. So they knows he ain't exactly objective when it comes to circuses.

No, yer ain't, Joey. Circus folks is—

See, now that's exactly what I means. Just cause yer *uncle* was a cunt—

OK, I'll give yer that. All *clowns* is evil, but—

. . .

Are yer done?

OK, then. So, Slick and Quip, they ain't *entirely* persuaded by Joey Picaroni's rant on how this Myriad Carnival is like as not behind it all, a nefarious conspiracy of a wicked summat coming thissaway, scrobbling scruffs to turn them hellion against their own will, hack at their Stamp till they has flippers for limbs, other freak show fuckeries; but they has to admit, that flier ain't quite right in this era. It looks awful antiquated, they agrees.

—Could just be a steampunk thing, says Quip.

—Could just be a fucking circus fucking front for fucking scrufftrading thing, snarls Joey.

6

—It's not, says Foxtrot—laters, once Joey's brung the flier back to the crib, Slick and Quip scurrying at his heels, now the boss and his council is gathered in his attic hidey: Foxtrot, Bananastasia, Squirlet; Flashjack and Joey; Earwigger; ickle Vermintrude playing with a dead rat in the corner. It's not, says Foxy, inconceivable.

—I'd know if the Trade was back, says Squirlet.

The scamp gives his monocle a polish, strokes his pencilled moustache as he muses.

—Earwigger, this Myriad Carnival . . . have you—?

—Dextricks Kitsclaw! cries out Flashjack all of a sudden.

—Pardon? says Foxtrot.

—Dextricks Kitsclaw, says Flashjack.

He were a scallywag what chummed around with Flashjack, see, *way* back in the day. Back when Georgie Porgie Brownprick Loonyburk was on the throne, like, and the Sodomites' Walk still run through marshy Moorfields. It were just before Puckerscruff come along, says Flashjack; him and Dextricks would go rough trading together round the molly markets, thruppence for a thump to any Mr Punch as had to thwack a pretty lad to get his pintle hard. Except one night Dextricks just Gone Offsky, never seen again, but Flashjack swears blind, that night . . . there was . . . this funfair on the Upper Fields.

—The Myriad Carnival? says Foxtrot. You're sure that was the name?

—Absofuckinglutely, says Flashjack.

—Really? says Squirlet. *You're* sure that was the name?

She don't sound too convinced. If there's one thing our hellion with his Stamp hacked to fuck *ain't* renowned for, to be fair, it's minding anything what happened much more'n a minute ago. But Flashjack's right insistent on this point. He minds, cause they sprung a whole load of scruffs from the Waiftaker General next day, and Dextricks shoulda been among em if the stickmen got him, but he weren't.

—Foxtrot, says he, you mind it, right?

Foxy scrunches his freckly nose. He ain't forgot nuffink, not for as long as he's had his cock and balls—which were the first tweak Nuffinmuch O'Anyfink ever made with his tinker savvy, they says, back when them two was just liberated by Scallywag Jack. So he thinks hard, rootling around in what he calls his memory rookery, and after a while he nods.

—Kitsclaw . . . indeed, says he. Hellion with talons for fingernails; Turnmill Street crib; disappeared . . . 1714? Presumed Scrubbed.

—That's him, says Flashjack.

—There *were* a few coronation fairs around then. And riots.

—The riots were sick! says Flashjack.

7

So that's how's Slick and Quip found themselves called into the meeting, briefed, tasked, oathed on their eyeballs, and toddling offsky the next morn, bright and breezy, for Battersea Park, where's this Myriad Carnival was advertising its *ASTOUNDIFYING AMUSEMENTS*. Them being fresh-Fixed and all, see, Foxy figgered they'd fit in as normal kiddies easy peasy, whereas yer hellion, well, they might needs to wear shades, having tweaked their Stamps to give themselves cat eyes, say; or yer urchin's spikes might give her away; or maybe like Flashjack they're still dressing like it's 1976 and they're sucking Johnny Rotten's cock.

Off the tube at Vauxhall they pops, and down by the power station and cats' and dogs' home, strolling in through the Rosary Gate on a day so sunny as Quip had to drag Slick past the pedolas on the boating pond, him saying, *Aww, just for a little bit? No?*

Soon enough, they're into the gather of groanhuffs and brats streaming in under a banner as announces this *MYRIAD CARNIVAL* in letters as is appropiately circusy . . . 'cept for the flourishes making em look like bones, reckons Slick.

—Only a bit spikier, says Quip.

—More *hooks* than spikes, says Slick.

Weren't long before it struck our snoops how this funfair seemed . . . a little queer—and not in the way what Slick and Quip is neither. There was dodgems and waltzers, an octopus and whatnot. There was hoopla and air rifles, coconut shys with cuddly toy prizes. Candy floss for sale and hot dogs, of course. But back of the Big Top, coming off the midway, why, bugger me if the steam train tootling of a calliope don't beguile em in, past a coin-operated jigging mechanical sailorboy in a glass case, to an whole warren of stranger booths and tents.

Stages and stalls held Psychics now, a Strong Man, a Mesmerist, an Illustrated Lady and a Burlesque Revue, a Wild West Sharpshooter, one poster says, as fought the cavalry at Little Bighorn!

—Not *in* the cavalry? says Slick.

—*That's* what you focus on? says Quip. Not the Little Bighorn bit?

There's a bona fide freak show, a bird-biting geek show—like Slick and Quip ain't sure's even *legal* now. Why if it weren't that Joey would've knowed the name, they might've thunk this the very carnival he run away from to take the Stamp, escaped from history into today.

8

—There's steampunk, says Quip, and then there's pickled punk.

—Is that fun house playing *Fun House*? says Slick.

And it were indeed. A few steps down from the *ANATOMICAL ANOMALIES*, brats was scrambling a two-storey obstacle course of see-saw floors and jiggly stairs, a barrel of love and a ball pit; and all's the while some fairground organ in its heart played a creepy instrumental cover of The Stooges' "Dirt." A midget in a red suit danced at the entrance. Red velvet curtains. A zigzag floor.

—This is, says Slick, a bit fucked up.

—You think? says Quip.

—Ten-in-One and one for ten, says the barker at the flap of the Little Big Top. One token for entry, ten acts for one token.

—How much are the tokens? says Slick.

Candy-striped waistcoat, dicky bow and boater, that barker would look right bloody Barnum if it weren't for the waxy greasepaint and the little lines down from the points of his grin as makes him look more like a ventriloquist's dummy than the glass-eyed tyke in a tux lolled on a chair beside him.

—Your call, he says. We take appreciation, affection or outright love.

—No fair, mutters Slick as they takes their seats. Twenty fucking quid I offer him, but *no*, all *he'll* take is the fucking wallet. My Ben 10 wallet. That I've had since I was, like, *eight.* It was a present too!

—That *was* the idea, says Quip. Token of . . .

Slick's glower shuts him up.

—And what does he take from *you*? A fucking playlist from your iPod!

—Your mixtape. It's the sentimental value, poutyface. Just means—

—He didn't even delete it, just took a fucking copy!

—Ssshhh. The show's starting.

And with Slick still muttering of *fucking liberties,* the spectacle begins.

A woman what eats razor blades; a man what breathes fire; a pinhead ballerina light and dainty as a hummingbird; a captive savage from Old Etonia—a terror in a tailcoat, ranting rabid in his cage; an human pin-cushion; an horsey what does sums; a flea circus; a dwarf and giant magic act; a two-headed man as sings "Je t'aime" to himself; and finally, to top it all, the barker as was interducing em presents the ultimate exotica, he says, a sight right out of Hell itself . . .

—The diabolical, he says, the demoniacal, dreaded Devil Boy of Dis!

9

And the lights go red now in the Little Big Top, what's hardly big enough for a few dozen punters in a horsheshoe round the sawdust floor. There's a pause, a hush, as curtains part, and all peers into the black beyond. Then *RARRR!* out from the shadows comes a flash of fiend, a 'splosion of scarlet, crimson, teeth and talons, like some zombie chimp frothing to chomp off yer mush, so Slick near shits himself, and shrieks, he does, whiles Quip jumps back so hard he near falls off his seat. Half the bleeding audience has heart attacks almost.

RARRR! it comes out snarling, slavering, pouncing fierce, and why, our scruffs being sat bang in the front row's centre, they feels its very spittley breath, as it slams to an halt just a nipper's pinky from Slick's nose. Slams to an halt, it does, not an inch too soon, and is yanked back hard, as the chained beast it is. For its handler's out now after it, they sees, a mound of moustacheoed muscle in a leather vest, its iron leash clamped in his fist, wrapped round his forearm and his waist. And back he heaves it—*Back! Back!*

Oh, the sight of it now! The sight of this *thing* what's hauled back to the sawdust, and whirls on its handler, hunkered, howling.

A Devil Boy it is indeed, with horns and hooves, batwings and claws, and red as blood every inch of it, naked as the day it were born, or hatched, or fuck knows what, thinks Slick, maybe spat from the gob of Satan himself. And it *flaps* its leathery wings, it does. This ain't no bleeding Comic-Con cosplay. Ain't no Hollywood hokum with CGI shite.

—Oh my fucking God, says Slick.

—Wrong alignment, says Quip.

The Devil Boy and handler prowls around each other, the handler raising a crucifix in his left hand, so's the creature spits and hisses, cowers back. A gangle-limbed gargoyle, it moves on all fours like Gollum playing Spider-man.

A devil? Neither of em Scruffians wants to believe it, cause Heaven and Hell's a big pile of bollocks, innit? But they *has* only recently been interduced to the implausible factuality of a bleeding great magical doodad what can read and write yer soul into yer skin, as operated by a secret society of unaging, indestructible ragamuffins. So there's that.

10

It's all a bit Exorcist though, thinks Quip, what with the *Power of God compels thee!* malarky the handler's chanting, and the Devil Boy ranting back in tongues, rising up to pull back in a yowl, spread its wings wide as they wheel around each other. Its head turns to the crowd, eyes wild, like half of it's hoping for a rescuer even as tother half's hungry for a soul to rip apart. A flick of an arm whiplashes down the chain to its collar, brings its fury whirling back round at its tormentor.

—The Power of Christ compels thee!

But all of a sudden, that Devil Boy don't seem quite so compelled, as it lunges forward, leaps right at the handler to catclaw his hand, tear the crucifix right from it, kick off backward from his chest into the air. The handler he tumbles back, only just keeps hold of the leash as the fiend soars into the air and round, a circuit round the tent, swooping over the audience's heads, shrieking down at em louder than they screams themselves, all ducking down in terror, panic erupting for an horrible moment till the handler has things back in hand.

SMASH! he brings it down to the ground like the bleeding Hulk playing cowboy with a steel lasso and an aeroplane. Wrenches it down to bite the sawdust with a force so hard the whole crowd gasps. Why, didn't they hear the crack of its neck snapping? But the Devil Boy only rises to its feet, and cricks that neck back into place.

And now they sees: it holds its prize, that crucifix, upside-down, like a dagger—or a banana, more like, as Devil Boy slips his gob over it, swallers it to the crosspiece with a wicked leer.

Yeah, that's right, scrags. The Devil Boy, he gives that sacramental stick-symbol a fluting what ain't even suggestive so much as outright exhortative. Or exertative maybes, cause he puts his heart into it. It's only once he's done making a right cock-lolly of it, does he drop it to the sawdust between his hooves, take a hold of his tadger to aim, and tinkle out an ickle stream of piss on it.

As yer might imagine, there's a fair whack of the audience jostling their way to the exit by now, but Slick and Quip?

Not so much.

11

But if Slick is kinda thinking how the beast's bod could conceivably, *arguably* be cast as *slinky* as much as *gangly*, how it ain't so far off scallywag Quip's fine sleek physique, and Quip is shifting himself a tad discombobulatedly on his seat in admiration of the Devil Boy's evident expertise in them fellatial faculties . . . if they both has a little moment as leads to a brief back-and-forth of furtive side-eyes, reddish cheeks and innocent *ahem*'s, they don't gets time to follow their fanciful notions far down that road, for the handler he brings out a whip.

The Boy Who Loved Death

No sooner is the Devil Boy snarling his defiance over a pissed-on crucifix, see, than the handler's turning to less devotional means of discipline. In a tick, he's spun to switch what hand he holds the chain in. In a tock, he's snatched a whip from his belt and flicked it out to full-length. In a trice, he's brung that whip around in a whirl overhead and *crack!* lashing full force across the Devil Boy's face. The whole crowd flinches in shock, none more so than Slick, and then it's *crack!* and *crack!* again.

—Jesus fuck! says Quip.

The show takes a nasty turn from then on in. The whip cracks this side, that side, and the Devil Boy cringes. Yer liturgicals might not cow him, but the lash sure does.

—See the Devil Boy dance! his handler crows.

And dance he does—and somersaults, tumbles, trick after trick. Roll over! Play dead! On yer knees and beg! By the end, the Devil Boy's tamed to lick a boot, flinch from even a backhand raised in threat. By the end, Slick is flinching with him, hand shaking as it crushes Quip's. Brings back bad memories, savvy? Real bad.

—Hang on a fucking minute, whispers Quip. Check out his chest.

And sure enough, as Slick snaps out of a dark place, bumshuffles forward in his seat to peer, he clocks that the scarlet of the skin is guising summat as is quite familiar to em now. Tain't so noticeable when all em squiggles and whorls is the same shade as the flesh they's carved in—rather than black as ink, eh?—but there's still the *crinkles* of the scars as writes the Devil Boy's soul on his skin. If yer looks close enough, yer can still see his Stamp.

12

—He's a fucking Scruffian, says Quip.

Outside the Little Big Top, after the show, he paces this way and that. Grabbed Slick as they left, see, hussled him sideways from the flap, between two tents, and now he paces, all stirred up and struggling to keep his voice a hush.

—A fucking hellion, he says. Like Flashjack or Ravewaif, only . . . fuck me, that's some *serious* bodymods. Fucking *wings*! I guess Gobfabbler *doesn't* exaggerate, no matters what that sourpuss Joey says—

He did too! Didn't yer, Quip?

See?

Well, *maybe* ain't *no*.

Honestly, yer so sensitive, Joey. Tain't all about you!

Anyways, Quip he's in full flow as to how he hadn't thunk to see an hellion as had tweaked their Stamp *that* far, and how he wonders if maybes Joey Picaroni were right—see? happy now, Joey?—if maybe the carnies fucked with how some scruff were Fixed to make this freak. And Jesus, fuck knows if there's even any sense left inside him. Could they tweak him to *think* he was a demon? All that talking in tongues, and did yer see the wild look in his eyes? he's saying. And . . .

He tails off at the sight of Slick.

—We have to help him, says Slick.

He's finished puking now, but his fizog's still as pale as a corpse's, white as the greasepaint on the bowler-hatted Laurell and Hardy lookalikes as toddle past their hidey, lumping a cello and a ukelele.

—We have to liberate the Devil Boy, says Slick.

—We'll get the others, says Quip. I'll text Foxtrot; he'll send Flashjack for sure. Or Squirlet to smuggle him out.

Quip rummages his phone from his pocket, unlocks it, and . . .

—Fuck, he says. No signal.

Then:

—Weird, says he.

—What's up?

—Slick . . . what time did we get here?

—It can't be half five, says Slick. Look again.

—You're right, says Quip.

—Well, there you go.

—It says 6:23 now.

They just looks at each other for a moment, shivers running down their spines like as someone walked over their graves . . . in the white sash of an undertaker's mute . . . kicking golden brown October leaves in the long shadows of late afternoon when it oughts to be a midday in July. They was only in there for an hour.

—OK, says Quip. We find the Devil Boy, liberate him and leg it, you and me.

—Before nightfall, says Slick.

13

Quip rises up from his haunches, teetery with the weight of the scrag sat on his shoulders. Wood decorated in a *myriad* of multicolourings, natch, the caravan's one of em old waggony ones as looks like a barrow boy's acid dream, so the windows is higher than with yer modern affair what might bounce at the back of a Skoda doing thirty on a sideroad some bank holiday weekend. Stinks like the barrow boy's been selling stale piss, right enough, so however pretty the paintwork, Quip dreads to imagine the nick of it inside.

—What do you see? he whispers.

On his knees, hands behind his back, leather wrist cuffs latched by a chain, the Devil Boy hangs his head right meek as the handler lays into him over his performance. Slick and Quip could hear the bollocking, to be sure, soon as they got close enough, but now Slick's sick to see the battering as goes with it. The punching, the choking, the cigar burns. Then the fucker's cock's out even, pissing in Devil Boy's gob—

What?

Oh, bollocks. Like them scamps ain't *lived* worse. I'll tell em the fabble of Keen and Able, and they'll sleep just fine.

He pisses on the Devil Boy for pissing on the crucifix, that handler, then he uses him as a punchbag for not swallering every drop. And he fucks his face, he does, grabs Devil Boy by the horns and fucks his face! Grunting and calling him allsorts! And when he's done, he orders Devil Boy not to spit, but not to swaller yet neither, to keep it in his gob; and then he goes off and comes back with a roll of Cellophane what he wraps round and round the scruff's noggin so's the scallywag can't even breathe! Then—

What?

I'm only telling it as it happened.

Yeah, it's *important to the story*. If it weren't, I wouldn't be fabbling it, would I? Them scamps has to be minded of what goes on in the world, or they'll never-grow-up thinking it's all posh brats solving crimes, and sailing dingies, and not getting back into the Magic Land of Christian Allegory on account of liking silky knickers.

Alright, alright. I'll skip the part where he's thrashing around on the floor, face going purple, thrashing and jerking and drumming his heels until after a whiles it all just stops. Satisfied?

14

—He killed him, says Slick. He . . . spiked his hot cocoa with fairy dust and let him slip off painlessly into the Land of Nod! He's a fucking monster.

—Well, says Quip, long as he didn't suffocate him or nothing, cause that would be a right gruesome and gruelling death.

—Yeah, that would be slow and agonising, says Slick. Lucky that weren't what happened at all.

—Course, he's still bleeding dead, says Quip.

—Yeah, I sees yer point, says Slick. He's still bleeding dead either way, and lying there on the floor in his own shit where his bowels let loose.

Anyway, they's huddled under the caravan now, Slick having whispered to *let him down, quick!* whiles the Devil Boy were being gently gathered into the loving cuddle of his tranquil demise, as that moustacheoed man-mountain turns to the window.

—Quick, down! said Slick.

And now they can hear him thumping about overhead, doing fuck knows what—*thump, thump, thump, thump*—as they whispers that the Devil Boy has to be Scruffian, don't he? So he'll bounce back from it, won't he? They knowed that were how it works when yer Fixed, even seen Flashjack's finger grow back. But still . . . still . . .

—I'm going to kill that groanhuff fucker, says Slick.

—Look, says Quip in a most delicate manner, I'm not arguing, but . . .

An ice cold glare.

—I'm *not* arguing, but you did see the size of him, right? He's like fucking Bane.

—So we wait until it's dark, till he's gone to sleep, then we sneak in and cut his throat.

—Or we fuck off back to the crib, get someone who's actually, you know, experienced in this shit.

—Go on then.

—What?

—Go on. If you're too fucking chicken, just fuck off.

—Come on, don't—

—Get off me!

—*Ssshhh!*
—*Fuck.*

The thumping's stopped now, all of a sudden. There's a muffle of mutter above, vague rustles and thuds, then the sound of footsteps on the wood, headed right towards the scrag and scallywag where they hunkers in the hidey what's formed between the front wheels and the steps down from the door. The door which creaks open now.

—Who's out there? growls the Devil Boy's handler.

Quip looks at Slick. Slick looks at Quip. Ain't neither can even swaller for the panic. *Fuck*, mouths Quip, as a boot comes down from the top step. Then another.

And Slick grabs em.

15

Well, I'm sure ye've heard that groanhuff saying, scruffs, how the bigger they are, the harder they fall. Me, I've knowed a few scrags as might incline to quibble, with yatter of Galileo, cannonballs, the Tower of Pisa, and themselves having fallen off this steeple they was topping with a cross, and it was plenty bleeding hard, thanks very much. But it were true in this case, cause as that handler tried to take his next step, why, Slick leaped and latched to his boot, so that handler he went twisting, toppling, crashing down like a giant's sky-high beanstalk.

Flailing his arms like an urchin freaking out at cobwebs, turned in the air, that handler hits the ground on his back, near brains himself on a surface baked in summer heat. He ain't out for the count, but he's flopping and lolling and moaning, and most of all he's down. So Slick is on him in a flash, out from under the caravan and diving onto him, to punch and slap, scratch at the fucker's eyes. He don't have much in the way of a shiv, but wait! He minds the penknife in his pocket now, fumbles for it.

Oh, that fumbling and the fankling it open though, that gives the handler time to get his head round what's transpiring, so even as Slick hassles the blade out, as he's hauling back now to stab that handler in his neck, that mountain of a man's all *What the fuckety?* And his arm comes up as the blade comes down, and Slick he ain't a dab hand with a shiv like some scallywag as has spent a century seeing stickmen off, and a century on top of that rumbling with razor gangs, so that blade don't stab nuffink but dirt.

Still, if that handler's wise to the scrag on his chest, playing Psycho with a Swiss Army knock-off, he's still somewhats astartle at the why and wherefore, see, still abaffle at being mugged by some demented moppet, so he just throws his arms in the way as Slick goes stabby little dervish on him now. It's only when that penknife slashes to decapitate a mermaid tattoo on one meaty forearm that he yowls and wallops Slick away with a monstrous backhand blow, sends the scrag flying and tumbling, and the knife slipped from Slick's grip to fuck knows where.

16

Slick scrambles out of the heap he landed in, legs akimbo and arse half up the tent behind him. He scrambles to a crouch, he does, thinking on the fabbles of Puckerscruff facing the Waiftaker General, or Flashjack in the dungeons of the Insitute, or vicious little Vermintrude. The very Beast of Buskerville's in his wild eyes as he looks this way and that for his shiv, and he don't see it anywheres, fuck, but he's a fucking Scruffian, he is, and this handler's the fucking reason, him and every fucking groanhuff like him as gets his jollies like . . . *that.*

So he don't even see the look of bewilder and vexation on the ugly mush of this fucker as he lumbers to his feet, don't even hear what words is coming from the man's gob, turning the air as blue and thick as the smoke of a cigar puffed deep for the sizzling of flesh. Slick he just scopes his vicinity for a weapon, any sorta weapon—and he sees it, grabs at a wooden tent peg driven in the ground beside him. OK, so this ain't a bleeding vampire, but still. He grabs it, heaves. Only it don't budge.

He heaves again, but it still don't budge, and bollocks! big dangly hairy bollocks! the handler's striding straight toward him now, a tower of muscle, a veritable monster of a man, like the Hound and the Mountain from yer Game of Thrones, and Bane and the bleeding Undertaker, and every Tom of Finland drawing ever, all rolled into one. And still the tent peg won't shift. And the brute stands over Slick now, all umpteen feet of him.

—What the fuck d'you think you're doing? he growls.

Which is when Quip takes him down with a sledgehammer to the shin.

Yeah, it's Quip to the rescue, running full speed with a belter of a roar and a panic on his face of *oh, Lord fucking Cock Almighty, what the fuck am I doing?* He might have falled flat on his back under that massive great mallet if he weren't moving, and it's his momentum as brings it swinging round and down much as anything, and with all the grace of Upsadaisy playing *Dance Dance Revolution*. But it does the job.

SMACK! it goes, and that handler goes down. And Quip's spinning, whirling his hammer up to strike again, when:

—OY!

17

—OY! comes a thundering holler from behind Quip. OY! it roars to rattle his scallywag bones with such a shock as, him being halfways through his spin, off his hammer goes flying like as Thor tripped over his own feet in the DVD bloopers. And as it goes one way, natch, Quip goes the other, which is backwards, stumbling over the handler where he's lying on the ground, bawling bloody murder over his clobbered leg, howling louder even as Quip bumflops over him to land with his own gangly legs atop the handler's and the rest of him atop Slick.

So he sees it coming, does Quip, flopped atop the guddly heap of two Scruffians and one hobbled groanhuff. He sees the snarling, slavering beast blast from the caravan, its wings bursting out to full spread for a single mighty beat what bullets it straight at him with a fury on its scarlet face like as he ain't never seen before. He ain't ashamed to say he near pissed himself, are you, Quip?

Aw, shusht, you don't even mind it.

He ain't ashamed to say he near pissed himself as the Devil Boy come rocketing at him in full fury.

Well, that scallywag just about has time to think how he likes his face as is, and his arms and legs and whatnot all in their places. If he'd a little more time, and it were a bit less of a brown trouser moment, he might think to himself, oh well, least I'll bounce back to the way I'm Fixed, eventually, albeit the dismemberment won't be too pleasant. But no, all's he has time for is to shriek, shut his eyes, throw his arms across his face, and then there's claws in his throat and the queerest sensation of flying.

Slick meanwhiles, all's he knows is that ungodly horror of a holler, and then Quip's smacked down atop him with a bash of bonces as puts stars in his eyes. As the fuzz and blur coalesces to a crumple of himself beneath the lumpen flomp of his gallant rescuer, as his daze kinda sorta resolves a bit with the ear-piercing shriek of aforesaid Quip, all's he sees is the mess of fluffy black hair as is the back of his boyfriend's bonce. And then blood. Lots and lots of blood.

Then, like Quip, he ain't seeing much at all.

18

Now, some of yer will have experienced this for yerselves, so you'll know what it's like, but for them as hasn't, yer might imagine that thing when yer falling asleep, so close to the Land of Nod as yer might even hear Able on the other side of its gates, whistling for ye to come and play for the night, and Apple's Mouses might be squeaking their songs in yer ear, and all yer worries of the day are dissolving to nonsense, when suddenly *BAM!* Fuck me, you were falling! And it made yer jump so hard yer wide awake.

Well, that's how it is when yer bounces back from the sorta . . . stupification with extreme prejudice as was wrought on Slick and Quip—which I won't go into the specifical details of on account of *some* arsey know-it-alls thinks yer ain't up to fables what ain't sanitised of all the piss and spunk and shit and blood gushing up like a fucking fountain from a neck what's had its head ripped off. So that were how Slick and Quip come to, with a right start and a *What the fuck?* to find themselves both blessedly in one piece.

It were Quip first, who came to with a shriek as finished off the one so rudely interrupted by the Devil Boy's talons. And that might well have pierced Slick's slumber, for it ain't an instant before the scrag's giving a sharp gasp and a *Fuck me!* And they's both so flustered, why, Quip don't even come back with a *Later, baby*, as yer might expect. No, they just looks around, amazed and unnerved to see . . . why, they's sat on a bed in the caravan, propped up with their backs against the wall.

—Ow, says Slick.

His neck being sore.

Across from them, the Devil Boy's sat straddlewise on a chair, arms folded on its backrest, glowering at em. And when I says *Devil Boy*, of course, I means *hellion*, as them two scruffs can clearly see now, by the Stamp what's clear as day and black as night, carved on his chest, visible now because . . .

—You're not red, says Slick.

—It's called greasepaint, says the hellion.

That's right, mates. That sideshow Scruffian were as pink as Puckerscruff's pants—well, maybe not *that* pink—under the makeup what our scallywag and scrag had seen him in.

—Hello, says he . . . *circus*.

19

Now, Slick and Quip they glances around, right nervous, but the handler ain't nowhere to be seen.

—If you're wondering where my *significant other* is, says the hellion in rather pointy tones—and his name's Ted, by the way, just so you know—he's at the doctor right now, getting his leg checked in case you *fucking broke it*. In case you broke my fucking Teddy Bear's leg.

—Oh, says Quip.

—We thought . . . says Slick. I saw . . . What he did to you . . .

—Oh, for fuck's sake, says the hellion. I look like this, you don't think I like it rough?

Now, has any of yer guessed what that scallywag's name were?

That's right, scamp, it were Dextricks Kitsclaw, of course, Or Dex to them as knowed him well, says he. Like Ted. His Teddy Bear. His significant other what had swept him off his feet the night they met on the Sodomite's Walk some three hundred years ago by the calendar and been his beloved ever since.

—Wait, says Slick. So he's a Scruffian too, or—?

—A Rake, you mean. Fixed as an adult? No.

—Then how . . . ?

—Myriad Carnival, says Dex. There's more magic in the world than the Stamp.

So, yeah, as Dex informs them two, and in no uncertain terms, far from being some helpless scallywag sex slave of some monstrously malicious groanhuff, he is indeed a sex slave to one monstrously big cock and the burly beautiful beast of a man as adorns it, but it's all perfectly consensual and loving, and having put no small effort into training his master to sate his hardcore tastes, he don't appreciate folks *trying to kill him.* Hence the sore necks, savvy?

—How did you know we were Scruffians? says Slick. That we'd—

—I didn't, says Dex.

—Oh, says Quip.

And no, he tells em, after our impetuous scruffs has blathered their explanations of their investigations, no, he says, the Myriad Carnival ain't some evil company of scheming carnies, scrobbling Scruffians and selling em back into slavery in restoration of a Trade what's been dead some hundred years, he's given to understand. Did they even watch the show where's Sophie dances Swan Lake so dainty and don't nobody ever point and laugh? Oh, they puts on some Gothic and Grand Guignol for the rubes, but the Myriad Carnival's an haven as much as any Scruffian crib. It's his crib now.

20

After that, with a rap on the door and a message as Ted's fine, Dex being keen to hear how tricks is for his old peeps, since, he says a bit mysteriously, the Myriad Carnival does tend to . . . travel around, so he don't get much chance to catch up, well, it all gets quite chummy for a bit.

—How's our scallywag Jack? says Dex.

—Flashjack? says Slick.

—That what he's calling himself these days? Heh.

—Ask Slick how he got his name, grins Quip. Slickspit Hamshankery. Puckerscruff was not a happy bunny.

—Puckerscruff?

—Flashjack's squeeze.

—He's hitched? says Dex. *Dawww!*

So, they sits and chats for a bit, as to whether Foxtrot's proper boss now, in so far as Scruffians is bossable, or whether Nuff's come back from wherever he Gone Offsky to, and is Squirlet still running her smuggling operation from her coffeehouse, and so on. But after a while it gets to be about 6:24 by Quip's phone—which might not be entirely reliable within the Myriad Carnival, says Dex, but yeah, it's most likely heading into evening now. And maybe yesterday evening. In Illinois. So they might wants to head off now, eh? Best follow him.

Off they toddles then, through a carnival what's closed for the night and being packed up, tents struck and rides dismantled, by carnies what all waves cheerily at Dex as he strides his wildly weavy path through the maze of it, not one of em circus folk so much as blinking or blushing at this Devil Boy naked as the sin what don't exist, who catches Slick's glance downward and his red cheeks as they says tata under the banner, and winks.

—Naked in the warm summer air, says he with a mischievous stretch. Nowt like it. It's so liberating.

And off into the night went Slick and Quip, thinking how there weren't no harm here, none at all.

Well, that were just stuff they did for fun.

No, it don't sound like fun to me neither, but then I ain't Dextricks Kitsclaw. And if yer asks me, that Myriad Carnival, whatever the fuck it is, might well be a damn sight safer space for a Scruffian than the streets and squats these days. Them circus folks looks out for one another, ain't an ounce of—

OK, Joey, I'll give yer that. *Clowns* is just wrong.

I'll give yer *clowns.*

Broken Hearts in Bullet Time

A Jaunt Across Folds

t's Casablanca, 1941, a bustling market square of refugees and rogues. A corpse with a bullet in its back, face-down in the dust beneath a poster of Petain. That would be me, of course, Jack Flash, your ever-loving agent of eternity's resistance, after a little astral jumping and a little not-so-astral jump-start; me playing possum as they drag my sorry skinsuit to a stretcher for a one-way ride to the morgue. Me doing my best not to retch even as the black centipede crawls from my mouth. One of Wild Bill Lee's exotic pets.

Ah, fuck. The critter must've come through with me in the cut. Better hope it doesn't bite any of the locals or things could get a bit . . . untoward around here. Psychotropic poison from a junkie's wet dreams, viral language in the victim's arteries, editing reality— Morocco wouldn't know what hit it. Well, least it's not a Mugwump; that would've caused a *real* fucking ruckus.

Question: If it's December, 1941, in Casablanca, what time is it in Interzone? Answer: Any time you want, babe. That's the answer to *everything* in Interzone. Makes it a perfect springboard for a jaunt across folds.

In the back of the ambulance, I check out my new togs. One linen suit, slight projectile damage, blood-staining on the jacket; I wiggle a finger through the hole, poke my wound. One panama hat, very chic, but more Guy Fox than Jack Flash; I flip it aside. One hapless schmuck, nixed from the narrative in the opening scenes, poor fucker; I pick up a shiny surgical pan for a gander at my mug—which ain't all that. Gotta pick up some fresh threads ASAP, I'm thinking as the ambulance stops. The door opens.

He's blonde.

—Peachy, I say.

Body two is more me, but . . . watching Louis and Strasser enter the Palais de Justice, I so want to jump the Nazi for his Gestapo greys. Thing is, I know what Fox would say: *Jack, sometimes you worry me.* Sometimes I worry myself. Anyway, I stick with the snaffled police blacks that'll get me as far as Louis's office, as far as an *Are you new?* answered with a *Fucking brand-new, mate*!

Louis arches an eyebrow.

—*Jack?*

—It's about those letters of transit, I say, from the murdered German couriers.

Louis, Louis, I'm thinking. Oh, baby. You gotta go.

Martinis and Cigarettes

"It Had To Be You," Sam kicks off as I walk into Rick's Café Américain. Funny guy, that Sam, always joshing. I flick him a salute as I head past, to the private gambling room up back. A wink at the fezzed doorman, and I'm through, scoping roulette and card tables. A croupier with a checkbook in hand, headed for . . .

I hang right, skirting Rick's line of sight, watching for the opportunity that comes as some uptight ass protests his knockback. While Rick's seeing the wanker off, I saunter to his desk, shift some chess pieces, a message:

Anomaly oncoming.

As he talks with Ugarte, there's not a hint of fazing on his fizog. Still, he always was a cool one, playing his cards real close to his chest— it's no mystery how a player like Richie built himself a sweet scene like this from scratch, in just a year and a half. And even as he takes the beady-eyed weasel for a verbal dance, I see him casually switching other pieces on the chess board, shaping his response. I'll check it when the police swoop on Ugarte, I decide.

In the meantime, I've got 20,000 francs to win.

—So what's this about?

We sit at his desk, with martinis and cigarettes, Ugarte gone and the goods stashed in Sam's upright. I reach for my queen. What's it always about? I think. A broad, a boy, a broken dream. Trying to fight the good fight, and paying for it when fate spits in your eye.

—Ethiopia, I say. Spain. And Paris, 1940. I left my heart there, Richie Rich.

—Didn't we all? he says dryly.

I make my move. All the pieces should be in place real soon.

—So where do the papers come into this, Jackie? he says.

I take a draw on my cigarette. He knows fine well these letters of transit are Class A Anomalies, breaches in the chaosphere. And he knows just what you can do with shit like that. He fought beside *me* in Barcelona, after all. Crazy times, they were, in every sense of the term.

—In what reality, I say, would letters of transit signed by *De Gaulle* be useful here?

But before he can answer, the door to the private room swings open, and a snatch of soft music from the bar brings Richie to his feet.

—Perfect timing, I say.

A Case of Do or Die

It *had* to be yours, I think as, slouched on a chair in the darkest shadows of the bar, hidden in the bottomless black of expressionist cinematography, I wait for the ritual to take effect. He's well and truly shit-faced now, my babaloa Blaine, world blurring in a haze of bourbon and tobacco. As the tinkling music plays, I can feel the papers in the upright activating.

—Build me a bridge to Paris, 1940, I'd asked him.

And here it comes, a montage of car rides and champagne glasses clinking, Nazi tanks in the countryside, newsboys in the city—

It's Paris, 1940, the street under my feet painted with a shadow that reads *Le Belle Aurore*. The beautiful dawn. And so it was, I'd thought, after a months-long night of hell, fighting my way back to Paris, across the battle-lines. (Across the folds of realities.) So it was, I thought, as I staggered, ragged and exhausted into the den of resistance. (As I do now.) It's been a fucking dark dark time, I thought, (I think now,) but I made it through. I fucking *made it*.

He looks up as I enter, eyes shinier than sunlight. Puck.

—I heard you were killed, he says. Five times. In five different places.

—I was, I say. I'm irrepressible.

I sit on the bar stool beside Puck's, elbows on the bar, both of us making eyes at each other.

—A glass of champagne, messieurs? asks Henri.

Over at the piano, the others are quaffing it like there's no tomorrow. Like there ever is. As Sam sings the song that brought me here, I slide a hand up to the back of Puck's neck. Downy. We *should* have champagne. Or . . .

—How about a case of do or die, Henri? I say.

—Come on! I shout.

I drag Puck behind me through the crowd in the railway station the mass of troops in the country march past a tank on the streets of Gestapo van with loudspeaker blaring to newsboy Puck and Nazi me in pyjamas with pink triangle stitched herded on to cattle trucks into concrete shower blocks and gas billowing steam all round the mob of us as I drag Puck behind me through the crowd in the railway station—You said we should stay and fight! he says—to the train— We did, I say—and a whistle blows—

A Bad Thing

—You died, I say. I was beside myself. And *outside* myself.

We stroll along a side-street of adobe walls and rough wood awnings, stalls set along it, hawkers selling Egyptian cotton at hiked rates, Persian carpets over-priced, spices I recognise and spices I don't—my gaze drifts to a mortar filled with black powder. Looks awfully like . . .

—Ras el hanout, monsieur, says the trader. Very special. Aphrodisiac.

—Don't need it, says Puck. He has my ass.

I pull him away as he licks his lips, tips the trader a lascivious wink.

—Come on, I say. The Blue Parrot's . . .

Low-ceilinged with slow-circling fans, The Blue Parrot is cooler than outside but not by much. Darker though. Downright shady.

—I like it here, says Puck. It has character.

—A character we're looking for, I say. Over there.

Ferrari stands by some potted plants, flyswat in hand, talking with—

—Isn't that . . . ? says Puck.

—Richie's chick and her Czech. Fucking Laszlo.

Puck gives a wry smile at my sneer. He knows my opinion on the glorious leader . . . who got nabbed two weeks into the war. Him and his brave *escape*.

—You're just annoyed because—oh, wait, they're leaving.
—Let's hustle.

—I like your fez, says Puck.
—How charming of you, says Ferrari. Are you *sure* you won't accept my offer of a position here?
—I have my own position, says Puck. Lots of positions. I'm supple.
—It would come with your own room, my delightful boy.
—Could I keep kittens?
—Could we keep on track? I say. The deal.
Ferrari swats a fly.
—If you can, as you suggest, persuade Monsieur Rick to part with his café, I hazard my gratitude would be most abundant. And with a word to the right reliably unreliable customer . . . tonight, you say?
—Tonight, I say.

As we head for the door, I clock a waiter bringing nibbles to a table. But not dates or figs or olives—no, a bowl of ickle crispy-fried black centipedes. A group of youths welcome their arrival, reach to tuck in, one pretty boy placing a critter between his cherub lips, for another to lean in, with a bat of eyelashes, bite it in half. I can't help noticing the greenish tinge to their smooth skin, the glisten of sweat on a chest revealed by a half-open shirt.
—Puck? I say. I may have done a Bad Thing.

A Reputation to Uphold

We find Louis at the bar, chatting amiably with a young Bulgarian couple on their way to the roulette—hoping to win the cost of a signature, no doubt. Louis's working his best louche charmer act, with just a hint of predator, a hint that she could pay in flesh instead of francs.

—Trust me? he's saying. Just ask Ricky, my dear.

Waving them off as we approach, he makes a show of admiring the girl's long legs, not even a glance at her handsome beau. If I didn't know Louis, I'd buy it myself.

—Twenty thousand francs, I say.

As he shushes us and points toward a quiet corner, I nod at the departing girl.

—Got to hand it to you, Louis . . . selling visas for virginities, it's a perfect cover. Isn't the bedroom scene a little . . . awkward though?

—Those last minute pangs of conscience, he shrugs. I don't know *what* comes over me sometimes. But the damsels are so terribly grateful.

—And so terribly on the next plane for Lisbon, with not a word to a soul about your . . . kindness.

—I do have a reputation to uphold. All of Casablanca thinks I'm an outright scoundrel.

—Richie included?

—Ricky especially.

—Ricky especially, says Puck.

He points a handful of chips toward the roulette table, where Richie's strolling up to the Bulgarians. Then cocks his head toward Louis, sat at another gaming table, watching intently.

—Ten to one Lady Luck smiles on the lovebirds, says Puck.

Sure enough, in two rolls of the wheel the couple have two visas worth of chips in front of them; and their benefactor's gone, with just a quiet word in the beau's ear and a glance across at Louis.

—Richie Rich is feeling generous tonight, I say.

—Or jealous, says Puck. What? Isn't it obvious?

—No way, I say. He's in love with the broad.

—Who ditched him in Paris.

—For the husband she thought was dead.

—Until you rescued him. And brought him back. And told her.

—*Which Richie doesn't need to know.*

—But she still loves Richie too, you know.
—So what?
—So she's not the only one with her heart torn between two—
—You're not serious.
—They're totally into each other. I can tell.
—You're reading too much into it.
—Your gaydar sucks. Maybe we should put *them* on the plane to Lisbon.
—Don't even think it.
—It would be *so* romantic.

To Fight and Fuck in Handcuffs

By the time we reach the resistance meeting it's a wager: Puck betting that Richie gives Ilsa the kiss off, me that he gives Laszlo over to Louis. If the plan pans out we both win . . . or both lose. Hey, the stakes are sexual favours, so who gives a fuck?

I rap on the door, whisper the password when it opens a crack, and one of the waiters from Rick's ushers us in. Laszlo's in full flow, speechifying to the motley troops of how every patriot in the room might die, but hundreds, thousands would rise to blah blah blah.

—He does go on, whispers Puck . . . a while later.
—See, I hiss. I told you.

I ignore the shushing from in front. Skulking beside the door, for a second I'm tempted to make a last minute alteration to the plan, one that would take the decision out of Richie's hands, but there are *some* limits to my . . . ethical eccentricities. That would be a Very Bad Thing. Though it's not like the figurehead flapjaw has any kosher beans to spill. But no, all I want is to put a little heat on him.

And that's when the heat arrives.

The door bursts open, but I'm ready, chair in hand, smashing the kneecaps of the first policeman in, clubbing the second with the splintered remnants as he trips and tumbles.

—Move! I shout.

Puck darts through the crowd, urchin-quick, hitting Laszlo at full speed, shouldering him through the window, shoving Richie's waiter after him. He blows me a kiss then dives through himself as I whirl to take the third cop down with a chair-back in the face. Dive out of a bullet's path, roll, come up with a paper baggy from my pocket.

Black powdered centipede, baby.

—blow poison dust in their eyes like pepper—cloud of hashish and tiger penis—red eyes watering—seeping jap's eyes red and oozing of pricks cum out of flies—spanish flies in the air—buzzing corpses dance like puppets—to fight and fuck in handcuffs and—truncheons to be used in innaresting ways my dear—no resistance here and no control—this is agent jack flash reporting on carnal carnage—send reinforcements all the boys are otherwise engaged in nefarious sodomitic orgy—sphincters puckering keen for centipede penetration—ejaculation—and what's a punk to do but go with the blow—

The Last Stage Out of Casa Blanca

—You know what that stuff does to you, says Puck.

Flash Jack's bottom boy's been bitching all day.

—I am an unrepentant napalm fiend, says Jack. There is no virus of logic in my veins.

—You know what that stuff does to *reality*.

—Call the director. The studio has been invaded by Venusian slime boys, and the situation is untenable.

—Yes, that's one way to put it. Fox'll have kittens if he finds out.

Word on the street speaks of the incident with dread and horror, gossip traded in the markets as filthy lucre for lust.

—Wait. Here they come.

The Boy Who Loved Death

The Breakheart Broad and Slick Vic the Resistance Tick come crawling upright through the mist—two-legged bugs, says Flash Jack's informed opinion, and damn them both for it. Time for the long con's end game, culmination of his secret schemes.

—I'll take the Czech, please, says Jack.

Fast Puck pulls his pistol and the dynamite duo step forth, transtemporal outlaws, kids or curs—who can say for sure? But those tickets for the last stage out of Casa Blanca have their disreputable names on them, names accursed on Laszlo's lip before Jack busts it with a hard right hook.

As the plane lifts from the rumble of tarmac under wheels, into the silk of sky, Flash Jack feels the buzz in his blood and balls fade, feels the Hunger crawling into his skin and guts. Coming out of the twenty-four hour comedown, finally, he shivers like a sick dog. Fuck this shit. Never again, he swears.

I need a new line of work, I think.

I gaze at the letters of transit in my hand, our names on them just like Louis promised—*if*, he said, your rather implausible scenario should come to pass. Good as his word.

—Are you sure we did the right thing, Jack? We did just strand the leader of the Czech resistance in Casablanca.

—He was heading for America. Like there's a fuckload of Nazis to resist over there.

—And it's nothing to do with his escape from the concentration camp?

—It was a *rescue*. I *rescued* him.

—Exactly.

—I have no idea what you're insinuating. Anyway, Rick and Louis are together, and that's what counts.

—Could be the start of something beautiful.

—Damn straight. Rick and Louis with the Brazzaville Free French. You know they take out Rommel in this fold, right?

The Last Straw

Report of Agent Jack Flash

I land on the red tarmac of George Square, roll, and come up on one knee, arms out for balance, with a natty Kung-Fu flourish of greatcoat, as my skybike spins on through a flap frenzy of scattering pigeons, clips the stone pillar of the Cenotaph, and crashes through the front doors of the City Chambers, blowing wood and glass and blackshirt guards out in a fireball glowing green and brilliant blue with all the super-saturated orgone-vapours of a Triumph V2's fully jizzed-up ray-tanks. Bollocks, I think. I really liked that bike. But, fuck, thing is, I had a little itchy trigger-finger issue with the missile I was meant to use just as I passed over Pitt Street Police HQ and left myself without too many options. Sometimes you have to make a sacrifice, I know, but it's still hard. I really liked that bike.

I flick the roach of my Afghan Black away, and stand to scope my circle of not-so-admirers. Fucking pipers.

After twenty feet or so of space cleared in awe of my lithe and limber landing, most of the square is filled with tourists, but I've landed smack-dab in the middle of the Big Show's backstage, so to speak. The inner circle of my own personal mosh-pit is lined by several hundred pipers, drummers and assorted instrumentalists from all corners of the Empire—but all of them white as Widdemore, of course—dolled-up in every colour of kilt and tunic, toppered with busbies, pith helmets and turban-like towers adorned with peacock feathers, ostrich plumes or sundry silliness. It's Albion's soldier sons come home for the Umpteenth Annual International "How Fucking Loud And Annoying Can These Bastard Bagpipes Drone?" Competition, and I can feel my hardcore hackles a-rising. The bagpipes are a weapon of war, baby; Christ, I never understood why the spooks of Guantanamo use Death Metal for torture when sixteen seconds of the 14th Royal Highland Falangists would have me naming every pet pooch in my family history as an Al Quaeda top dog.

So I'm glad I've already got my Curzon-Youngblood Mark I chi-pistol in my hand, because if any of these biscuit-tin kaffer-killers so much as lets a breath out in the direction of a chanter he's getting a discharge of the most dishonourable kind, I tell you. I click the juice on full to let them know that I mean business. No mistaking that salty-ozone scent-and-tingle of orgone energy that fills the air. Sex pistols, honeybuns. Can't beat them.

—Easy, tigers, I say. You know how fast I am. As fast as you can say—

—Jack Flash! shouts the brightest spark among them, and I spin, brighten him a tad more with a chi-blast in his sporran. First prize, beefcake. Ding-a-ling, ding-a-ling. And your next question, for the cuddly toy, is: how the fuck do I get out of this?

No answer. Shit.

I can see over the heads of fleeing tourists that militiamen are pouring in from the side-streets round George Square. The thopters that nearly brought me down over the M8 are now flitting like bats overhead. And it's only the mob of bandsmen that are blocking the blackshirts from a clear shot at Imperial Albion's Public Enemy Number Nothing, Jack Flash, terror of the tartan traitors, scourge of the Scottish fucking Fascists.

The pipers are gearing up for a charge, I can tell, idiot grunts ready to fall for King and Country if it helps bring down a swaggering faggot anarcho-terrorist who's wreaked royal havoc, I'm proud to say, in the Second City of the Empire today. *Today of all days*, I can see them thinking as they twitch, inching forward at the corner of my eye. *This is our day. This is our big day.*

This is Empire Day.

They lunge for me, but instead of trying to take them all I backflip, spring-heeled jackboots firing me high over the head of the first to reach me up onto the shoulders of the one behind. I don't stop there, kangaroo-kicking myself back into the air, but forward this time and into the thick of them, leaping, loping from shoulder to shoulder, piston heels punching me up through the air and them down to the ground behind. I hurdle, somersault and twist this way and that through the gunfire of the militia, headed for the still-smoking rubble of the once-grand entrance to the City Chambers, but with all the directness of a drunken flea.

With the bastard pipers getting mown down by their blackshirt brethren I could play this game all day, but I've got a job to do and the Fox will yap if I don't do it right, so I snatch a glinting gold baton from a bandleader as I crunch him underfoot, give it a twirl just to annoy them all the more as I set my sights on the goal. Problem is, of course, by now the doors are a kill-zone of cross-fire from inside and out. They know where I'm headed, who I'm headed for—a special visitor for a special day, here to award the winning band with shiny silver trophies and shit. But they don't have a fucking clue what Jumpin Jack is capable of. I make a high jump, tuck and roll, come down, coiled like a cat for one surprise spring, hit the ground and—

—hear that imaginary applause as—

I land on the stone balustrade of the balcony, crouched and grinning like a gargoyle at the Foreign Secretary, Jack Straw, who stands there gawping out at me through the French windows. The Provost is ranting wildly at four Special Support men about—well, I can't hear his words but I'm guessing that I've pissed on his parade. I raise my Curzon-Youngblood in a mirror image of this other Jack's rising hand, slowly, surely, until we're both pointing at each other, his finger trembling, my gun-barrel accusation steelcast-steady, chi extending in a straight line from my shoulder to the centre of his forehead.

I give him a second to feel the fear.

Let me drop-kick you an update on the dream-state of the nation. We got ID cards and internment, fucking Special Support forces with their lightning bolt insignias. The thought police I'm fighting are in your head, snuggle-bunnies, and it's time you all woke up to that. The conspiracy is society and every one of you is a fucking sleeper agent of your own worst enemy, the status quo. Scary thought? Scary worldview? As Nietzsche said, all great things must first wear masks of terror in order to engrave themselves upon the hearts of men. You know, I always loved Freddy's one-liners; man would've made a great stand-up. God is dead, *badoom tssh*. That kills me every time—*and* makes me stronger too, but then I have a hardy constitution. Others are not so lucky.

The Foreign Secretary, the Jack Straw that broke this camel's back, points at me in silence for an exquisitely eternal second, then his mouth is opening, he's mouthing his horror, and the Provost and the SS men are turning . . . so I blow him a kiss. And then I blow his fucking brains out.

That one's for Puck, motherfucker.

Charge Sheet for the Arrest of Tamuz Masingiri

```
Strathclyde Militia
CHARGE SHEET

Defendant's Copy

Division: X
Station Charged:  Partick Police Station
Date of Arrest:  24 April 2006

Full name:  Tamuz Alhazred Masingiri
Born:  1  April  1984  in  Tell-el-Kharnain,
Palestine
Sex:  MALE
Religion: Heathen

CHARGE(S)
You are charged with the following offence(s).
You do not have to say anything, but it may harm
your defence if you do not mention now something
which you later rely on in court. Anything you
do say may be given in evidence.
```

```
1  F1900405—refusal  to  produce  ID  card  on
request.

On 24/04/2006,  in Kentigern  in  the  Lanarkshire
Region of Caledonia,  refused repeated requests
to  produce  identification  card,  contrary  to
Section  28,  Clause-22  of  the  Sedition  and
Security Act (1984)

Reply: I told him I didn't have it with me. It's
in my flat.

Time charged:  16:46
Date charged: 24/04/2006
```

Report of Agent Guy Fox

The subway station at Calvingrove is busy with commuters and militia at this early hour. The latter in their black shirts and their day-glo yellow flak jackets form a gauntlet of security, standing in pairs up at the turnstiles, at the bottom of the escalator, and at various points along the platform, checking ID'S and scrutinising faces. I hand my chipped card over at the bottom of the steps, wait as it's scanned, then take it back with a polite smile and a tip of my bowler, then stroll out onto the platform just in time for the arriving train. This close to the Rookery—that square mile of ghetto fortress at the heart of Kentigern's West End—it's no wonder that security is tight, the Rookery a haven to the dregs and debris of society, the type one really doesn't want travelling too far beyond their own thieves' den. Sadly, these blackshirt goons are mostly trained to look for punks or razor mods, common-or-garden crims up to the more banal forms of *no good*. They're really not equipped to deal with a master soulsmith like myself, moving in an identity forged from the skinsuit to the credit history. I've been Thieves Guild from the age of four and those thirty years have stood me well in my life of subterfuge and subversion. Even the smartpaper nerve-gas pack I'm carrying under my arm is indistinguishable from the newssheet folded round it, by any but the highest range of scanners. The wonders of this modern era: so many gadgets offer so many ways to hide a bomb.

I get off the underground at St Enoch's, leaving the newssheet and its contents on the seat, no more conspicuous than the half a dozen *Sun*s and *Metro*s lying scattered around the compartment.

A short detour through City Central Terminus takes me past a postbox where I dispatch the latest batch of anthrax-loaded envelopes addressed to various stars of sports or screens who've publicly endorsed the Blair regime. Craven apologists for fascism every one of them—one can only hope they're shallow enough to open their own fan mail. Outside the front entrance of the wireline station, I climb into a black hack and give the driver a destination that's halfway to the Rookery, doubling back on my tracks; it never hurts to throw a little randomness into one's movements.

I text in a quick bomb threat as the taxi heads up Woodlands Road—using recognised keywords so the authorities will know to take it seriously—then ask the cabby to pull over at a garage for a second. I buy a softpack of Gitanes and pay with a forged twenty, tapping out a memorized number on the phone and sizing-up the chap behind me in the queue while I wait for my change: a normal-looking fellow in a business suit and cashmere overcoat; it seems a shame to land this on him but needs must when the devil rides. I hit *send* on the phone and fumble it towards my pocket with a fistful of coins and notes, clumsily bumping into cashmere man as I turn.

—Sorry, I say. All fingers and thumbs today.

He mumbles his own apology and steps past me up to the counter, no idea that the phone now sitting in his pocket is not his own, or that in five minutes time he's going to be standing in a circle of heavily armed militiamen all shouting at him to *get down on the ground NOW*. Poor soul.

Another hack back to City Central Terminus, a quick change of suit in the public toilets (switching the black I'm wearing for the pinstripe in my briefcase, the bowler for a fedora), then an airtrain over to the South Side, a third taxi, and I'm walking up to the reception desk at the main entrance of Southern General Hospital, handing over an Imperial passport in the name of Dr Reinhardt Starn. This is a long-term sleeper self I've been working on for five years now: a German defector, based in the American Dominions, showing up at conferences around the UK, publishing papers in the journals, corresponding with learned colleagues based in Albion, and awfully eager to at last meet, in the flesh, my fellow expert in the field of biological defence, Dr Shipman . . . who just happens to be giving the Health Secretary, Jack Straw, a tour of his bleeding-edge research facility on this very day that I just happen to be in town.

—I've told him all about your work, he'd said. He'd love to meet you.

—Well, you know, I'd love that too, Harry, I'd said.

I take directions and a clip-on visitor's pass from the receptionist and, chatting casually with my blackshirt escort, stroll along the corridor to the staff lift, swipe my pass through the electronic lock and, inside, hit the button for Sub-Level 5.

—So with these nanites in his system, says Shipman, a serviceman in Iraq, say, will be able to deal with any of the viral agents or neurotoxins we're currently using on the field. No more incidents like the Basra Barracks fiasco. I understand your people are working on something similar, Reinhardt?

I nod. It's true, actually; my people *are* working on nanotech personal defence systems; it's just that my people are not actually refugees from the Futurist Reich working for the Pentagon, but rather Arturo Guevara and his team, down in the Republic of Venezuela, trying to come up with something that might help the New International Brigades in their struggle for freedom. It's a pity the Starn identity gets all the glory, really, because Arturo's work is quite brilliant.

The Foreign Secretary stands gazing through glass into a quarantine room where cleansuited doctors are injecting all manner of microscopic horrors into a test subject.

—And when will it be ready? he asks.

Not soon enough for you, I think. Arturo's bitmites, coded to his stolen DNA pattern and transferred with a casual handshake on our meeting, should already be starting to work their wicked ways, replicating through his system, eating Mr Straw from the inside out. In about six hours time he should look like an Ebola X victim, bleeding from every orifice.

Puck wouldn't have approved, I know. He'd much rather have had the bitmites rewire Straw's pleasure centre with an irresistible scatophilia that would have him eating his own shit, time-coded to kick in with maximum compulsion at some public dinner with the Governor Generals of every Dominion and Protectorate in the Empire. That's what Puck would have wanted.

But Puck isn't here.

Interview with Tamuz Masingiri

DCG: Interview commences 17:04. Present in the room are DC Powell and myself; Cameron Mackie, solicitor; and Tamuz . . . Masingiri. Right then, Tamuz Masingiri. So why wouldn't you show me your ID card? It *is* Masingiri, isn't it? The fingerprints aren't going to tell us that your real name's Mohammed or Moussaoui or something, are they?

TM: No. That's—

DCG: Because you know we can check these things, don't you? You're not in the desert now, Tamuz. This is civilisation, son. We do have computers, you know?

TM: I'm not your son. And, yes, that's my name. I'm not lying to you.

DCG: Alright, alright. No need to get stroppy, son. I just want to know that you're who you say you are. Cause if you're not, you'd be better to tell us now than have us find out from the records.

TM: This is stupid. Why would I lie about who I am?

DCG: I was just asking the question, Tamuz. This is just routine. Just for the record, can you confirm that you are Tamuz Masingiri.

TM: Yes. I am Tamuz Masingiri. For fuck's sake -

CM: DC Griffin, do you have an actual question?

DCG: All I want to know is why you wouldn't show me your ID card, Tamuz. You haven't answered that yet.

TM: I told you. I didn't have it with me. I just—

DCG: And why didn't you have it with you?

TM: I forgot it.

DCG: You are aware of the law, aren't you? You know you have to carry it? Someone like you, I'd've thought you'd know that.

TM: What do you mean *someone like me*?

DCG: Just answer the question, please. You *do* know you're legally bound to produce your ID card if requested by a police officer? But, you don't think the law applies to you? Is that it?

TM: No.

DCG: You don't carry your card for political reasons—

TM: No.

DCG:—because you object to them?

TM: No.

DCG: You don't think you should have to carry an ID card just because the government says so? That's it, isn't it, Tamuz?

TM: I told you. I just forgot it.

DCG: Where are you from, son? Palestine, right?

TM: What? Look, I've stayed in Scotland since I was four years old. I stay in Glasgow.

DCG: Scotland? Glasgow?

CM: Hold on. I'd like to talk to my client in private for a second, DC Griffin.

DCG: This is *Caledonia*, son. This is *Kentigern*. You've been hanging around with the wrong sort of people if you're calling it *Glasgow*?

TM: Sorry?

DCG: Are you a rook, Tamuz?

TM: What? What are you talking about?

DCG: You were picked up on the edge of the Rookery. Is that where you live, Tamuz?

TM: I stay in the Halls of Residence on Southpark Avenue. What's the Rookery?

DCG: Oh, pull the other one.

CM: DC Griffin, I need to talk to my client in private now. Please, stop the tape.

TM: Just check with the university and they'll tell you. Take me to my room and I can show you the bloody card.

CM: DC Griffin.

DCG: OK, OK. Interview suspended 17:07.

Report of Agent Joey Narcosis

Joey clicks the radiovision camera into the tripod stand, flips out the view screen and swivels the fitting with the lever, angles it down to centre the hostages in the frame. They're all crying. They all know that one of them is going to die.

Jack and the Fox don't have the emotional detachment for killing innocents up close and callous. Sure, Jack takes out the odd passenger-laden wireliner now and then, but it's usually in the heat of battle with a horde of thopters on his tail and militiamen trying to blast his skybike from the air. And, sure, Guy has his schemes of strikes on subways and other such public places, sex-bombs blasting orgone energy through City Central Terminus, prime-time commuters losing their senses to their lust in instant orgies that leave them puking and naked, horrified at the De Sade style excesses perpetrated by their unleashed subconscious; but most of his lethal plans are either carried out at a distance or targeted at the top dogs, the knights and bishops of the Empire rather than the unwitting pawns. When it comes down to it both Jack and Fox need to think their victims deserve what they get, even if it's just for their complicity in the system. Joey Narcosis has no such sensitivities. His actions selected in accordance with the calculus of survival, Joey's so deep-chilled that he even files his reports in third person.

—You can kill Straw, he'd said, but they'll just pull another one out of the vat, burn the meme-pattern into his brain, and bingo-bongo, we've got a new Home Secretary just the same as the last one.

They'd been sitting in Club Soda, two weeks after Fast Puck's disappearance, the evening that the word came back to them about a Tamuz Masingiri being picked up on the edge of the Rookery by the blackshirts in a routine streetsweeping operation. The boy should have had more sense as far as Joey is concerned, should have been pristine clean and with his skinsuit airtight to the dotted i's on the paperwork, but then the fascists might have just been looking for an ethnic to fit-up on a drug-bust—easy way to boost the arrest figures for a slow week. Still, Puck knows when to duck and dodge, should have slipped through the sweep like water through a sieve.

Idiot kid got himself lifted though, and now Jack wants action.

—So I'll kill the fucking next one too, Jack had said. And the one after that. We just keep fucking killing the bastard until there's no more of him left.

—It won't bring him back, Guy had said.

—But it'll send a fucking message, a fucking chi-beam text right in the fucking ajna eye.

—Assassination is just a post-it note, mate, Joey had said. They'll look at it for half a second before they bin it. Christ, who gives a fuck about these muppets anymore? There's always another one to replace the last.

—Unless, Guy had said, we take them all out.

The Boy Who Loved Death

Joey looks at the five hostages huddled on the floor, all dressed in their Guantanamo Bling, as they call it on the street—orange jumpsuits and full body-shackles—wrists locked to the steel belt at the waist, ankles cuffed with a few inches of chain for shuffling. The black hoods are off their heads for now; Joey removed them so he could look into their eyes, figure out which one will give the best performance for the camera, the most frightened. It'll go out live over the aether and, routed through Don Coyote's pirate station in the sky, Radio Birdman, the signal should jack every radiovision set in Kentigern. So he wants it to be good, does Joey, insofar as you can say that Joey Narcosis wants anything.

He scans the line of identikit Straws, looking for the most snivelly and snot-nosed. Frankly they're all much of a muchness. Vat-grown, crèche-raised, they're not meant to have individuality; their job is just to eat and shit and sleep until the day comes when they're called upon to do their duty for King and Country, Edward and Albion. That blank idiocy should make for more impact in the footage, right enough, the terror on the face heightened by incomprehension. With the speed of growth, the clones don't get to a mental age of more than five in the time it takes their bodies to mature, so Kentigern is going to be watching a retard beg for his life, for his Nursey, for the safety of the Institution. Add to that the fact that the Straws were snatched en route from the crèche to the acceleration tanks to slumber through their breakneck adolescence, and what you have is a retarded *child* begging for his life.

It should make for a good show.

One of the Straws has a wet patch at his crotch, Joey notices; the little bastard must have pissed himself. Well, the fascists do like their Nietzsche and their natural selection, so it seems only fitting to play the game by their rules, show them what will-to-power and might-is-right really mean. He grabs the kid by the shoulders and drags him forward into centre-frame. The image on the viewscreen is clear and, with a zoom out just a smidgeon wider, the black flag with the white Circle-A—nailed to the concrete wall of the basement—should be visible enough. He checks that the balaclava is tucked tight into the collar of his shirt, straightens his tie and flicks a speck of dust off the shoulder of his black suit jacket. He picks up his katana from the top of the cardboard box in the far corner of the room and walks back to the camera, hits record.

—You getting this OK, he says. Sight and sound?

The laptop sitting open on the box beside the tripod gives a beep, and Joey crouches down, clicks to open the window with Coyote's response. *Loud and clear.* He takes his position behind the Straw and waits for the second beep. There's no need to read it; it means *On The Air.*

He sweeps the sword out of its sheath in an elegant arc that curls round and up and to a stop, to a pause, a stillness among the screams and sobs of the Straws, before he slices the blade down through the neck of the mewling cretin child on its knees in front of him, this symbol of servility.

Perfect timing for the Six O'Clock News.

Interview with Tamuz Masingiri

DCG: Interview recommences 18:00. Present in the room are DC Powell, myself, and Tamuz Masingiri. Right, Tamuz. Mr Mackie tells me you've been spinning him a right wee dreamworld. He thinks you're in need of psychiatric help, but myself and DC Powell here, see, we think there's more to you than you're letting on, my lad.

TM: Where's my solicitor?

DCG: It's gone past that now, lad.

TM: What do you mean? What is this? Is this some fucking TV prank show? Did Jack put you up to this? It's a set-up, right?

DCG: Don't try and play games with us, boy. The schizo routine won't wash. We're not daft, son. We've seen it all before. Wee rook gets caught flying home to his nest, thinks—you know—just flap your wings hard enough, act like a mental case, and we'll call in the shrink instead of Special Support. What was it, Tamuz?

TM: Come on, this isn't funny any more.

DCG: Your prints aren't in the database, Tamuz. You know that? So you're either a ferry-rat with no business being in this country or you have some contacts in the identity trade and a dirty past you wanted cleaned. Either way you're in deep shit, boy. Suspicion of sedition. For the record, Mr Masingiri is shaking his head. Come on, Tamuz. What were you up to when we picked you up? Grazing wallets? Casing houses for the Guild? Drug run? Data courier? Nah. You're old enough to have graduated from the kiddywork long ago. You're into something deep, boy. That's what this loony tunes routine is all about, isn't it?

TM: You're the ones who're fucking loonies. This is all—

DCG: Are you a good Muslim, Tamuz? Pray five times a day? Fast for Ramadan?

TM: I'm not a Muslim. What's that got—

DCG: You don't expect us to believe that.

TM: What? Just because I've got darker skin than you I must be a Muslim? Man, this is sick. This isn't fucking funny—

DCG: Sit down.

TM: Let go of me.

DCG: Sit down. I said, sit down!

TM: Ah!

DCG: You sit down when I tell you to, lad. Now. You have two choices: you can ditch the act and tell me who you really are and what you were up to; or I walk down to Special Support right now and tell them I've got a suspected subversive in the interview room. If I were you, I know which option I'd prefer.

TM: This is all wrong. I don't belong here. This isn't—

DCG: Too fucking right you don't belong here, Ali Baba. You belong in the desert with all your suicide bomber chums. Or maybe it's the Rookery you belong. Come on.

TM: *Ah!* Hey, you can't—*fuck!*

DCG: What are you, Tamuz? A political or a religious? What are you mixed up in?

TM: I'm not answering any more questions. This is fucked up. This is fucked. You're crazy. Where's my fucking solicitor? I know my rights.

DCG: You don't have any fucking rights, son. You don't exist. Suspicion of sedition, Tamuz. That's what it is now, and that means you're up shit creek. Now, I'm giving you a chance, son. You can talk to me or you can talk to Special Support. Your call.

TM: This is bullshit. This is fucking bullshit. Let me out of here.

DCG: You're making a big mistake, son.

TM: Let me out of here. I'm—*ah!* Jesus fucking—*uh!*

DCG: Interview terminated 18:03.

TM: Let me go. Let me go. Let me—

Report of Agent Jack Flash

Crouched on the flat gantry on the roof of the wireliner, the thrum of the Cavor-Reich engines all round, I click my Zippo again and again, trying to spark it into flame to light my hash cheroot. It's just too damn breezy up here, the ray-tanks of the monster machine sweeping up to each side of me forming a perfect wind-tunnel, billowing my greatcoat peachily but thwarting my best efforts at full cool. Bastards. In the Society of the Spectacle, style is the psychic weapon of choice, and this is like having your voice crack on you at Rourke's Drift with the Zulus bearing down: men of Harlech, hack cough splutter; sorry, mate, frog in the throat. Can we take it from the top?

Unlit joint dangling from my lips, I clunk my way forward along the gantry, muttering dark curses and radiating Bad Vibes, man, as I slap the Semtex packs left and right, flick the detonators on. Twelve charges, six for each side, is overkill, I know—twice what we planned—but if there's no stone for Jack today, well, a boy's gotta get his buzz some way.

At the front of the wireliner, my wings are waiting where I left them, clamped down with magnetic grapnels. Light as paper, stronger than steel, ray-tanks in the harness to counteract my body-weight, the twelve-foot in span synthe pinions lift with the wind beneath them, fighting to take off on their own. The modified waldoes are one of my favourite toys and I slip in under them, latch the harness shut under my arms and around the waist, shove my hands into the gauntlets, like a knight of yore putting on his armour. Up ahead I can see the junction of the wire, already jacked to take the wireliner off course and south-east, towards Ibrox and the football stadium where the torchlight procession should just be arriving. Thirty years ago that stadium's where the Jews and Asians of the South Side, the Catholics of the East End and the academics and bohemians of the West End were all gathered for the Purification; there's no record of how many had their souls stripped down, their bodies stolen to the service of the Empire, but if Straw had been from Kentigern—it's kind of ironic that this is where they would have brought him to die the first time. Now I can see it off in the distance, getting closer fast, a golden glow from the massed ranks on the pitch lighting up the night. I'd swear I can hear the roar of the crowd, the rhythmic chant, the *Seig heils*, the *God Save the King*.

As the wireliner lurches left on its new course, aimed directly at the stadium, I flex the wings and release the clamps, lift up into the air. In the gondola bridge below they'll be pulling levers now, spinning wheels, trying to radio the signalman with a frantic *what-the-fuck*, but the inertial dampeners, the wirebrakes, the retro-jets and the radio—all of that shit is already taken care of.

I spiral up to a safe height on an updraft, hold my position in the air like an eagle scoping the treetops for its prey. I figure distance, height and momentum, hold for the perfect moment before I hit the detonation button.

The *Heidelberg* goes boom.

A few hundred tons of metal and fireball heads down in a parabolic curve, hitting the near end of Ibrox Stadium fast and hard, taking out a solid quarter of the terraces and raining a shrapnel meteor storm on another half. Baby, I can definitely hear the crowd roar now. I flick the wings back, aim myself at the far end of the stadium, at the Director's Box where the Culture Secretary, Jack Straw should be standing behind bullet-proof glass, trying to register the carnage below, the flame and the smoke, the rows and columns of blackshirts on the pitch all broken into pretty chaos, the celebrants on what's left of the terraces piling over each other in panic, the landslides of flesh, living and dead. High up on a scrap of terrace, through the billows of smoke, I spot a lone figure with a camcorder held up to his eye, a vulture in Babel.

I hope Coyote's picking up my own broadcast. He fucking well should be; my senses are acid-acute right now, so this report, this vision of devastation, should be beaming out white-hot over the astral airwaves, a psychic EMP in the aethernet of Kentigern's dreams. Radiovision, no matter what Joey thinks, is so Twentieth Century. Old news. This is the Kali Yuga, mate; in a war for hearts and minds, the subconscious is the battle ground. You can switch off the news but you can't switch off a nightmare.

I blast through a billow of hot black smoke a-crackle with orgone blue-green sparks and come out with the Director's Box dead ahead, tuck my wings in tight, a human harpoon aimed at the heart of the Great White Empire. There's no glass made by man can stop this bullet, motherfucker.

Shards spray into the room around me as the window shatters. Wings jerked back, nearly ripped off in the impact, I whiplash forward but manage to pull off the landing neat and square, down on my knees in a jitterbug slide that takes me right to the shiny shoes of the last Straw, the Culture Secretary, minister of bread and circuses for the masses. I rise to my feet, hands out of the waldo-gauntlets now, Curzon-Youngblood in the right, a Scorpio .99 in the left, flicking my arms out in a crucifix of armament, firing left and right, to take down the bodyguards at the corners of my vision without once losing eye-contact with Straw. I holster the guns and take the jack-knife from its sheath at my waist.

He knows we got his vatlings. He knows this angel with shredded wings means not just death but extermination. He knows he's not a human being here, just a poison pen letter to the Blunketts and the Blairs and the thousand other motherfucking muppets waiting to take his place. And we're going to make it nice and personal, signed . . .

Yours truly,
Jack

Death Certificate of Tamuz Masingiri

Certified Copy of An Entry
Pursuant to the Births and Deaths Registration
   Act 1953

DEATH **Entry no: 2313**

Registration district: **Greater Kentigern**
Sub-district: **Kentigern West**
Administrative area: **Lanarkshire**

1. Date and place of death: **Twenty-fifth April 2006 Partick Police Station Kentigern**

2. Name and surname: **Tamuz MASINGIRI**

3. Sex: **Male**

4. Maiden surname of woman who has married: **N/A**

5. Date and place of birth: **First April 1984, Tell-el-Kharnain, Palestine**

6. Occupation and usual address: **Unemployed No fixed abode**

7(a). Name and surname of informant: **Nicholas Griffin (D.C.)**

(b) Qualification: **In Loco**

(c) Usual address: **c/o Partick Police Station, Dumbarton Road, Kentigern**

8. Cause of death: **Asphyxiation**

Certified by **J. Tyndall M.B.**

9. I certify that the particulars given by me above are true to the best of my knowledge and belief

D.C. Nick Griffin Signature of informant

10. Date of registration: **Twenty-fifth April 2006**

11. Signature of registrar: **Derek Beackon**

Certified to be a true copy of an entry in a registrar in my custody.

Join the Club

had to shave my head to join the club. Village culture can be like that, even when the village is actually a neighbourhood within a city. It wasn't explicit. I wasn't refused entry by the shaven-headed men in their shiny black bomber jackets. I was served at the bar . . . eventually. Nobody took me aside and asked me to leave. But it was made very clear, in their eyes. Yes, physically I was in the club, but I didn't really *belong*, not with that haircut. I had to take the razor, shave my skull to suede or smooth skin.

I had to get a tattoo to join the club. The first few nights I went—Saturday this week, Friday the next—it was just a matter of paying at the door, getting an X in black ink on the back of your hand. So you could go outside for a smoke, you know, and get back in. Then they began to use a little stamp, something not unlike an X, but a little more intricate, less easily copied. Then they brought in one of those library book date-stamps. The tattoo was just easier, they said eventually. Permanent membership.

I had to wear a badge to join the club. Everyone was wearing the badge, the same way everyone was wearing their heads shaved, the same way everyone was wearing those shiny black bomber jackets with tartan lining, and the tight jeans, and the shiny black boots. These were all markers of identity, of pride in oneself—a fierce defiant pride. Because no matter what anyone said, we had the right to be what we were, and together we could stand up to Them. The badge declared our Truth. Was it a pink triangle or a Union Jack? You decide.

I had to march with a flag to join the club. There were those who hated Us, those who had to be shown that their conspiracies against Us would not win. They had infiltrated all corners of society, the media and the government. They were spreading lies about Us, plotting our deaths in fire. We had to march down the streets where They lived, past the corner-shops where They might well work, selling the newspapers that were little better than propaganda. We had to chant in unison to show Them that we were an army. Organised, resolute, unafraid, rising.

I had to board a train to join the club. That was where the march ended up, at the train station. One club, one village, one city wasn't enough. We had to spread out across the land. We had to gather in camps in distant places inaccessible to most, places where we would be safe, with our own kind. I had to follow the others onto the train. I had to lead them, drive them on. It wasn't a time for doubts, for questions. Questions were to be met with violence, murder. We had no choice. We had no choice.

The Boy Who Loved Death

White Stones Like Stars

Once far ago and long away, in a sleepy little village on the edge of nowhere, a small town turned commuter zone city suburb, miners' houses swallowed into Seventies schemes of pebbledash matchboxes, Lego blocks of buildings nestled soulless on winding roads all lined with parking bays and patches of grass trimmed lobotomy neat . . .

Once, once upon a time, down a pathway of tarmac black as space and dotted with white stones like stars, night sky bound into banal functionality for trudging hollow-hearted to an identikit bungalow's door . . .

Once far ago, there lived a boy in love with Death.

Falling Ever Inwards

Death had come to the boy one day, as he walked home from school through catcalls and jeers he no longer even cringed at, a shape with the body of an ape and the skull of a wolf where its head ought to be. As he walked out the school gates, across zebra stripes on a busy road, from one glowing yellow lollipop to another, Death had come to him in his heart, had eaten that heart from the inside out, all life, all love falling ever inwards as light into a black hole, leaving only skinsuit, a hollow child.

Hal Duncan

The Golden Fires

Come with me, Death had whispered to him, and the boy followed Death down through the golden fires of Hell, fires that did not harm a hair on his head even as he combed it back, that hair, slick with adolescent grease and ancient Brillcream of a beatnik father salvaged from the bathroom cabinet, the boy admiring in the mirror his fantasy of a Hollywood hitman. He leaned in toward the mirror on the cabinet door and kissed Death's yellowed canines, whispered a promise, an offer, a deal.

He would bring Death every soul he could before they shot him.

Warpaint for a Wingless Angel

He walked into school the next day, armed to the teeth under his trenchcoat the colour of ash, the grey of concrete holocaust memorials, grey of clay bleached bone-white as birdshit, bleached of earthen red by moonlight's acid, mixed with soot to a shade of steel or slate, and smeared on a face as warpaint for a wingless angel. He needed no wings, the boy, the upturned collar and furl of coat catching the air enough to mark him as the right hand of the god he loved, here to bring the beautiful word, the gospel of murder's salvation.

As in Benediction

His first victim was John MacDonald, aged 16, who approached him as he entered the school gates, nudging a friend, Hugh Williamson, also 16, and pointing at the boy, mocking his attire, pointing and laughing at the sad fool.

The boy reached into the inside pocket of his trenchcoat and slowly, calmly, with the smooth robotic calculus of a reptile's step, he drew out his hand, clenched into a fist with forefinger, index finger and thumb extended as in benediction. Eye witnesses report that he aimed this makeshift weapon directly at MacDonald's face, unblinking as he quietly, calmly, said, *Bang*.

And Yet

Four years later, authorities confirm, MacDonald was killed by a bomb in Ballykelly, while serving with the British Armed Forces in Northern Ireland, when five pounds of commercial Frangex explosive hidden behind a support pillar were set off on a timer by the INLA inside the Droppin Well disco, a regular haunt of British soldiers stationed at the Shackleton Barracks.

Any connection between the two incidents is unproven. The probability seems remote. And yet while most died under fallen masonry, MacDonald sustained fatal brain injury from shrapnel.

And at the boy's quiet *Bang*, eyewitnesses say, four years before, he screamed.

Cold Iron Gates

It is not known why MacDonald's friend, Hugh Williamson, the second victim, also screamed—did not laugh at an absurd make-believe of murder but rather screamed—falling backwards to scrabble himself away from a handgun formed of two fingers pointing, thumb as hammer. It is not known why, trapped by cold iron gates at his back, he cowered away from the weapon, begging for his life.

All we know is that the boy shot him once in passing, in the chest, and forty seven years later, at the age of sixty three, Hugh Williamson died of a heart attack.

Semaphore of Slaughter

Panic blossomed as the boy strode in through the double doors of the school's main entrance, drawing left hand out now from his trenchcoat, this too shaped in the flesh and bone icon of a pistol. Cruciform arms swung to semaphore of slaughter, this way, that way, *Bang*, *Bang*, *Bang*, *Bang*.

They fled from him, slipped on flooring shiny with mopwater, stumbling over one another in their terror, four more victims in the corridor:

Jane Ferguson, aged 12, leukemia at 18.

Brian Williams, aged 14, heroin overdose at 28.

Sean and Jessica Doherty, both 13, dead at 21, car crash.

Through His Lover's Eyes

The boy watched the rest, the whole routed crowd, fleeing past the stairs leading only to the Maths classrooms on the first floor, Chemistry on the floor above, running for the far doors that would lead out to the playground and B Block: English, History, Art. He waited for the squeeze of bodies in the bottleneck, then whispered, *Boom*. Dozens died in the future uttered, in the years that followed. None escaped.

Death smiled to see it through his lover's eyes as the boy turned to enter an assembly hall packed that Friday, and already in uproar at the horror.

Impossible to Comprehend

It is impractical to detail the carnage fully, impossible to comprehend the piss and shit stench of fear, the hall echoing cacophony of shrieks and sobs, every plea ignored by the boy who loved Death, who walked from huddled wretch to wretch, putting handgun fingertips to foreheads, murdering with every quiet, *Bang*.

Nine hundred and fifty eight pupils died that day or in the days to follow. By accident or cancer: lung; lymphatic; bowel; breast; testicular; etcetera. Whatever.

Only the killer walked away, his handgun pressed to his own chin clicking, clicking, the boy already taken by Death.

Already dead.

The Death of a Love

1

The death of a love is a hard thing to take. Most loves die of natural causes, of course, just fade away slowly over days or weeks, months or years, until there's just a scrap of a ghost, echoes of the good times and the salad days, haunting a home like the tobacco-stink of last night's party, or trailing after two ex-lovebirds as they go their separate ways, clinging to their clothes like each other's perfume or cologne, whispering in their ear when they listen to a certain song. Most loves just have their natural lifespan and after that they weaken and they die. That's the way of things. But it's hard to take, so it's weird but maybe not surprising how a lot of times you see those 'birds stay together after their love is dead, after all that's left is a shadow.

You look for that fat little pink-skinned cupid with its white wings, but it just ain't there. The little fucker is dead and gone.

I mean, sometimes it's not what it seems. Some of those ghost loves, you find they're not really dead at all, so much as . . . dissolved into every little thing that makes up a life together. You're interviewing the parents of a suspect, say. Sitting in some floral-patterned armchair, right? Watching them sit there on the sofa across from you. They don't hold each other's hands. They don't even sit that close to each other. Hell, maybe the wife will be sat down on the sofa while the husband's over at the drinks cabinet, pouring himself a malt whisky. You look around the room, and you see the photographs and the knick-knacks, everything perfectly in place, and it just seems so fucking hollow. You think: this couple, their love died years ago; there's no passion here, no deep desire, just fucking habit. Once upon a time they might have had a cupid fluttering back and forth between them, lighting on her lap now and then, or his shoulder. But that love's flown the coop long ago.

That's what you think.

But then . . . then you notice the wife's gaze drifting across to the photo of the kids. Or maybe the husband will walk across the room and rest his hand on her shoulder. Or something, you know, something like that? And you feel this . . . presence in the house. You can smell it—roses and chocolate and popcorn, maybe, or some other set of smells, sweet and soft or rich, ripe even. You catch a glimpse out of the corner of your eye, a flutter of feathers or a flash of flame, a reflection in a mirror or the glass of a picture frame. Or you hear it—echoes of laughter maybe, a faint hint of a fairground tune. That's when you realise that their love isn't really dead at all; the little bastard's just gone quiet, hid itself in every corner of their life. It's kind of sweet, when you think about it. Like it's become a secret between these two, their silent invisible love.

They're still 'birds, you know? They just sing quietly, just for each other.

That's what my folks were like, you know? Before the old man died. I didn't realise it till after, always thought their love was long-dead of neglect, what with the old man hardly ever home, always working nights on this case or that, and closed in on himself whenever he *was* in the house, drinking to forget those cases. It was only after his death that their love sorta . . . came out of the woodwork, I guess you could say, when my mother needed it most. Fuck me, if I don't go round to visit one day and hear her in the kitchen, chatting away to some chirping canary or some such, I think; only when I walk in, turns out it's their fucking love, this cute little bastard of a cupid, flying round her as she washes dishes, chattering away in this language of whistles and chirps that only she and it understand. Where the fuck was *that* hiding all these years? I thought. Where the fuck was that when I was laying in bed at night, listening to them argue about how the force was killing him.

But, you know, after a while, watching the cupid perch on the refrigerator that he'd grab a beer from, or the kitchen chair that used to be his, or the counter-top where he'd lay his badge down, I understood it was *always* there; I was just too dumb to notice it as a kid. And if there's only two of them speak that weird birdsong language now, it used to be three.

It's a different story for a lot of 'birds, like when the love turns to stone—that I've seen as well. I mean, you can be in the exact same house, with the exact same floral-patterned armchair, exact same sofa, exact same fucking *scatter cushions*, and I tell you, if you don't catch at least a hint of something still going on between the husband and wife—you take a close look at what's around you. Ten to one what you'll see, up on the mantlepiece or on some fucking dresser in the bedroom, is that little butt-naked cupid frozen forever like some plaster cherub. You might even think it looks cute at first, but look closer, at the face. Sometimes they're blank, but a lot of time they're sad. Sometimes they're fucking screaming. Like Han fucking Solo in carbonite.

Swear to God, that type always have their dead love on display somewhere, like a fucking statue. I don't understand those fucks, really I don't. You let your love go cold and still, let it turn to stone, and you put it up on a shelf like a fucking trophy. What's that about? You want to have your grandmother's ashes up on a shelf, that's one thing. You want to send Old Yeller to the taxidermist because you can't stand him being gone—fine.

But your dead love . . .

2

Shit, one time—the Armitage case—I was interviewing this yuppie couple—mid-thirties at the oldest, in-laws of the suspects—and they had their love sitting up in a glass-fronted cabinet, in this Chesterfield kinda thing, right between a model of the Eiffel Tower and a fucking snowglobe of Lady Liberty. The husband, he catches me looking at it, and you know what he says? *It's beautiful, right?*

The Boy Who Loved Death

What kind of fucked-up shit is that, I ask you? Fuck, I know you can't always blame the 'birds for their love going south—shit happens—but these fucks, they don't even question that maybe it's their own fucking neglect killed what they had; they don't even get what they've lost, I realise. To them everything is A-OK and they're proud of it. Never mind the Sixties, I remember thinking, these fuckers have barely caught up with emancipation; to them that love is still something that *belongs* to them, a fucking piece of property, not a living, breathing, laughing, crying *being*. Or the stone-cold mortal remains of one. That kind of attitude to their children and we'd be calling Social Services on the bastards.

That was damn near my first case, actually. I was such a fucking rookie. I remember mouthing off to my partner afterward, Jackman, in The Lizard Lounge, elbow on the bar, waving my beer as I fucking testified: *How can they be like that? What the fuck kind of robotic assholes are these people?* Fuck, I was a real hothead about it; I was so sure that kind of creepy shit put the finger on them, that these heartless freaks had to be the perps, *had* to be.

I don't know. Maybe a little of it was I still thought my folks were that way, an empty shell of a relationship with a dead love inside; I didn't see what they really had going between them, so I hated the old man for a while because I thought he'd let their love die. And maybe that's what made me follow him onto the force as much as anything, made me push for this department. I wanted to sort that kind of shit out. I was a self-righteous little bastard.

Cause all that's just the fucking cherry on the icing—the shadow loves and the stone loves, the cupids dead from lack of due care. What you bite down on in my line of work, every single fucking day of the week, is the big-ass hunk of cake made of chocolate-coloured bullshit, bitter lemons and sour grapes. Cause most loves die of natural causes, sure, and even neglect is natural at the end of the day. You gotta let that love live for itself, find its own way, even if that freedom is the freedom to fade away or go cold; a cupid's progenitors don't *own* it, you know? So you gotta let it be what it's gonna be, live and die by its own will.

But those that don't die natural . . . ah, shit . . . it makes me sick to my fucking stomach sometimes.

You talk to Homicide, Narcotics, Vice, they'll all tell you that they deal with the worst of it—the psychopaths, the drug-dealers, the kiddie porn peddlers; but they ain't got nothing on Erocide. *You* stand on the wharf, I tell them, you stand on the fucking wharf as they pull a three-day old floater out of the water, some poor fucking cupid with its wings all ragged and torn, half the feathers missing and what's left filthy with oil and shit, used condoms and fuck knows what all caught up in them. You look at that baby-soft pink skin all purple and blotchy now, I say, half-eaten by the fishes. You take a good fucking look at that bloated belly and the tongue so fat it spills out of the mouth, like a sick fucking caricature of the podgy little imp it used to be. You look at the fucking strangle marks round its neck, and you tell me that's not a million times worse than any of the shit *you* have to deal with. That's some couple's love, their fucking heart and soul, their hopes and dreams, murdered and dumped like a stray dog. That's a dead child, a crack baby and an abuse victim all rolled into one. That's the worst there is.

And nine times out of ten, it was one of the victim's own 'birds that done it. Shit, *more* than nine times out of ten.

Sure, every so often, every once in a while, you find it's some vicious bastard with an axe to grind, a family-member or so-called friend, some twisted little fuck who can't stand for your two 'birds to have what they don't. Believe me, I've seen them all: the father who don't think his would-be son-in-law is high class enough; the mother who can't let her baby boy love anyone but mommy dearest; the stalker who's sure their cupid is just hiding until this upstart is out of the picture; the angry ex-boyfriend who knows, who *knows* that him and his girl never really had shit together, just a flap of white feathers overhead when they were fucking, but still he blames it all on this bitch who broke his heart. Sure, you get those bastards, the ones who hide their bitterness, stay close to the 'birds and do their damnedest to destroy the love they hate, smiling all the time.

3

That's what I thought we had with the Armitage case, with the in-laws—that yuppie couple with their dead love in the fucking souvenir cabinet. They had to be all fucked-up on the inside, I thought, even if it didn't show; she had to be jealous of her brother and his new wife, what they had together; he had to feel like less of a man than Armitage, not being able to keep his love alive. I couldn't shake that image of the stone cupid in the cabinet, couldn't see how anyone could be that twisted. *Fuck, Jackman*, I remember saying, *would you pickle a fucking cot death and put the jar up on display?*

Don't remember Jackman saying anything to that, just raising his glass to his lips, taking a sip of whisky.

I'd learn.

Those types of love-killings are rarer than you'd think, I'd learn, swear to God. A love can be a tough little bastard when it comes to outside influences set on breaking it up. Disapproving parents might drive your Romeo and Juliet to their deaths, but likely as not they'll just drive them out of town, and those 'birds will fly off into the wilds with a passion that's stronger than if the dumb-ass parents hadn't tried to split them up in the first place. The stalkers and the jilted, they can try to poison the love they hate with lies and rumours, but most likely it'll just come back and bite them on the ass—literally— a bona fide pint-sized angel of vengeance with teeth and fingernails sharp as a cat's claws.

Fuck, most pathetic thing I ever saw was an attempted erocide by an old harpy whose sister met the man of her dreams one day. These two spinsters are both in their seventies, been living together all their lives—fucking Patti and Selma we called them—then suddenly, bam! Selma's got a cupid fluttering round her every time she sees this guy she met down at the bingo, every time she talks about him; and this cupid is getting more and more solid with every date. Patti, she sees herself ending up alone, and she can't stand it. But she doesn't let on. No, she plays it like this is the best thing ever, makes like she adores the little sprite, she's so fucking happy for her sister. She's making nice with it, cooing and petting it all the time. Of course, turns out every night she's creeping out of bed, sneaking into her sister's room, and trying to smother it with a pillow while it's sleeping at the foot of her bed. What makes it so pathetic is the more she does this, the stronger it gets. See, somehow, somewhere in her heart, Selma can tell that there's something not right here. All Patti's fussing, it starts to seem kinda creepy, just a little too intense, so slowly but surely Selma starts to back off from her sister. She starts talking about it to her fella, of course; hell, it just brings her and him even closer together. Anyway, it all comes to a head one night when Selma wakes up to find Patti fucking *gone*. In the head, I mean. She's lost it, totally bat-shit fucking crazy, all her old maid weight on top of the pillow as she tries to suffocate the cupid, screaming at it over and over: *just die already, just die, just die!*

Almost felt sorry for her when we carted her away. That cupid looked as bright-eyed as a prom queen's first crush.

Point is, more often than not, that sort of shit just backfires completely. You put a bullet in someone's love and if they know it was you . . . well, that love might spend a night in intensive care but it'll be all the better for it in the morning. Unless you can persuade your victims that one or both of them is to blame . . . hell, I've seen loves rise from the deathbed like Lazarus, fucking fireworks lighting up the sky, soon as both 'birds found out it was all a mistake. No, he didn't really cheat on her. No, she never said that about him. It was just some scheming little shit trying to wreck their relationship, and not the almighty mindfuck by their partner they'd been led to think it was. Boom! Fwoosh! Fucking happy ever afters like a fucking Disney movie.

Just not that many of them.

See, that's not the usual story. Nine times out of ten—*more* than nine times out of ten—it *is* one or both of the 'birds to blame. Because people are fucking dumb, and they're fucking greedy. They're blind, and they're selfish, and they're just plain fucking crazy. I learned that with the Armitages. There I am, this fucking rookie, railing on at Jackman about how it had to be the creepy in-laws. My second or third case, it was, I think. Jackman, he just shakes his head. *You didn't watch the 'birds*, he says. *I told you to watch the 'birds.*

That's what he'd said to me when I asked why it was us going to notify the victim's progenitors, why they didn't just send two uniforms? And what the fuck were we going to say anyway? Shit, how do you tell a couple of bright young lovebirds that their cupid is down at the city morgue after being pulled out of a dumpster? How do you tell them that its face is pulped so bad they may not recognise it, skull caved in to a different shape, compound fractures to its forearms where it tried to stave off the assault, wings hacked off and as yet unlocated—dumped separately, we were reckoning, in the hope that the body might be misidentified as a human child's? Like you could ever mistake the scent of a cupid, no matter how fucking rank the smell of petrol and burnt flesh coating it. Like you could really mask that beautiful aroma of coffee and home cooking, of rosewater and bergamot, of a thousand other things you just know mean something wonderful to someone. To *two* someones, rather.

You let me do the talking, Jackman had said. *You just listen and watch the 'birds.*

But I didn't listen, and I didn't watch them, not properly. All I saw was two progenitors devastated by the news of the death of their love. All I heard was the hollow echoes of broken dreams recited in broken voices. How they'd been childhood sweethearts. How they'd been living together for two years now, engaged for one. How they had their wedding just there in June. All the things people say mechanically as they realise they don't mean shit anymore. I took some of it in; I noticed the way she cried and he just looked at her helplessly, the way she didn't even turn to him for comfort, the way that even when he moved in to hug her there was a distance, an awkwardness between them. Like they were going through the motions. But their love was dead, right? That thing they'd had between them, that fusion of souls that had once made them reach out to each other without thinking, in times of need, to console or be consoled—that was gone, battered to death by some sick fuck with a tire iron, a crowbar, fuck knows what. How the fuck you expect a couple to be there for each other after that?

4

That's another thing makes Erocide the fucking worst. Can you imagine what it's like to lose a child, but for the one person you share that grief with to be taken away and replaced by a stranger you don't know at all, a complete stranger sitting across the breakfast table from you, looking into your eyes and feeling nothing, just as you look at them and feel nothing? Can you imagine what that's like? I don't know that I can. I don't know that I want to.

They said they'd sort of known—the Armitages, I mean—said they'd felt something was wrong when they got back from the movies and their love wasn't around; but they didn't really admit it to themselves. They'd gone to bed tired, feeling weird, disconnected, but it wasn't until they got up the next morning that the absence really dug its nails into them. That was when they'd phoned in the missing person's report. Cupids go AWOL all the time, play hide-and-seek with you, wander off on a whim, disappear into the shadows only to leap out when you least expect it. They're fucking *capricious*, right? But the Armitages, they said they'd felt that this was different. They'd known.

I remember Jackman nodded at that. But me, I didn't pay attention. I didn't listen and watch. So when we start interviewing the friends and family, when we meet the in-laws with their stone cupid in a cabinet, I think we've got the killer or killers in front of us. The two couples are close, have keys to each other's apartments. This pair are fucking freaks and they're getting their noses rubbed in it by the newlyweds. Who are away at the movies leaving their little cupid home alone. That's means, motive and opportunity, right? And, come on, who the fuck is going to off their own love then call in a missing person's and draw attention to it? When you could just lay low for a month or two then tell everyone your love just faded away? That was my genius logic.

~~~

Sometimes people are dumb or greedy, Jackman said to me. This was in The Lizard Lounge after I'd been laying down How I Saw It. *Sometimes they're blind or selfish or just fucking crazy. But sometimes afterwards they're smart enough to know that if a dead cupid gets traced back to its progenitors that whole story's going to fall apart.*

He was right, of course, more right than I knew. I've been working Erocide now for about as many years as he had been then, and in those years now I've seen all sorts of fucked-up shit from perps trying to make cupid corpses unidentifiable: burning off fingerprints with acid so you can't match them to the 'birds; gouging out eyes so you can't do retina scans for the progenitor's imagos, cutting out their double-hearts and scattering the bits so you can't piece together IDs from the shared memories. At the end of the day though, a couple's love is built so much out of the two of them that their fucking names are coded in its bones. Some solid forensics and some good old-fashioned footwork . . . sooner or later you're most likely going to find your way to the right door. Doesn't mean we can tie a love-killer to the crime, of course, but if they've been telling all their friends about the slow wasting of their late love to a frail wraith . . . and we've got an all-too solid skeleton . . . well, then they have some explaining to do. Sometimes the perps do have the sense not to dig too deep a hole for themselves like that. A lot of the time. Shit, if there's no missing person's report matching your body, and the perp has done their best to make it difficult to identify, most likely what you have is a cover-up, where the love you're dealing with was as hidden in life as it was in death. A love that was fucked from the beginning.

I don't know what the worst case I've dealt with was, but it's a good bet that it was a cover-up. I mean, mostly they're just run-of-the-mill . . . snuffed-out affairs, aborted flings. Some Joe Schmoe has a mid-life crisis and sparks up an affair with his wife's best friend, you know? He's been with his wife for ten, fifteen years though, so when their love starts to fade suddenly he gets cold feet. He doesn't know what he wants. He wants the best of both worlds. He's confused, torn. Guilt makes him compensate, try to rebuild the love he has with his wife. But all the while he's trying to hide this other little cupid, too greedy to give it up but trying *really* fucking hard not to let it show, not to think of the best friend, of the times when they're together, of the thrill of it all. You ever tried *really* fucking hard not to think of someone? It's a surefire way of getting them stuck in your mind like a bad jingle. So slowly but surely Joe drives himself crazy. One day he just loses it while he's with the best friend. *I can't do this anymore*, he says. *This is fucked-up. I love my wife.* Then they get into an argument—maybe it's just the first of many—and sooner or later he's pacing this way and that, shouting all sorts of bullshit at her. They start blaming each other for everything under the sun, cause the guilt is eating away at them both. They're screaming in each other's faces. Finally . . . finally he grabs that cupid by the throat and he strangles the life out of it right in front of her.

Those are the ones we fish out of the river, or dig out of a shallow grave, with their eyes gouged out and their fingerprints burned off. The perp, he panics, but then he gets to thinking, nobody knows about this, just the two of us. Nobody else needs to *ever* know about it. And sometimes, I'm sure, nobody else ever does.

I think my first ever case was a drowned cupid that never did get IDed. Fingers cut off with secateurs or some such, eyes gone, heart never found. The bones gave up names alright, but they were all pet-names—Sweety, Honey, Kitten, Pumpkin, Baby. Forensics said there might be a John or a Joan or a Jean or a Jan in there, but that was the best they could do. *Love*, I remember Jackman saying, *doesn't generally give a fuck what's on the driver's license.*

Sometimes, the cover-ups are as easy to trace as the Armitages, the names shining out of the bones for all to see. Sometimes not.

5

Those are just the common-or-garden cover-ups though, the one-offs; there's much worse than that. You get a serial philanderer with the right fucked-up mindset and you can end up with a backwoods cemetery of shallow graves filled with murdered loves. One old guy we brought in, turned out he had a hundred and forty-three fucking bodies in bits under the floorboards of his apartment. He'd never married; it wasn't that he was trying to hide anything. Psyche evaluation said he wasn't even a psychopath by the normal tests; he just "couldn't face commitment". So over the decades he'd get himself into one relationship after another and he'd destroy them, one after another. Soon as each cupid appeared he'd grab it, chain it up in his closet. *Chain* it up. He needed the love, you know, so he'd let the relationship grow, but he couldn't fucking handle it like a fucking human being so he'd keep that love hidden from the women. The women, they didn't understand what the fuck was going on. It felt like love but there was no fucking cupid. And then eventually, with each of them, he'd reach a point where it was all just too fucking serious, so he'd kill the little bastard. Next time the woman comes round, there's nothing between them; it's like there never *was* anything between them. And she walks away, wondering how she ever fooled herself into thinking they had something. A hundred and forty-three bodies. It was a fucking slaughterhouse that smelled of hot dogs in the park and vanilla incense.

It was the closet case cover-ups Jackman hated the most, and I can't say as I blame him. You could usually tell them right off, because a couple's love always looks sorta like a mix of the two 'birds—one eye of his colour, the other of hers, his fingerprints on one hand, hers on the other, and so on—and that goes all the way down to most cupids being hermaphrodites. Most, I say. If you find a cupid that's wholly male, you can be pretty sure you have a closet case on your hand. You know at least that its progenitors were two gay guys, and if it's a cover-up . . . well, when someone's hacked away at the genitalia in some botch-job attempt to disguise what's going on down there, it's not hard to put two and two together and work out why that love ended up dead. You trace that shit back and half the time you find two frightened fifteen year olds who just panicked before anyone could tell them nobody really gives a shit these days. Don't get me wrong; it's still an erocide and Jackman and me, we'd work the case just like any other. It's just that it brings the bullshit of it all right home to you. Like the Sanchez/Rodriguez case—two kids from the projects, running with the gangs and hard as nails, but scared shitless their compadres would discover they had a thing for each other. So they dealt with their problem the simplest way they knew, emptied the clips of their automatics into it. Thing is, it wasn't that they were horrified at wanting to do the down and dirty with each other; they didn't give a fuck for any idea of what's sinful and sordid; they just bought into a game, and having power in that game meant sacrificing soul for status. They still fucked every day, they told us in the interview room; they just took down the billboard that advertised the fact. That's what Jackman hated about it, not the poor little repressed gayboy bullshit, but the fact that it was so fucking senseless.

Dumb or greedy. Blind or selfish. Or just plain crazy.

Sometimes seems like it's all of the above.

I don't know if it's the worst, but the cover-up case that got under my skin the most was the Henderson cupid, a body that was little more than a bag of broken bones, found in an abandoned subway tunnel. It was Forensics' finest hour, that case, but it still gives me the creeps. All the flesh had been stripped from the skeleton, and a hammer and a hacksaw taken to it; this cupid had been taken apart into a fucking human jigsaw puzzle. That's not the bad part though. The reason this cupid had been taken apart so thoroughly became obvious as the reconstruction job went on and the skeleton began to take shape—or misshape, rather. You get disabled cupids, of course; there's no reason that you wouldn't. They all look pretty much like your plain old-fashioned cherub, but then so do babies; and they all inherit a fair amount of their physical features from their progenitors, just like babies. Now I ain't exactly a paid-up member of the PC Brigade, but that sort of shit never meant anything to me. Some people, they still think in terms of Romantic bullshit, like a beautiful cupid is a beautiful love or some such, and as much as they might deny it they think a cupid with a hunched back or a gimp leg is some sort of sign of malformed love. Frankly though, once you've seen them laid and splayed on the autopsy slab, they're none of them that beautiful a sight and "malformation" is just a matter of metabiology. It doesn't mean shit. But this one was strange in a different way, all out of balance, this part too large for that, that part too small for this, some of the limbs and digits more fitted to a doll than a cupid. I don't remember who it was suggested we had a kiddy-fiddler, but as soon as the suggestion came up it seemed the obvious answer.

Here's the thing though. Forensics pulls all sorts of shit out of their ass, gives us a mugshot and a name, Frank Henderson, even points us at the right neighbourhood. So we do some checking, and we haul this creep in, and he cops to it straight off. It was his cupid, sure enough, his and his niece's, and he'd killed it because he knew it was a fucking freak, that *he* was a fucking freak, that he was *enough* of a fucking freak, even, to twist a young girl's affection for her uncle into something that could spawn this . . . thing. I don't know that I believe his claim that he never touched her, even if we did lean on him hard enough to raise brutality charges in this more enlightened day and age. I don't know that I really care whether he's a sick fuck that acted on it or a sick fuck that didn't; either way he's a sick fuck. What gets in my head is the death of that love, cause I sure as hell don't think it's a fucking miracle of the human heart. Fuck, what gets in my head is I'm not even sure that cupid *was* a love; or if it was, what the fuck does that tell you about love? Some of the boys in the squad, they said it wasn't; that sort of shit just doesn't fucking qualify. But that just leaves me thinking, I've seen some pretty fucked-up loves in my time in Erocide. What else doesn't qualify? Cause I've damn sure seen some shit that walks the line.

Dumb or greedy. Blind or selfish. Or just plain crazy. People kill their love because that's what they are, Jackman used to say. But I wonder if it's maybe even more fucked up. Maybe that's what *they are* because that's what *their love is.*

Fuck, I don't know.

6

As a rookie, on the Armitage case, I thought I had it all figured out though. Love is desire that just keeps growing, right, becoming more and more solid by the day? It's wanting something, and wanting it even more after you've got it. So if someone's taken that away from you, most likely it's because of jealousy, because if they *can't* have it they don't see why you should. I had it all worked out.

I was right that it was jealousy, but wrong in every other way. When we brought the Armitages in to give their statements a day or so after the visit to the in-laws, the husband rolled immediately, gave himself up almost faster than we could get the fucking tape rolling.

He told the whole story with a strange calm, like he'd locked all his feelings so deep inside he wasn't even connected to them anymore. It had been going wrong for a while, he said, since before they got married. He'd gotten moody and brooding when they weren't in company, barely spoke to her in the house; there were money problems and job worries he just couldn't open up to her about. She was diagnosed bipolar, so there were wild ups, but there were wild downs he couldn't deal with, times she said he didn't love her, just the idea of her. She knew he was kinda insecure, worried that he'd lose her to someone better-looking, more exciting. Fuck, it was a long and complicated story of two people letting their relationship fall apart for a huge sorry mess of reasons, of friendship and intimacy gradually crumbling into silence and distance. And yet their love didn't fade, both of them as sure as ever that they loved each other. It just seemed that, no matter how they felt, they couldn't *be* together. It didn't work. So he'd decided that he had to finish it.

She confirmed his story, eventually. They'd gone to the cinema and come back. She'd gone to bed and listened to him smashing glasses in the kitchen. Then something else shattered and she didn't just hear it; she felt it, in the atmosphere of the apartment and in her own heart. She got up, walked through to the kitchen, found him standing over the corpse of their love, the bloody baseball bat in his hand. And that was that.

He'd taken care of the body, and they'd sat up most of the night talking about what exactly they'd lost, what they were going to do now. She'd been ready to lie for him just to try and get them both through this sorry-ass shit-fest. Hell, they both *did* lie, when they called in the missing person's report, and when Armitage and me showed up to notify them that we'd found the body. They kept up the whole charade for two days, and I'm still not entirely sure why he caved so suddenly, changed his mind just like that. I remember him shrugging when I asked though.

I don't know, he said. *I don't know if I was sane then and I'm crazy now, or if I was crazy then and I'm sane now. I don't know anything anymore.*

So, yeah, you talk to Homicide, Narcotics, Vice, they'll all tell you that they've got the worst of it—the PTSD, and the alcohol abuse, and the relationship problems; but they ain't got nothing on Erocide. You look into the eyes of someone who's murdered their own love, I tell them, and there's a whole level of mindfuck you can't even imagine. A few bad dreams and a bit of a drink problem is chickenshit. But, fuck, show me a cop on Erocide who's even *got* a fucking relationship and I'll show you the next in line to put his weapon in his mouth and pull the trigger, blow his fucking brains out. The death of a love is a hard thing to take, but the worst thing is when you learn how to deal with it. Because the only way to deal with it is not to fucking love at all.

Fuck.

You walk long enough through the death of love, after a while you get to thinking . . . maybe those loves should never have lived at all.

The Toymaker's Grief

Once Far Ago

Once far ago—or maybe twice or three times—there lived a toymaker with a beautiful wife and a charming daughter. Then there lived a toymaker with a charming daughter. Then there lived only the toymaker, alone in a quiet house after the funeral, after the mourners had all left, dressed in his finest black suit, sitting motionless on a smooth bed, in a cold room, in an echoless house, simply sitting there, gazing out the window at a sky as blue as the eyes that would never again confirm their love with just the slightest, most momentary, smiling glance.

The Corner of His Vision

He stood then, the toymaker, largely because he didn't know what else to do, and he left the bedroom, closing the door behind him with a soft *click*. He walked down the stairs to the ground floor, pausing at the bottom of the steps, where the front door faced him and the doors into the living-room and kitchen waited to his left, in the corner of his vision, on the threshold of his memory, closed and with a thousand joys beyond, those joys and all the sorrow wound within like coiled springs.

The toymaker turned right and entered his workshop.

The Magic of the Workshop

The magic of the workshop was gone for him, of course, every half-built toy upon the shelves and surfaces an image of another, an original built for his girl: a teddy bear of golden fur and black felt eyes; multi-coloured building blocks with letters on each face; a rag-doll in a gingham dress with wool for hair; a wooden marionette in lederhosen, red cone for a nose; a clockwork ballerina in pink silk, wound by a key to turn *en pointe* and *port de bras* to tinkling tines, delicate as—

The toymaker leant against a wall and wept a while.

The Single Fibre of a Squirrel-Hair Brush

The doll's house was unfinished, just a painted plywood shell of angled roof and four walls hinged to open out, two floors divided into rooms, a stairway made with matchstick banisters. It would have been ready for her birthday, wallpaper patterns painted on with the single fibre of a squirrel-hair brush, each room curtained and carpeted in finest fabric, furnished with bed and dresser, or basin and bath, or sink and cooker, or sideboard and suite and television set and coffee table and china dogs upon the mantelpiece.

Largely because he didn't know what else to do, the toymaker began.

As the Toymaker Worked

As the toymaker worked he didn't notice the minutes becoming hours, the hours becoming days, no light of sun or moon to mark time in his windowless workshop filled with every clockwork toy you can imagine but without a clock. He noticed hunger and he ate, he noticed weariness and slept—at first, at least. After a while he didn't even notice these. He didn't notice the days becoming weeks, the weeks becoming months. The last thing he remembered noticing was the doorbell, a neighbour with concern upon her face, food in her hands.

—You're sure you're coping? she'd said.

A Door Without a Letter-Box

As the toymaker worked, each time he came close to completion of the doll's house, he found reason to be . . . unconvinced by it. The painted-on front door seemed cheap, a trick, when it would hardly be impossible to craft a working frame, a door with hinges, and a pin-head for a doorknob. The windows needed glazed—no, needed to slide open, up and down. The walls were bare without framed paintings and bronze ducks. The floors required Persian rugs. The dresser needed perfume bottles, photographs. And that front door . . . what was a door without a letter-box?

It wasn't good enough.

Shrunken by Sorrow, Consumed by Work

As the toymaker worked—and how he worked—striving to make the doll's house perfect for a memory, he didn't feel the wasting of the years. His hands did not seem frail for all the delicacy of their age; if anything they trembled less, trained by this work of such devotion to such exquisite minutiae. His eyes were sharp as in his youth now, as he worked on tiny letters to sit on the writing bureau in the living-room.

The Boy Who Loved Death

Shrunken by sorrow, consumed by work, he only felt a little weary as he curled up on the stool to sleep.

The New Screwdriver

The doll's house, he decided, needed an extension to the kitchen—no, a garage off to one side. No. A workshop.

It didn't take long to build, barely a year. The hardest task lay in the crafting of the tools to line the racks, and the toymaker had some practice here. He had long since built new tools to work at the small scale of detail he required for the perfection that he sought: a half-scaled hammer; a hacksaw at half the scale of that; a vice scaled down by half again.

The new screwdriver sat well in his grip.

A Little Something Missing

From inside the doll's house the work was so much easier now. He only had to stoop a little as he moved from room to room to squeeze himself through the miniature doorways. He could kneel to paint the skirting boards, or to carve in gaps between the floorboards where he had pulled up the carpet, or to screw in the power sockets for the wiring he had laid. And the doll's house in the workshop of the doll's house in the workshop was nearly complete, only a little something missing, he thought.

A letterbox for the door, he thought.

Hal Duncan

And Long Away

Once far ago—or maybe never, maybe never—there lived a toymaker without a beautiful wife and a charming daughter, alone and lost, somewhere in a doll's house within a workshop of a doll's house within a workshop of a doll's house within a workshop, and so on. And so on. He had lived there for so many days and weeks, months and years, in the houses of his grief, that he had quite forgotten how far ago and long away the outside world was.

Is this the end of the story?

Let it not be the end.

One day . . .

Styx Water and a Sippy Cup

Babycart at the River Styx

Three hours later and my shout of *bored now* is still echoing round the caverns of Erebus when the darkness finally splits and, out of the streaming light of the temporal plane, the Angel of Death hands me the stillborn babe. It's screaming loud enough to wake the dead—no pun intended; I was nodding off waiting for the fucking portal, but the kid's caterwaul is audio adrenaline, delivered by syringes in the ears. I wrap it—*him*—in the swaddling clothes and rock him in my arms.

—No name, says the angel. They hadn't decided yet.

—Bollocks, I say.

~~~

—Ah, shusht, I murmur.

I hold the wrinkly runt in the crook of one arm, reach the other into the pram, groping for the bottle.

—Yeah, death sucks, I know. But this'll fix you right up.

The formula feed is basically cold water, but the babe still locks his cherub lips around the rubber teat like it's the mother's breast he'll never now taste. They always do, right enough. Who doesn't love the sweet salt tang of the Cocytus, river of lamentations? Who in Hell doesn't love the liquor we all live on, the quenching, quieting tears of the bereaved?

~~~

What? It's good for them. The Acheron spring water heals the holes in their hearts, the diseases in their blood, the damage in their genes. And the Lethe takes away all those nasty memories of being born and dying . . . or dying and being born, I guess . . . or just plain dying.

As the babe sucks down on it, I lay him in the pram so I can slip my hip-flask from my pocket. I prefer a little vodka and kahlua in *my* mother's milk: the firewater of the Phlegethon, hot as wrath; and the rich dark hatred of the Styx.

—It's not so bad here, I say to the kid as I trundle the pram onward through the cavernous wastes of the underworld.

He looks up at nothing in particular, eyes unfocused, tiny hands grappling air.

—Well, not *here* per se, I admit. Erebus is pretty fucking crappy. But where we're going it's not so bad. You'll see.

Cold grey catacombs of rock riven by chasms. Spines of stone that arc through the hollows of the afterworld. Slopes of bone scree that descend to plains of dust and ash. I'm glad I know the shortcut to the River Styx.

A Conversation with Charon

—And if you look out on your right, says Hermes Trismegistus, you'll see the Old City, founded by Ereshkigal in the Eighth Millennium BC—and if it looks desolate now, you should've seen it in its heyday! Men, women, *children* in cloaks of feathers, feeding on mud and drinking from ditches, languishing in lamentation! And it wasn't a whole lot better, so I hear, even *after* Queen Ereshkigal found love in the form of Nergal, back in the Fifth Millennium. That was before *my* time, of course . . .

—Fuck, I say to Charon. How many times have you heard this spiel?

Standing in the door to the bridge, babe cradled in my arms, I look back over my shoulder at Hermes—spiff as ever in his tour guide's blazer, radiating charm and sincerity to his audience of however many pram-toting nurseryfolks on stork runs, some listening intently, others looking bored, chatting, snoozing. Oh, and one Amazonian tribesman in a Coca-Cola t-shirt. Poor confused bastard; given you only qualify for Limbo if you never had the chance for salvation . . . well, I'm guessing he's no more offay with riverboats and Sumerian deities than with the Gospel of Jesus Hallelujah Christ.

Hermes is onto the War now, the palace coup pulled topside by Japheth—or Jove or Jehovah or whatever He wants folks not to call Him. How He exiled the previous incumbent down here, with his giants and whatnots. To the abyss at the heart of the city.

— . . . the Phlegethon flowing into it, says Hermes, a crashing cataract of fire! It was quite a sight, the King of Gods dragging his fallen foes in shackles through the city of death, hurling them over the Gehenna Falls. Just imagine it! Titans tumbling down in flames into Tartarus . . .

Fucking marvellous, I think.

Charon stands at the wheel, guiding the riverboat downstream, steering for one archway of Perdition Bridge—with its endless parade of damned souls, all trudging on under the scourges of hideous angels and beautiful demons, all headed for the New City, the prison built into the walls of the pit itself, the panopticon Pandemonium.

—Originally, of course, Hermes is saying, the maximum sentence for the Chosen People was twelve months, then it was off to Olam-Ha-Ba. But since the Reforms . . .

I try again with Charon.

—I said, You must have heard this spiel how many times?

Charon shrugs.

Hal Duncan

The Fields of the Lord

—Isn't it pretty? I say to Junior, holding him up to see the shimmering coast of Elysium, the low rolling hills of green and gold fields where work crews in orange jumpsuits toil in eternal summer, harvesting the asphodels. Off in the distance, even Mount Purgatory itself is kinda . . . industrial picturesque, slopes built up in a collage of concrete factories, sandstone and adobe dwellings, like some little town of Araby or Europe, I'm told, only city-scaled, with a mooring tower for its minaret or steeple. Silver zeppelins rise from the smog haze, sail off into the blue, for Heaven.

I wait patiently on deck with the other nurseryfolks while Charon lowers the gangplank and Hermes, still spieling, leads the Amazonian tribesman down onto Limbo's docks, introduces him to his Purgatory liason, here to sell the poor pagan the salvation scheme he missed out on in life. Fucking Purgatorian vultures. Might at least give the heathens time to settle in before trying to shill them with your Short Shrift Gospel. I clock an old couple headed for the Amazonian, waving. Get in there quick, I think, before your boy buys a quick trial and a long walk over Perdition Bridge.

I shouldn't be so down on the Purgatorians, I guess; this city of the innocent and ignorant would be Stone Age misery without their labour and trade, without all those new inmates and their new ideas . . . riverboats and shit. It's just weird for us Limbo kids. You can't help but wonder who you left behind, where they ended up. Sitting sweet in Heaven? Suffering in Hell? Slaving sixteen centuries on His holy asphodel plantations?

I dig a softpack of Ambrosias from my pocket, spark one up and earn a hard stare from a nurseryman beside me.

Fuck you, I think.

—Fuck you, I say to the Purgatorian as I bump the pram down off the gangplank and over his foot. Save me the *suffer the little ones* speech.

—Friend, he begins.

I cut him dead.

—No sin but being born. *Fuck. Off.*

It's the one loophole in God's Law, the original sin exemption clause—which, given His nutjob notions of sin as a stain of temporal temptations, makes for one almighty fuck-up. Apart from dying unbaptised, legally speaking, my immaterial ass is incorruptible as gold even if it farts the Lord's Prayer backwards.

So much for His almighty omniscience.

A Pram on a Tram

—Coming through, coming through. Come on, delivery for the nursery here.

I flick my cigarette away and, with no small palaver, haul the pram up the steps into the tram, flash my pass at the driver. Shit, a city built around a nursery, and the public transport system is a fucking obstacle course. So, yeah, all the cool storks are using those papoose things these days. I am *not* wearing a fucking baby like a fucking backpack. Or frontpack, whatever. I'd only end up blowing smoke in their eyes, flicking ash on their heads by accident, or some such shit.

—Hey, bro! says a voice behind me.

—Sis!

I give a back-slapping hug to my old dorm-mate, Suze. She scruffs my hair just like she used to—what?—sixty years ago or more? Must be five or ten since we last met. She still looks like the twenty-something punk kid I used to mosh with in Club Oblivion, albeit in indie hipster togs now.

—Another for the brood? she says.

—They keep coming so I keep collecting, I say.

—If you're that committed, she teases, you know they have those foster schemes these days.

—Fuck that shit.

∾∾

I'm a traditionalist, I guess. Or maybe I just click with the old-fashioned ways because that gives me a sense of . . . paying it back. Like, Aunt Euphemia did this for me way back when, and for all I grump that she'll never let me forget it, crabby old broad, I'm glad she was my stork. And glad, weirdly, that my first memory is her rooking me at Texas Hold 'Em.

All that hugs and kisses nurturing shit? Schooling and scolding? That's what the nursery's *for*.

Fuck it, OK. I just don't have the patience to be an actual parent.

∾∾

—Don't blame you, says Suze. If it goes in as asphodels, what comes out don't smell flowery. A decade of diapers? Not for me either.

I shrug as the two of us lean in over Junior.

—Meh. This one's a spurter, I reckon. Look at him grasping, the curious little sucker. Don't worry, Junior. Law says you grow as you grow. Can't starve you of experience if you're hungry; that'd be cruel and unusual.

Suze arches an eyebrow at me, grinning.

—You so totally want to raise him.

—Bollocks, I say. You remember how long we were eight-to-ten?

The Nursery of Limbo

I push the pram down the Avenue de Pèpiniére, grumbling all the way at the juddering cobble-stones and high curbs, the distance from the tram stop to the nursery, the pram-rattling ridges of tarmac ridged and ripped-up by tree roots underneath—but kinda happy, to be honest, to be back on my home turf, humping the pram up steps—that really shouldn't be there—to the great ornate iron gates of the nursery. Those gates. They're not pearly but they don't have *Abandon Hope* over them either, and the most important thing is they're always open.

Always.

Kids running and playing. The Nursery of Limbo was founded in the 4th century or so, maybe before—not that it really matters. Kids shouting and shrieking. It's kinda like a city within the city, huge and sprawling, buildings built onto buildings, a labyrinth of dormitories, refectories, libraries, its boundary ever-expanding. Kids fighting and laughing. Courtyards and cloistered quadrangles and archways between them, stone steps leading up or down. Kids crying and skipping. Gardens with signs that tell you to walk on the grass, go on, you know you want to, dance on it barefoot, with a water-pistol.

Kids.

In the motherer's office Aunt Euphemia is in full flow, arguing with the Dormitory Mater, waving away protestations with her usual disregard. It's something about Styx water and a sippy cup, I think, but my arrival and the ensuing fuss cuts it short. She stands, arms folded, as I lift Junior from the pram, hand him over to the ermine-uniformed motherers. (Or *smotherers*, if you're Aunt Euphemia.)

—No name, I say. Parents hadn't decided yet.

There's much tutting. (And a nod from the old stork towards the door.)

—I'll catch up with you, I say as we slip out.

—Unca Sal! Unca Sal!

 —Did you go to Hell again, Uncle Sal?

 —Did you bring us something back?

 —Uncle Sal, what was it like? Did you see Sharon?

 —It's *Charon*, dummy.

 —Uncle Sal! I won at Blackjack!

—What was it like, Unca Sal?

—Cold and dark as God's heart, I say. Cause it's where he buries what he hates.

—Except *we're* right under His nose, aren't we, Uncle Sal?

—Damn straight, I say.

I tweak a freckly sniffer between two knuckles.

—Uncle Sal, the kiddies' pal, says Aunt Euphemia, who's standing at the door. Who knows me all too well.

Last Drink Bird Head

Last Drink Bird Head is the state of mind achieved in walking home from a party that began the scorching afternoon of the summer day before when you were sitting in the park with friends, smoking a spliff rolled by your mate and drinking beer out of the can, perhaps, or red wine from a plastic cup, and as the sun lowered with the evenfall, between you all an obvious and often-made suggestion was approved—the pub?—and you, the three or four of you, or maybe more, walked the short distance laughing, staggered in and ordered food, and sat there chatting, arguing and joking until closing time when you all realised two things, that you'd run up one fuck of a bar bill, and that none of you really wanted to go home, to call it quits, just yet, so in the end you grabbed a taxi, headed back to your mate's house to drink more, smoke more, talk and toke more, listen to loud music, maybe take some pills or tabs and go through thrills and chills and stabs of shiver rippling down your spine so fine and twined like a snake around and right back up it to a judder of shoulders and a *fuck me, man, it's really kicking in now*, and the world began to shudder apart again to trails of red and green streaming dreams down curtains, round the edges of it all, friend's faces glowing golden, leonine and haloed, a kaleidoscope of meaning in your head, a glorious insanity, a rapture of the charlatan subconscious that crashed in a clash of symbols, washed in waves, and peaked, peaked with a vision of wise nonsense, peaked in the truth of being here and now, and slowly faded, slowly faded to the after-effects, the grit of teeth and ache of bones like you'd been over an assault course, strangely comfortable—fuck, almost *sensual*—but enough to make you grab another beer, accept the spliff passed to your hand, and let yourself unwind with alcohol and hash, relaxing in the splendid afterglow, returning to the gab and giggles till eventually, eventually, you realised it was getting light outside and so you took a slug of beer, of that last drink, a last drink for the road, and grabbed your coat, said your goodbyes and took another slug, then swirled the can to check how much was left and—*fuck it*— drained it and, now long past drunk and out the other side, you headed out into the break of day, dawn chorus greeting you with birdsong light and dancing as your mood, your head with that last drink become a reeling flutter of a myriad starling thoughts awhirl in the blue sky of a gorgeous day, riotous night and tranquil morning, the cerulean of your quietude broken only by the sweeping, swooping flock of moments that the day and sleep have not yet scattered into dreams, not yet, not yet.

The Beast of Buskerville

1

The Beast of Buskerville? Now there's a tale! Why, it's only the tale of old Whelp, eh? The tale of the most frightsome hound as ever haunted London, and of Yapper, the Scruffian as learned to speak dog, the Scruffian as *tamed* Whelp . . . well, as near to tamed him as that snarling, slavering, scurrilous cur of a canine ever could be tamed. But more'n that, scamps, this here's a tale of the single most villainest villain ever to prey on the likes of us, the vulture of vagabonds, the buzzard of beggars, the scavenger of Scruffians . . . the Waiftaker General himself.

Now, you all's seen the Waiftaker General with yer own peepers, so there ain't no need for conjuring him, right? Back when this story took place, he'd the same beak nose of a bird of prey, the same beady eyes with pin-prick pupils, the same scrawny neck to angle his head this way and that, to size up a Scruffian just Fixed or all set for a Scrubbing. Only thing different back then . . . though his hair it were slicked back to his skull the same, so's he looks a true hawk—back then it were black instead of white.

So. It began on a day as seemed like any others for the Waiftaker General, as he rose from his fancy four-poster bed, bid his butler hold the piss-pot for him whiles he drains his bladder, then pour water—piping hot!—for him to wash his fams. Why, that butler even buttons up his breeches, he does; helps him on with his big black frockcoat what flaps like wings when he pounces on yer; and knots his white silk cravat so *sartorially sophisticated* . . . what only makes his neck look scrawnier, poking out as a vulture's from its ruff.

All the whiles he were dressing, of course, he were already at work, calling in his lieutenant to tell him how many waifs was took for Fixing in the dead of night, and was they Jews or gypsies, paupers or carnies? Was they boys or girls with black mops or blond curls? What ages and stages of starving was they? So what was their worth at the going rates? And all of this writ in his little black book. And then lastly he spins, with a smile cruel as sin, and asks, How many *scruffs* did the stickmen bring in?

2

Now on this day, after all these accountings of the night's business, there's a few more things for the Waiftaker General to be asking after, yeah? This weren't no different from no other day, mind, cause he'd always have what he calls *extraordinary business*. One day it might be a partic'lar Scruffian as is vexing him sorely with spritely shenanigans—Lightfinger Larker outdoing himself as prince of the pickpockets, or Flashjack Scarlequin playing scourge of the stickmen. Others it might be *truly* extraordinary—rascalry from Rake Jake Scallion or some other Rake as *looks* like a groanhuff but's Scruffian inside.

Today though it were the Beast of Buskerville to be dealt with, and for some reason—a reason what nobody in all his staff knew, not his butler nor his lieutenant, nor one of his stickmen, nor a single sausage in all the lodges across London—this partic'lar *extraordinary business* did seem to get the Waiftaker General's feathers extraordinarily ruffled. What news of the Beast of Buskerville? he snapped, soon as the tally of snaffled scofflaws was noted. Is there sight or sound of it? Sniff of spoor of it? What news of that bothersome, blackguardly brute of a Beast?

See, there ain't no borough more troublesome to the stickmen than Buskerville anyways, on account of it having its streets *all over* London, it being patched from the pitches of all em organ-grinders, penny-whistlers, Punch-and-Judy-men and whatnots. Worse, it's always on the move, always shifting, and that's a thing as no stickman can stand. Can't get their heads round it, can they? Course, every Scruffian knows Buskerville the way a sailor knows knots; there's rich pickings to be made among the toffs as dawdle on its corners, wipes and tickers just waiting to be plucked.

So if there was anywheres in London as caused the Waiftaker General grief, it were Buskerville; and lately that Buskerville botheration had gotten sorer still, with reports of routs—panic in the streets—all sparked by vicious attacks from a dread fiend of the four-legged faithful-friend variety. Nobs was being savaged, and their brats was being mauled, by some demon dog as like to go for a throat as for a toffee apple. A demon dog, says they, as had been shot, stabbed, scorched, you name it, and weren't nothing could keep it killed. Could it possibly be . . . ?

3

—A Scruffian dog? says the Waiftaker General as he steps down from the carriage that's took him all the way from his Kensington townhouse to his Westminster workplace, that dark, domed crematorium of a construction they calls the Institute. Perhaps, he says as he swipes his cane at some hawker stood on the steps with a lad on a leash—an urchin to be Fixed, no doubt, and an owner as needs learning in the protocols of propriety, to bring his purchase to the *appropriate* entry.

—Perhaps, he says to the lieutenant as scurries after him. Perhaps some . . . failed experiment.

—An investigation must be instigated, of course, says he. An inquiry must be initiated, an inquest inaugurated. If this monstrous mongrel is indeed a product of our hallowed Institute, why, this is a scandalous misuse of our facilities. Scandalous! Tell the PM he may rest assured: we *will* uncover the culprit of this crime, and deal with him severely. *Most* severely.

Oh, there was a black scowl in the Waiftaker General's beady eyes as he says those words. There's few groanhuffs can brood as bitter as the Waiftaker General, foul-tempered fucker that he is.

—Heads *will* roll, says he.

—But of course, says he as he aims another swipe at the hawker (who don't seem to be fathoming the correctitude of conduct as is being imparted to him through the medium of whacking, who's still worrying at the sleeve of the lieutenant as is s'posed to open the Institute's front doors for Himself, holding him back from doing his dutiful.) Of course, says the Waiftaker General, our priority of primacy must be the apprehension of this foul abomination, the extermination of this vile vermin, the Scrubbing of this Scruffian canine. If indeed that is the nature of this . . . this . . .

Oh, there was a right sour twist to the Waiftaker General's thin lips as he spoke. Might have been a slight bite to em too, me scamps, the bite of lip on a man as wants to say more than he ought to, a villain as has an awful urge to rant and rail, but has a damn good reason not to blather his bile too wildly, eh? But if there were, it wasn't such as the lieutenant were like to notice with the hawker tugging at his sleeve and Himself exploding:

—The side-entrance, you cretinous oaf, he shouts.

The Boy Who Loved Death

4

Now, that were the first the Waiftaker General truly noticed the nature of this hawker as was harrying his man. And if ever there was anything made to revolt him to the depths of his soul—anything as wasn't an escaped Scruffian, that is—it was this pitiful peddler. Hunchbacked and hook-nosed, he was, a Rumpelstiltskin as rag'n'bone man, wearing the black-glassed spectacles of the blind, with straggly hair and matted beard as might be grey or even white underneath all the filth. Togged in tatters too, layer upon layer. And the sight weren't nothing to the stench.

But now as the Waiftaker General had actually noticed the peddler, he couldn't help but notice the urchin as was with him too; and if the peddler had him wanting to wash the filth from the Institute's front steps with a firehose, why, that boy made him wants to purge it with purifying flames first, for he'd never seen no Scruffian as scruffy as this in all his puff. Barely clothed, the boy was, in rags as hardly kept him decent, the number of holes they had in em. Why, the dirt made a better job of covering his flesh.

More'n that though, the Waiftaker General, he saw then that this weren't no urchin being brung for Fixing, but a Scruffian already Fixed, the scars of the Stamp upon his chest for all to see, under his buttonless shirt, when the boy sat back on his haunches—as he did just at that moment. He weren't just on a leash that lad, see, a leather collar round his neck and a chain held tight in the peddler's liver-spotted hand; he even walked on all fours like a dog, sat down like one too, at a yank of his leash.

Now the Waiftaker General weren't inclined to be intrigued by this. Was he bollocks! No, all the more reason for him to rail at this noisome nuisance, cause Scruffians to be Scrubbed *definitely* wasn't for the front doors. But with him proper noticing the hawker now, well, nows he noticed what the man were saying. And that *were* intriguing.

—If ye please, yer vorshipful 'onour, says this hunchback hawker. My name is Lionel J. Reakesack, and fer all as I'm blind and beggarly, yer eminent regality, I'm come here vith me Scruffian to 'elp yer catch the Beast of Buskerwille.

5

There's wicked and cruel men who would have simply laughed then, scoffed at the notion of such scum being of service, being useful in any manner other than maybes keeping rats in check by hunting em for mealtime morsels. But that's a kind of wicked and cruel as has a sense of humour in all its nastiness, and the Waiftaker General, he ain't even got that to be said for him. Ain't never so much as a snigger passed those lips, not a chortle nor a chuckle. So all's he done was sneer down the beak of his cocked snoot.

—To help us catch the Beast of Buskerville? says he. And just how does a piddling peddler such as you, an aptly-named *reeking sack* of misshaped penury such as you, propose to be of assistance? You do understand that as the Waiftaker General I have the entire Institute at my disposal, not to mention the constables of every lodge across the whole of London? How precisely do you fancy yourself, a blind cripple, facillitating the capture of that cur?

—If ye please, yer esteemed reverence, says Reakesack. If ye please, I've come to offer me serwices as a tracker.

—Well, in truth, says he, if ye please, yer magnanimous magnificence, it ain't so much *my* serwices that I'm enwisioning as may be of some walue; no, it's the serwices of me Scruffian 'ere. Now, blind as I am I can't see yer scorn, but as a certainty I can imagine it, sir; for sure and this creature must look as vorthless to you as to the sot I bought 'im from; and truth be told that drunk had so little use for 'im I got the lad for a bottle of gin. Got 'im to be me eyes, sir.

—But ye see, says he, if yer please, yer resplendent nobilitude, the boy were a vild child, found in a forest or summat, never learned to talk nor even walk upright. Fixed for to be a guard dog, growling being 'is only apparent skill. Veren't much use at that neither; 'e's a craven whelp as cowers at a kick—see? Oh, but bless the good Lord if old Lionel J. Reakesack didn't find a use for a boy raised as a dog, and not just as me eyes. As me nose too, sir. Oh, my Yapper'll *sniff out* yer Beast.

6

Now the Waiftaker General hadn't never heard of no feral child being Fixed, but old Reakesack 'splained as the lad were from way back, according to the sot what owned him afore. Guarded the family business for generations, stretching back to the days of his grandfather's grandfather, so he says. Kept with the dogs for a century or more, until he come to think he was one, even come to know his way by his nose just like a dog. Course, then that sot drunk away that family business, and what use were a guard dog with naught to guard?

—Now mark me, says Reakesack, for I'll not lie to ye, yer blessed grace; it's a fishy story, of a truth, if ye please. For as ye see when I kicks 'im—see?—or when I smacks 'im with 'is leash—see?—or even if I just clips 'is ear—see?—he don't growl at *nothing*. So I reckon as that sot was spinning a yarn and thinking to pull a fast one on old Lionel J. Reakesack. But bollocks to that bugger, hee hee, if ye'll pardon me French, for I got the best of 'im in the end.

—A Scruffian vot ain't got no words to be always asking questions, says Reakesack. A dog vot 'as the smarts to answer. Yes and no. Two yaps for yes, and one yip for no. Ain't that right, boy?

And blimey if that boy didn't give two little yaps in answer.

—Ye'll be a good dog for yer master, won't yer, boy? says Reakesack.

—Yap yap, says the lad.

—Knows the Beast of Buskerwille's stink, don't yer, lad?

—Yap yap.

—Yer can sniff yer way to 'is lair, boy, can't yer?

—Yap yap.

—And ye'll not lead us astray, eh?

—Yip.

So the Waiftaker General he peers at the scamp, angling his head this way and that; and the scamp he's just sat there, tongue lolling from his mouth. Then he peers at old Reakesack, angling his head that way and this; and old Reaksack *he's* just stood there, tongue licking at his lips. The gleam of guineas in his eyes, he has, thinks the Waiftaker General, the greedy grubbing avarice of a right Jew.

Oh, but the Waiftaker General, he has his own hunger rising in his heart. It just ain't wealth he's wanting.

The Waiftaker General, he wants *blood*.

7

—Look sharp! he snaps at his lieutenant. Sound the bell! I want ten men, with pistols, nets and ropes, here *now*! Go on! he roars. I want them ready for the hunt, ten of the best, snapped to attention, spick and span—you know I'll stand no less—and if this blistering breath has ended by the time they're here, by God, if I have time to catch another breath to blast, I swear my next will signify your last, I'll have your badge, your balls, and all the seed they've sown, you laggardly, lollygagging, lazy . . .

—Very good, he says.

So there's a baker's dozen of em as sets out in search of the Beast—the lieutenant counting himself as one of the best, natch—an unlucky thirteen of em, as they might have had good sense to pay some mind to: ten broke-nosed, brawny stickmen with coshes, all dolled up like a boxers' wedding party in their grey bowlers and tin flutes; the Waiftaker General at the head of em, his topper on tight, his cane tapping sharp with his stride; Reakesack up front, scurrying on, stoop-shouldered; and this lad, half-pauper, half-pup, leading the pack.

They starts the hunt in Covent Garden, where's many a Scruffian snaffles treats and trinkets; though there ain't many a Scruffian in sight soon as em stickmen stride in. Why, one whistle from a lad sat watching Jack Ketch hanging Punch, and half the audience is offsky in a flash, scattered into the mob like mouses to their holes, and scarper signals by the score sounding all through the market. But for once the beak-nose bastard ain't a-flap and screaming shrill, to *grab em* and *nab em*. Oh, no; it ain't scruffs is on the Waiftaker General's mind today.

—This . . . marketplace, says he, voice dripping with disdain of all em flower-girls and fruit-hawking costermongers. The last sighting of the Beast was in this . . . vicinity, was it not?

—Indeed, sir, says his man. Last night, no less, stealing sausages from some servant's—

—How most like a Scruffian, sneers the Waiftaker General. Well, Reakesack, set your whelp to work; and pray it does as promised, else . . .

—Of course, yer 'igh-born 'oliness, says Reakesack.

And down he bends to pinch the lad's ear, hiss his orders in it, seal em with a curse and cuff.

And then they's off.

8

At first they ain't going nowhere fast, Yapper leading em in circles, snuffling at the stalls and cobblestones, wandering left and right to weave his way amongst the mob of serving-maids with shopping baskets and whatnot. First it's all zig-zags and criss-crossings, now this way, now that, like as that lad were scribbling out the very Stamp scarred in his chest, in all its convolutions. 'Fore long though, Yapper, he's straightening out to sniff his way along one wall, stopping to cock his head. Then with an almighty howl, that Scruffian lad starts straining at his leash.

Out of Covent Garden he pulls em, scrabbling keen along the kerbs, up Bow Street and around, down Drury Lane, with all its plate-glass-windowed gin palaces—and there's more'n one rogue there eyes em stickmen as they pass, pipe in his teeth, hand drifting to them scars he never shows nobody—his Stamp. There's more'n one Rake gives a queer peer at Reakesack in partic'lar. And slinks back into a doorway as the Waiftaker General marches past.

Along and around, nipping down this alley here, this back-street there, off Kingsway and back on it, Yapper leads em.

Every turn as can be took along High Holborn, Yapper takes it, and some more besides, winding wigglier than the Thames itself, and never tiring, so it seems, even as morning passes into afternoon, even as the proud stride of the Waiftaker General and his stickmen gets less puffed-up and more puffed-*out* what with all em hours of walking. It's early-afternoon afores they even reach the Old Bailey, mid-afternoon by the time they's jostling through the crowds of Cheapside, Reakesack casting glances at the glint of signet rings and scarf pins in the jewellers' shop-windows.

As the afternoon stretches on, Yapper starts to lead em north, he does, up through Petticoat Lane with all its stalls of clobber top-notch or tatty; and the Waiftaker General he scowls at the traders with their sidelocks and wide-brimmed hats, mutters about immigrants and churches turned to synagogues. On and up they goes, more directly now, as evening sets in, using bluster and bullying to carve a clear path through Spitalfields Market as the traders is closing up their stalls for the night. Up to the edge of Bethnal Green and Shoreditch.

To the Old Nicol Rookery.

9

—Of course, says the Waiftaker General as Yapper halts, starts whining, cringing from the kicks what Reakesack aims to send him on, but stubborn as an animal as smells its own death in the abbatoir ahead. Tain't no abbatoir as is in front of em, that loverly little neighbourhood marked out by Half Nichol Street and Boundary Street, Old Nichol Street and Nichol Row, that cesspit of a slum owned by the pious and rented to the poor, three families to each house. Tain't no abbatoir, but it might as well be, how it treats em animals as enters it.

—Gerron, yer warmint! snarls Reakesack, whipping his Scruffian forward with the chain.

—A most suitable habitation for a mongrel scruff, says the Waiftaker General as he brings out his pistol. On your guard, men.

Into the lair of the Beast they goes then, into the rookery's maze of blackened tenements, more'n a score of narrow streets, all reeking with the stench of tripe and tallow, cow's shit and cat's meat, dead dogs' corpses in the mud. Dark doorways gape on either side, doors long-since gone for firewood. Eyes peer at em through broken soot-smeared windows.

In they goes.

Three men the Waiftaker General sends down a side-street, to circle round. Three men he orders down another alley as might hide a hound. Three he sends off yet another way entirely, three in each team cause even pairs ain't safe in the Old Nichol, not even the beefiest bruiser stickmen, with the heftiest coshes they can carry. But yer don't catch nothing in the Old Nichol lest ye can box it in. So they needs to be smart, he tells them, leave the Beast nowheres to run.

—Sound your whistle if you see it, men, says he. Immediately.

Course, with old Reakesack and his Scruffian hardly counting in a scrap, well, the Waiftaker General, all's he's got is his lieutenant now, but he ain't one to be trembling with no stickmen at his side. Don't you be fooled by all his fineries into thinking he's a fop. Don't you be thinking, as he's heartless, why, he must be gutless too. Evil don't come so neatly wrapped, me scamps, all tied up with a dainty ribbon. No, that there waiftaker were a man with ice in place of blood, a man as hadn't *never* known fear.

Until that day.

10

On through the rookery they goes, eyes watching em all the way, children and drunks being dragged in off the streets, quarrels cut-off with fists at faces, songs stilled to silence halfways through a verse, *all* ruckuses dying in their path, like as the Angel of Death has come to Egypt, come to take their firstborn. Men as would murder for a sniff what slighted em step back to let the vulture of vagabonds pass.

The Boy Who Loved Death

Only once had a Waiftaker General come to grief in any London slum. Tales are still told of the tithe took by his heir.

Sudden and sharp, a sound cuts through the air—a whistle! Off to the west it is, and the Waiftaker General's after it in a jiffy, pistol in the air—come on! This way down an alley, that way now, he runs, the slap of steps echoing off the walls as the whistle blows again, then cuts off dead. He's still running when another whistle sounds—to the south now.

—Quick! It's on the move!

A third whistle! This time to the north—too far away, surely. He whirls, coat billowing, his lieutenant stumbling not to run right into him.

Now the second whistle blows again, no more'n yards away; he sprints to a corner, pistol aim sweeping round at . . . nothing. Another whistle! The first again? But to the east now? How? And he ain't barely off his mark, the lieutenant, Reakesack and Yapper in tow, when a shrill tin shriek sounds far behind. Now all three whistles sounds at once, here, there and elsewheres, notes drawn long, and longer still, going on and on until . . . they stops.

All's silence.

Silence except for Yapper's whimper as he slinks back, cowering, quivering, peepers fixed on the black maw of a doorway.

—Sir, says the lieutenant. Sir! The Scruffian!

The Waiftaker General, he's got the gears of his noggin whirling right now, figuring how's the rookery scum's ambushed his men, called a reckoning upon themselves too, interfering in his extraordinary business; but he's quick to catch the drift of his lieutenant's fluster. The hawker ain't slow neither, finger pointing.

—Is 'e in there, boy? says Reakesack.

—Yip!

—'E's in there, sir! The Beast!

In the Waiftaker General's noggin, a tiny niggle—*yip*, one *yip*—catches a cog only to be whirled away. No matter.

At last the Beast is within his grasp.

11

The Waiftaker General goes in first, pistol in one hand, cane in the other. His lieutenant follows, cosh and net at the ready. Ain't a flicker of light in the tenement close. Only hints of gloaming seeps through the cardboard and rags what patches a window on the stairwell, halfways up to the first floor. Ain't no lights in the ground floor flats neither, nor a peep of human habitation. In a rookery as has folks living twenty to an home.

—Search them, sir? asks the lieutenant.

The Waiftaker General points at where Yapper's nosing.

—Up the stairs, says he.

On the first floor landing, it's darker still, without even the light from the close's front door. They peers into flats with windows boarded up, but all's they make out is rotten floorboards smeared with filth they smells more'n sees. Up to the second floor they goes, into deeper blackness, like as someone's sealed up every crack what might let in the slenderest shaft.

—Ah, vait just a tick, yer grandiose vorthiness, says Reakesack. I've a glim here, sir, I'm sure. Hold this.

He gives the lieutenant the leash, rummages out a candle, strikes a light, a phosphorous flash, and-

Of a sudden, Yapper barks and bolts, leash spinning the lieutenant like a top, yanking him round and off-kilter even as it's ripped from his grip. The lieutenant stumbles, snapping a curse that's killed in his throat by a black shape shooting from a doorway. Then the match is dropped and snuffed, and the afterlight in their peepers makes the darkness worse. All's they hear is the savaging, the gurgling screams, the thumping and thrashing. There's another flash, with a bang this time—the buzzard's pistol—but it's wild, shook by Reakesack clutching at the arm, screaming, mercy! mercy!

—Damn you, man! Let go!

The Waiftaker General clubs the peddler with his cane, struggles free to fire another half-aimed shot at the sounds of horror, gets a glimpse of eyes and teeth and blood. He falls back as it hits him, feels the cane thrash in his grasp, hears the hound's blood-curdling wrath in his face, smells its breath, feels its slaver. He don't hardly know what he's doing as he shoots and swings, and rolls and shoots. Then the cane's torn from his grasp, but he feels the lieutenant's net beneath him, grabs it, flings it.

12

Now there's something on him again, but it's Reakesack, panicked to a wild and howling scrabble like as he wants to get up on his shoulders and behind his back all at once. And now the pistol's knocked from his hand, and it's the Waiftaker General's turn to howl in rage, not a string of curses at the bloody Beast and peddler, the accursed darkness and damned chaos, just a single wordless bellow of wrath. He's no fool to be lost to his ire though, not that vulture. He's already figuring where the Beast is from its snarl and struggle.

He throws Reakesack off him, stumbles back, hand slapping on a rickety banister that near collapses with a mighty crack under his weight. Yes! With a roar he slams himself into it, splintering wood. Now he rips out a balustrade for a bludgeon, throws himself at the shape in the shadows, wild as some monstrous ape. The rotted wood shatters in his hand, but there's bone cracks too, he's sure, from the hellish yowl as the Beast gives out. Tain't even nearly down and out though, and its lurching brings it twixt him and the way out down the stairs.

But the peddler's already sorted *his* solution to that, fleeing past the Waiftaker General, screaming as he goes.

—Upstairs! Upstairs! Follow the Scruffian!

And it's near drowned out by the Beast, but sure enough Yapper's frantic yelping can be heard above. The Waiftaker General, he don't stop to think, knows that the Beast ain't more'n stunned, that he has to fall back, find a weapon, higher ground. He turns, leaps the stairs three at a time, spots light ahead of him now—yes!—on the landing, from a flat, a room, an open door—snarling at his heels—a door!

And he's in, with the door slammed shut at his back, the Beast pounding into it on the other side, shuddering it, a demon crazed with hunger for his blood. But he's safe. A chair sits just beside the door, and he hauls it round, jams its back tight under the handle. He looks round the room for anything else as might help his barricade, but all he sees is Reakesack panting and the Scruffian . . .

He sees the Scruffian stood at a bare brick fireplace, leaning on the Waiftaker General's cane, spinning his leash, and grinning, casual as can be.

13

There ain't many as has had the Waiftaker General lost for words, but Yapper he got that bugger gawping like a goldfish. It might have been him nicking the bastard's own cane, and it might have been him playing dandy with his own chain, but I likes to think it were mostly just the sight of Yapper standing on his own two feet as dumbfounded the Waiftaker General. Whatever it were, the buzzard were so blowed over, it were Yapper had to speak first.

—One yip *always* means yes, says he.

—Reakesack? growls the Waiftaker General.

—Yer hubristicality? sneers Reakesack.

The Boy Who Loved Death

Now as the peddler strolls over to stand beside Yapper, the Waiftaker General looks around a room as is empty of aught but that one chair holding back the slavering Beast. Floorboards and fireplace is all there is, and windows with ragged-edged grills nailed, screwed and bolted over em, crude but crafted for a purpose as is all too obvious. A cage, he thinks.

—Reakesack, I swear-

—He ain't the one to be swearing at, says the Scruffian.

Oh, how the Waiftaker General glowered at that. The filthy *scruff*...

—You, he says. Who do you think you are that- ?

—Yer don't *really* has to know my name or story, says Yapper. Fact, yer don't *get* to know my story. All's yer need know is that I'm awful fond of dogs. Ain't a dog in the world that's not a little bit Scruffian in its heart, so *all* us Scruffians loves our poochy pals, yeah? But even me crib-mates says I'm downright daft for me mongrel mates. So what? says I. So what if I likes to go down to all the strays in the backstreet bivouacs and feed em any grub as I've got spare? It's mine, innit?

—So what, says I, if this Beast of Buskerville everyone's gabbing about is fiercer than a ticked-off tiger? I talk dog, don't I? Tain't that hard if yer lives with em for long enough; it's mostly *feed me* and *bad men* and *cats*! Anyways, if it's true that Beast's been Fixed, says I, ain't we obliged to offer it a crib? So I had a little shufty for him, yeah? Took yonks to find him, but in the end . . .

—Blow me if he ain't indeed a Scruffian dog, says Yapper. A Scruffian dog! But you already knows that, eh?

14

The Waiftaker General glowers at him then, saying naught with his lips but blathering the bleeding works of Charlie Dickens in the glare of his murderous peepers. A Scruffian dog and he knows it alright. Blow me if he ain't got the look all em groanhuffs gets when's they been rumbled for a rook, that look of hate hiding guilt, like as they can smother the shifty with the surly. It's the look of them as don't wear their story proud, pinned to their chest in a name like Gobfabbler, yeah? The look of them as is ashamed of it.

—Oh, he's a wild one, right enough, says Yapper. Whelp—that's what I calls him—Whelp, he don't half get his hackles up if a stranger come too close. First day I goes back to me crib, I had three fingers missing, bit right off. Lucky the Fixing sorts that, eh? Me crib-mates swore blind I was bonkers, but I kept at it. Lost more fingers than I has to count with, but afters a while, Whelp and me, we got to talking. Thing is though, dog . . . tain't exactly made for fabbling, so getting his story were another matter.

But the Waiftaker General, he don't need to speak dog to have a fair notion as to what Whelp is saying right now, on the other side of the door behind his back. And tain't nothing to do with *cats*. *Bad men* and *feed me*, maybes. Maybe even *feed me bad men*. But a lot of that barking, why, it's almost in plain English, it is, as best a mutt can articulate all em complicated consonants with its slobbery muzzle. But, well, it ain't like there's too many consonants in: You! You! You! You!

Yapper he smiles and carries on.

—Most I could get from Whelp was *river, river, river*! Which weren't getting us nowhere. Then I has an inspiration. Go ask Rake Jake Scallion, I thinks. He's a good mate to us Scruffians—well, ye'll know that on account of the grief he causes yer—and *he* weren't Fixed for the usual reasons. He don't talk about his own how and why, but maybes he'd have a notion why the Institute would be Fixing an animal of all things. So I done just that, and blow me if Jake Scallion don't know the whole story of the Scruffian dog.

15

So now Yapper spins his yarn, how he stopped by Rake Jake Scallion's hidey-hole in—well, yer don't needs to know that—and how Jake brung him in, give him a glass of hot gin as welcome, and listened keen as Yapper told him 'bout this mad dog he was wrangling out of rage. And after he was done, Rake Jake Scallion gazed a whiles at his latest forgery, a perfect copy of some fine Old Master's painting of David with the head of Goliath—only Goliath's face looks right familiar in a beady-eyed buzzard way. Then nods.

—See, once upon a time there was a spoiled brat of a boy who'd an awful tendency to torture his pets to death. Went through a dozen mice, he did, a half dozen cats, and a good few dogs. His old man keeps bringing him new ones, but he keeps on killing em, till one day his father says enough's enough; this is the last, and if it's killed there'll be no more. Only that father happens to be the Waiftaker General, and the brat knows all about his old man's business. About the Stamp, and how's it Fixes things.

Old Lionel J. Reakesack, he's got his arms folded now, but the Waiftaker General, he sees a thumb come up to drift across the man's chest, like as he's minding an itch what's been scratched raw. Like when it hurts too much to scratch more, yeah, but it's still a right sore bother, so's you can't help but stroke it? And it don't exactly help none, but somehow yer can't help but trace the pain with a gentle touch, as if to soothe it with yer thoughts, to let it know it ain't forgot.

Yapper, he just twirls his leash.

—So this brat has a bully idea, see. Sneaks his pet into the Institute one night, not a stickman even asking why the spiteful little turd is there, for fear of him running to his old man, getting em dismissed for imaginary insolence. He knows where the Stamp is, how to use it, how he's *going* to use it: he's only going to Fix the dog, ain't he? So's it won't ever *have* to be replaced. No matter *how* he harms it.

—Only he don't reckon on how Fixing hurts. He don't reckon on the dog going . . . well . . . barking mad.

16

—Now that dog don't like the little fucker to start with, and it don't trust him an inch, so when he brings the Stamp out, it does its damnedest just to get away. He has to catch it, muzzle it, tie it down while it's Fixed, and by fuck, the moment the pain starts, that dog snaps. It goes from struggling to snarling, howling and growling with all the fury it's got. Is it any bleeding wonder? It don't know what's going on, but it sure as fuck knows it ain't good. That dog was Fixed fighting for its life.

He feels the door shuddering at his back, does the Waiftaker General, slamming and rattling under Whelp's unending onslaught. He minds how he'd felt when his lieutenant first brung him news of this Beast of Buskerville, his wave of a hand—hardly our concern, man. But then how the sightings and stories grew and grew, till he gots to wondering whether it *were* just another rabid cur after all. If it had really been shot in the face and survived. If it were truly the fury they said it were . . .

But it couldn't be, he'd thought. It just couldn't be.

—Course, even this brainless little brat knows it ain't suitable for a pet now. Man, it near enough skins its own legs getting free of the straps as holds it down; it's all's he can do to beat it back into a cage; and once inside, well, when it manages to smash its muzzle off, there's no sodding way he's going in there to try and Scrub it. So what's the boy going to do with an immortal, indestructible beast Fixed furious at him? Except maybe order two stickmen to dump the animal in the Thames, cage and all.

It weren't from panic, strange as it might sound. As the Waiftaker General stood there scowling back at the scruffian and the hawker, as they slowly moved in towards him, that were a certainty in his heart, a truth as made him hate them more for their not knowing that part of it. He were a reckless child, but it were cold anger as made him hasty in . . . disposing of the dog, not fear. He were like ice as he give the order, he remembers, calm as can be. But the white light of his ire did blind him, maybes.

17

Now the Waiftaker General he rallies himself. Bold and defiant he is as he steps forward, fists up for a fight. An old man and a scruffian, he's thinking. He looks from one to the other, both right close now.

—Years passed and that boy grew up to be a man, says Yapper, inherited his father's office and all. But that was all Scallion had to tell, he said, 'cept that if I ever met him I should pass on a message.

Only now Reakesack stands far bolder than the buzzard. Tall.

—Sod it, says he. I'll do it myself.

And Reakesack punches the Waiftaker General right in the gob, spins him around in place, knocks him so hard, why, all the letters of the name Lionel J. Reakesack go whirling up into the air, and when they comes back down, you knows what they spell, dontcha: Rake Jake Scallion.

Why, he plants his punch on that beady-eyed bugger square as the Stamp were pressed on his chest, breaking beak and busting teeth; and the Waiftaker General, he gets the message loud and clear as it whirls him off his feet in a stagger and crumple to the floor.

—Scallion, he hisses, blood bubbling at his lips.

The old hawker looks a foot taller now and a fair few decades younger as he peels off the straggly beard and shnoz, sends his hat sailing off through the air with a flick of his wrist, wig and spectacles too. Why, even with the greasepaint, glue and grime as still disguises him, Rake Jake looks more beau than beggar now.

What's that, scrag? Well, of course not. Come on! Yer didn't think we'd be having an *actual* money-grubbing, child-slaving Jew in this here fabble, did yer? Not bleeding likely.

No, Rake Jake just knowed that him playing Fagan Shylockowitz were the best way to work the Waiftaker General: give him a hook-nose to hook his hate to, so's he don't think to sniff too deep. It ain't always a matter of fooling a mark into trusting yer, is what Jake says to Yapper, see? Sometimes it's a matter of fooling them into *dis*trusting yer . . . but distrusting yer the wrong way, for the wrong reason.

Tell the truth, there were likely a pinch of bitter joke to it for Jake too. The Jake is short for Jacob, after all.

18

—So we heard you was looking for Whelp, says Rake Jake Scallion. Thought we'd arrange a meeting.

—Why? says the Waiftaker General He don't say no more than that, but they can tell as he's asking about it all. Why the whole charade? Why the Scruffian should care about the dog? Why the Rake should care to help the Scruffian? Why they'd risk a Scrubbing for this savage *thing* snarling on the other side of the door? Why they'd play this game as will surely bring a terrible reckoning upon them? Why, if any harm should come to him . . . ?

—Why?

Scallion crouches down to him then, leans in close.

—If yer asking as I got the Stamp before yer time, says he, so why should I hold it against you personal like? Well, as far as I'm concerned, mate, one Waiftaker General is *all* Waiftaker Generals. But more than that? You don't get my story no more than you get his. Know this though: the only reason I'll not kill you, no matter the villainy you were begotten in, is you're as much your mother's as your father's son. And she would have loved you, I'm sure . . . had she lived.

And now Yapper hunkers down, steadying himself with the cane.

—And if yer asking why we'd risk the wrath poured out the last time a Cuntlicker General came a cropper, he says, well, yer ought to know we has a little leverage amongst the Lords these days, peers with . . . peccadilloes they'd rather keep shtum. And with you to blame for the Beast and all . . . only reason I ain't bashing yer fucking brains in with this stick of yours is, the way I sees it, it wouldn't be right to let yer die when it's living is how most Scruffians suffer.

It weren't quite then that the Waiftaker General felt fear for the first time in his life, as he realised all his stickmen didn't matter a squittery shite. It weren't as he looked into his enemies' eyes and saw not an ounce of fear in Scruffian nor Rake. It weren't as they snatched him, sudden and rough, hurled him into the centre of the room, knowing that neither was feared to finish him; for they'd both said they wasn't gonna. It were when Yapper spoke his next words, cool and quiet.

—But neither of us speaks for Whelp, says he.

19

The bloodcurdling howl that rang out across Old Nicol Rookery then, when Yapper and Jake opened the door to let the Beast of Buskerville meet its maker . . . well, only Yapper and Jake knows for sure which of the two that horrible sound come from, and they ain't saying. Ask em and they just smiles.

—Maybes it come from the monster, Yapper'll say, from that fiend as still stalks the alleys today, that vicious brute. Or maybes from Whelp.

—We was already halfways out the door, Jake'll say. Giving Whelp some time to . . . renew his acquaintance with his old master, savvy?

Yeah, that's right, scrag, you heard right. Three whole—what? Dunno. *Nobody* knows how Whelp kept him alive that long. Or *why* for that matter. Maybes the dog brung him dead rats or summat. Maybes he were thinking like Yapper, that killing were too quick. All's we know is Whelp played guard-dog to his prisoner, kept him caged in mortal terror and no small amount of pain most likely, till one day . . .

He let him go.

Yep, just like that. There's some as say not all of him got let go, right enough, that Whelp kept a few . . . souvenirs.

Oh, yeah, there's some as say he's short a few fingers under his fancy kidskin gloves, or that his lanky-limbed stride is . . . ungainly now cause half his toes ain't on his feet no more. Or on account of him being one bollock shy of a pair. When he finally staggered out of Old Nicol, so they says, every hair on his head were white, but it run deeper too. Maybes he hides it, says they, like as a Stamp hid by a buttoned-up shirt. But yer can see the fear as in a nipper's flinch.

Fixed in him.

The Boy Who Loved Death

~~~

Maybes some madness too. See, it weren't the hideous stumbling state of him as made passers-by recoil in horror. No, for all the blood and shit filthing his mauled and naked form, it were the ungodly howling as shook em, when he grabbed them by the lapels. Cause he weren't talking the Queen's English at em, but the Beast's Dog.

He's had many years to mend his mind a little, but he ain't mended his ways, the fucker.

But you mind if yer has a run-in with the Waiftaker General.

You just gives him a little growl, hear?

Die, Vampire, Die

Just Like Galileo

Ah, Thomas, come in. I trust you had a comfortable journey? Good. Good.

Yes . . . Rolls Royce Silver Shadow.

Mostly original. Glad you like it. A bit more stylish, bit more modern than a hearse, eh?

Quite. You know how I feel about all the coffin nonsense.

Yes, that's a little something of my own design. Can't very well spoil a car like that with black paint on the windows. It would be an absolute sin.

Well, I'm sure that can be organised. The modifications aren't that difficult; it's just the manufacturing of the glass.

Well, you'd think so, wouldn't you, but you know what the elders are like.

Yes? In a crate? Oh, that's rich! Talk about pathetic.

Anyway, have a seat. Can I get you a drink? I have a nice Californian blonde at the moment, special import, exquisite bouquet and you can almost taste the sunlight.

Him? Oh, Thomas, you're as bad as ever, the original sucker for a pretty face. Never could keep you away from the help. No, I'm afraid he's one of us already, aren't you, Jack. Well, not one of *us*, obviously. Not Chosen. I'm not looking for a brood anytime soon. No, no; he's just a shabti.

Quite tame. Don't want to risk ending up like the old man, after all.

Yes, honestly. He's a shabti.

I know. Quite remarkable really, bit of a freak. Come here a second, Jack. Show Master Thomas your trick . . .

190

Bravo, Jack. Bravo. Very graceful. Thought you'd appreciate that, Thomas. Yes, I think it's called *capoeira*.

You can go see to the experiments now, Jack. I'll page you if I need you.

Yes, it's quite remarkable, as I say.

No idea. Presumably he had the skill before, but . . . no. Just showed up in one of the shipments. Didn't seem to be anything special. A bit strong-willed but nothing extraordinary; fought like a tiger when I let him out of the cage, punched, kicked, scratched, but after the first few feedings he was quite compliant.

No—I mean yes, I did *use* him in an experiment but it was quite unrelated. I've repeated it since and, well, the other subjects just . . . well, you know what shabtis are like. Most of them you're lucky if they can shuffle without drooling, never mind—actually, I'm running it again at the moment; you may find it quite interesting. So, no, I wish I could take the credit but he just sort of turned out that way. I'm tempted to do some work on him, but I find him terribly useful. There's some things you just can't use humans for. You'll see. I'll give you the grand tour in a minute.

The old man? Oh, he's fine. Safe and sound as always. He was asking after you, you know . . . but then you always were his favourite.

Well, OK. Not so much asking after you as cursing your name.

God, no. Why would I want to do that? The vault's sound-proofed and who's going to hear him anyway?

Oh no. Jack's under express orders to stay away from there. He's smart but he's still a shabti. Does exactly what he's told.

Well, *obviously* I take precautions, but he does have to be fed.

Yes, I blind them.

Yes, I puncture their eardrums.

Handcuffs.

Well, I cuff them behind their backs obviously; I'm not that foolish.

Oh, really, Thomas, I think hamstringing is taking it a bit far. I have no intention of carrying them to him and holding them up while he feeds. Look, even if he did use the Hold on them, I can snap their necks at any time. Honestly, I have it all under control. You can see for yourself.

Well, it amuses me to hear him going on.

Oh, don't be such an old maid, Thomas. It doesn't suit you. Leave that to the bloody elders with their coffins and their crypts and their ridiculous-

Nonsense! They can't hear us, you know. They may be immortal but they're not omniscient.

Oh, please! I thought you of all people would be-

Oh. You had me going for a minute there, damn you. Thought you'd lost it completely. Thought maybe you'd spent so long hanging around with Malik and his little clique that you'd actually started to believe his overblown claptrap.

Well, I'm glad to hear that.

So how *is* the project going? Any closer to the truth? Any hints about who sired who?

Really? Not *another* one. How many secret origins of the Chosen can there be? What is it this time? Another Egyptian pharaoh feeding on the blood of slaves? A Phoenician sorcerer making some dark deal with terrible demonic forces?

Oh, Mesopotamia . . . *again*. Funny how that one only started popping up in their interminable stories fifty years ago or so—just after Kramer published his book on the Sumerians. Curious coincidence, that. Honestly, Thomas, I don't know how you put up with all the pseudohistorical, self-mythologising, self-important hokum.

Heh. Quite. Yes, I can just picture you playing the wide-eyed young newblood eager for tales of ancient times. You should have been on stage, you know. Who wouldn't trust a face like that? Oh! Do you remember the look on the old man's face when he realised you were in on it as well? I mean, *me* he expected, but *you* . . .

Oh, yes, that too! It was, wasn't it? Ah, those were the days. Poor old Reynard.

But no clues yet about his sire? Malik hasn't let anything slip amongst all the flim-flam about—what did you say it was—the Blood of Ishtar?

Whatever.

Is that so? I thought the old leech had to be in the bloodline somewhere.

You're not sure? What exactly did he say?

The Boy Who Loved Death

Hmm. Yes, I see what you mean. It's not quite proof, is it? Damn it. You could be hanging off his every word for centuries and still not be any the wiser. Well, no matter. You have your methods; I have mine. Science, Thomas, science. It's the way of the future. No . . . correction: it's the way of the *present*.

Well, yes, I have made quite a bit of progress, actually.

No, I'm afraid, not that much progress. It would be nice, though, wouldn't it? Some sort of DNA test so you could track your bloodline back and make sure they're all . . . safe and secure, so to speak. Unfortunately not. I did look into it but the lack of, well, DNA rather put a damper on that line of inquiry.

No. No DNA at all.

Yes. Didn't I tell you? Didn't Malik pass on my-

You hadn't heard at all? Bloody Malik! Bloody luddite—I don't believe he—I told him—this is just too much.

What else has he just decided to keep to himself? I mean, he did at least tell everyone about the rain, yes?

Well, that's at least something. God, Thomas, sometimes I feel like Galileo. They're worse than the bloody Vatican. I mean, I took the blood to get away from that sort of nonsense; I thought we were supposed to be the faithless, the unbound, the free. And we're worse than them. It's the bloody 21st Century and they're still—tell me, is Malik still having his Black Masses every Sunday? God, it's like a bunch of O.A.P's all toddling off to church on their zimmers: Nearer My Satan To Thee; and our sermon today comes from the Maleus Maleficorum; and would you like a peppermint sweety, deary? Cretins!

I'm sorry. I'm sorry. It just drives me crazy, all their spiritualist nonsense. They're not living in the 20th Century, never mind the 21st. Here I am, working on saving the race and they're dithering around, making sacrifices to Beelzebub. You know, if they really dated back to Mesopotamia, you might at least expect them to know that their great elder god was only called Beelzebub in the Bible as an insult. It's a corruption of the original Baal-ze-Baal, Prince-of-Princes, applied to half the deities across the Middle East.

Yes, it's quite true. Well it's not hard to find. A little reading is a wonderful thing, Thomas. Stops you from looking like a blithering fool.

No, I don't know. I mean, it's possible that it's all part of their shell-game, just another way of keeping the newbloods under the thumb, awestruck and obedient. But, I don't know. Sometimes I think the elders are just so . . . senile that they've actually started to believe their own nonsense.

Well, it would be funny, but this is our survival at stake here. Sorry, no pun intended.

Damn it, where was I?

Yes, my research. Well, obviously Malik has been happily burying everything I've sent him under the nearest stone. Actually, he probably burned it, knowing him. No matter. You and I, Thomas. You and I. We're men of the modern era. We're not afraid to step out in the rain. That's what umbrellas are for. Technology, Thomas. Science and technology. That's what's going to save us. Not some mediaeval gibberish chanted to a horn-headed lump of stone in the basement.

Come with me. Yes, I'm glad you're here, old friend. What do you say we pay a visit to the old man and I'll show you what I've been up to on the way?

Follow me.

Reticent? I'll Bet!

Through here, yes. After you. Yes. Ah, hello, Jack. How's everything running? Good. Good. No more suicides amongst the humans? Good.

Yes, it is quite impressive. Ex-army facility. Wartime crisis shelter for the government.

Oh, a few here and there. A couple of cabinet ministers, a general or two. You know what they say: keep one shabti right beside you, and a thousand slaves around the world.

Quite, quite. Actually, that is one of the things I've been studying. You know how we've never been quite sure how long you can sustain a human in the pre-death stage? You know, just a small feed here, a little nibble there, let them recover for a week or so, then same again.

Well. Short answer: indefinitely. And the longer you do it, the more loyal they become. You'll see.

But as I was saying, the first, most obvious question has to be, just what are we? What exactly *are* the Chosen? Yes, I know the clichés, the euphemisms and the nicknames. Vampire, virculac, nosferatu, the risen dead, the undead, creatures of the night, and on, and on, and on, and on. These aren't answers. These aren't explanations. These are just . . . words. Trite, tired, banal. And *wrong*.

Yes, wrong. Well, take 'undead', for example. What does that mean? How empty and pointless can a word be? What's that table over there? Oh, that's an untree. It was a tree, but it's been mysteriously transformed into something else, some dark, unnatural thing that can only be an abomination in the eyes of God because it is not tree. The horror of it! And look, is that a bookcase? My God, it's also untree! It's an untree bookcase.

Undead. What rot. What utter—No, Jack, I don't want you to kill the bookcase. The bookcase is not a threat to us. I was merely illustrating a . . . why on earth am I explaining myself to a shabti? Just get on with your work. Have you fed the humans today? Well, go and feed them then. And I said, feed them. Not feed on them. You understand? Good. And stop biting your nails. It's a filthy habit.

What was I saying? Yes. Undead. Tell me, Thomas, do you remember dying at any point? Did you, or I, or any of the Chosen actually die and rise from the grave?

Exactly. We're not bloody shabtis. Oh, the humans might not make any distinctions between Chosen and shabti, but then you don't expect them to be any more than ignorant animals. But you and I know. All the Chosen know. There's a world of difference between the—what was it you used to call them . . . shamblies, yes . . . very droll—between them and us—

Well, you have a point there.

Yes, I can see where you're going. Carry on.

Well, yes, that's all very well. Yes, I do remember my heart stopping. No, I don't have a pulse. But let me put it this way . . .

I don't suppose you keep up with the latest medical journals, no? I like to keep my eye open for new developments. Well, you probably won't have heard but a short while ago, maybe last year or the year before, they developed a new artificial heart. Now up until this point most artificial hearts have been modelled on the natural organ . . . four chambers, a rhythmic pumping action. But this tends to make them somewhat large and unwieldy. So someone took a lateral step. He thought, all this heart needs to do is push the blood round the body. It doesn't *actually* have to beat. It doesn't *actually* have to pound like a little metronome in the chest. Why not just use the sort of pump you get in, say, a washing machine? A whirring, buzzing pump like you would get in a washing machine. You can make them much smaller, they're far less complicated, less prone to breaking down. And one small side-effect of the artificial heart that he developed—which, I understand, works quite perfectly—is that the recipient has a steady flow of blood . . . no pulse, no heartbeat. Now, I ask you, is that person dead? Is that person undead?

Isn't it? I think it's exactly the same thing.

No, no, let's just leave the shabtis to one side for the moment. Let's look at you and I. Let's look at the Chosen.

We didn't die. Yes, our hearts stopped beating at the first taste of blood. Yes, I remember it well. But do you remember the hunger, the agonising excruciating hunger that just built up and built up after that first taste of Reynard's blood? Do you remember the taste of your first kill in your mouth? Do you remember the sheer ecstasy of it? The way you sucked in a breath and you could feel it in your chest, holding it there, and you could feel your heart beating in your chest with the excitement, and it's just like everything inside you freezes in that perfect, orgasmic moment? Do you remember? Do you remember looking down at the body on the ground in front of you and realising that you were still holding that breath, that your heart hadn't just skipped a beat—it had stopped entirely? Do you remember?

And that's my point. You remember.

You were aware the whole time. You never stopped being aware.

You never stopped being alive.

Crazy? No, Thomas, it's called science.

You see, I believe in taking a logical approach to these matters, a *rational* approach. I suppose, underneath it all, I'm just a man of my time. I remember the Enlightenment. Malik and the others spent most of it, as I recall, hiding in their cellars, waiting for humans to go back to burning each other at the stake for witchcraft, petrified that this 'atheism stuff' might make humans more resistant to the Hold.

No, science is not our enemy, Thomas. Knowledge is not our enemy. Logic. Reason. Remember that argument I had with Malik just before the Prague incident? You remember?

No, you were there.

No, no, you were *definitely* there.

Honestly.

Yes. Definitely, take my word for it.

Anyway, I remember Malik said something that day that got me thinking. What was it? *Surely we ourselves are proof enough of God's existence. You cannot have Absolute Evil without Absolute Good.*

And I remember thinking that was rather presumptuous of him. You know? Grandiose.

It doesn't, by the way. Atheism. It doesn't affect resistance. I mean logically speaking it's a specious argument, anyway. You might equally suppose that atheists would be *less* resistant, having less faith to bolster their weak wills. In reality, it makes not one jot of difference. I have done substantial work—and I do mean, substantial—on natural variations in human resistance to the Hold. Come here, I can show you. Yes, this way.

Yes, you see, these are the induction rooms.

Induction.

Not personally, but, yes, pretty much all of the test subjects. You have to get their personal details—religion, class, physical conditions, mental health issues. You have to take all these things into account in order to be sure you've got a representative sample.

Questionnaires, mainly.

Oh, I got one of these market research companies involved.

Yes, that's one of Jack's helper shabtis; they're quite capable of reading questions and ticking boxes.

Well, they don't have much choice, do they? They can be a bit reticent at first—the youngsters particularly—some of them could scream for England—but it's amazing how co-operative these humans can be with a little persuasion. We try to avoid using the Hold and generally—as you can see here—physical methods are quite sufficient. We—excuse me a second.

Hello. Yes, yes, the master is pleased. But you may want to loosen that a little. That's better. Don't want to kill the poor girl. Very good. As you were.

Sorry about that. You know me. I've never been good at delegation; always had a hands-on sort of approach. But when you're working on this sort of scale, you just don't have any choice. But you do have to step in occasionally.

Anyway, so we build up pretty thorough files on all our test subjects; that way we can cross-reference various environmental factors with their behaviour in our little studies. So I can tell you with absolute certainty: atheist, Christian, Jew, Muslim, Hindu, Buddhist, bloody Zoroastrian—it doesn't matter a bit. There's a standard bell curve distribution across all sections of the population. Some people will fall at your feet if you give them a nod across a crowded room; others will spit in your face even after you've been feeding on them for a week. It's-

Yes, that's where we put them when they first come in. I call it the Tank. Ah, the door's open. Jack must be in already.

Oh, only about a hundred or so at a time. Any more than that and it would be just unmanageable.

Mostly the Middle East, ex-Soviet countries, some from Latin America. All over, really.

Prisons, orphanages, refugee centres. These new refugee camps are ideal actually. Or asylum centres, or whatever they're called.

I know, but you've got to expect that; the poor things are petrified. You get used to the smell after a while. Actually, it's the ones that don't soil themselves that you have to look out for. Feisty.

No, surprisingly easy. I mean, not as easy as it was under Stalin, but, to be honest, in this day and age, you don't have to be stuck in some god-forsaken gulag in the middle of Siberia. When you're living in the global village, your castle can be pretty much anywhere.

Well, it's not as if it's my money, eh? God, no. That's what slaves are for. I mean, with all their pet industrialists and pocket dictators, you'd think the elders would be doing more things on this sort of scale. Capitalise on your resources, that's what I say. But no, they can't think further than a luxury crypt with a temple to Ashtaroth in the basement and a larder full of Filipinos.

Yes, well, Malik would say that, wouldn't he? Honestly, Thomas, nobody cares. What's a few refugees here and there? Read the papers. Nobody wants them, anyway.

I'm just telling it like it is, old boy. The humans are no different to us, really. They talk about sympathy and caring but-

Ah, good man, Jack. No casualties? Good. Well, you know what to do. Just pick the first ten and take them downstairs.

Well, do that afterwards.

No initiative, you see. A shabti's a shabti, no matter how intelligent they are.

Talking of which, if you'll just follow me. We'll take the stairs; it's quicker.

Yes, this is where I keep the shabtis.

If It's Not Too Much Bother?

. . . basic consciousness and brute appetites motivating them. I mean, they're really little more than animals, loyal to a fault but, well, the lights are on but nobody's home. We mustn't let this stop us studying them though. That's the mistake we've been making, I think. Some of us don't seem to want to delve too deeply into either our natures or the shabtis' just in case we were to find out that, horror of horrors, we're actually the same. We're not, of course. There are fundamental differences, but the elders would rather live in total ignorance than even run the risk of learning something that made them feel uncomfortable. It's all this undead nonsense again, is what it is.

No, of course that's not what I'm saying. But there's more to these creatures than just a corpse that's risen from the grave. Here, for instance.

Yes, these ones are actually still alive, still human. In fact, they're completely untouched. This is one of the mesmerism experiments I was telling you about. We measure their resistance to the Hold by having them administer electric shocks to themselves. I try to do this with all the subjects before they go into the experiments with more . . . permanent effects. Obviously there's *so* many factors to take into consideration, you really need to do this sort of thing over and over again, if you want to know whether resistance is an innate or a learned behaviour.

Well, from what we're getting back, it does seem to be innate; there's no obvious correlation between this or that belief-system, personality types or what-not. Pretty much standard deviation

Yes, what we do is we repeat this experiment each time the subject's fed on.

These cages over here.

Yes, you can see it, can't you? Their whole demeanour changes. You can actually see the Hold in progress. I mean this one—come out of the corner, yes, come to me—this one you can see is in the early stages. Three feeds, I believe. Look at him shaking like a leaf. This one, on the other hand . . . five—yes, five—feeds and already he's stopped crying.

Well, yes, you'll know yourself from practical experience. Give me a child for seven nights and I'll give you the slave, as they say.

And this one here. Ten feeds, I think. Totally submissive, totally subservient and—Silence! Yes, that's one of the things we've found. After eight or so feeds on consecutive nights they start to get a bit too submi— I said, *Silence!*—a bit *too* submissive. The death fixation kicks in and you get all the endless whining and begging to be killed. *Master* this. *Master* that. It really gets quite tiresome. So . . . needy.

Oh, a week or so recovery period. Just leave them for a week— even two—then move on to a fortnightly feeding schedule just to keep them happy. This one's due for total draining though. I have plenty of slaves out there at the moment. Don't need any more.

Yes, that's right, the master is going to kill you. Yes, I thought that would make you happy, you pathetic little creature.

Oh, God no. I don't feed on them myself. I don't think I could if I wanted to. I mean, do you realise how many of these creatures we go through here? This experiment for example. I'm looking to graph the relationship of exposure to the consciousness level of the resultant shabti. So we have a set of, say, ten subjects. We terminate them in a series of feeds. Drain one in a single feed. Do the next one over two nights, the next again over three. And so on. What we're basically looking for is any relationship between time spent with the sire and mental development of the shabti. We all know some shabtis are worse than others. Well, we can measure this. We can look at linguistic ability, mental and manual dexterity; we can use IQ tests; there's all sorts of things we can look at here.

But we do need to run this basic experiment many, many times to get any meaningful data. You need to repeat the exposure patterns, vary them—I think, yes, this one's an exponential series, doubling the feeding period with each subject—one, two, four, eight, sixteen and so on up to one thousand and twenty-four, believe it or not. Oh, you should see the humans after a thousand nights of feeding on them, by the way. The devotion! Honestly, if you think this one's servile . . .

Honestly, yes, a thousand nights. Well, it's all in the name of science, after all.

Anyway, after the exponential exposure pattern, there's linear exposure patterns—one, two, three, four, five, etc.—and, of course, those you have to vary to run over different scales and cover different areas. Ten to twenty. Thirty to fifty in steps of two.

There is a link actually, by the way. If you look at total desanguination in one or two feeds the shabti that you end up with is mute, bestial at best—lucky if it can put on its own shoes never mind tie the laces. As you increase the exposure, you do get limited comprehension displayed, minimal linguistic skills . . . still, little or no independent thought. I was wondering if we might see a direct correlation between exposure and intelligence, the one increasing along with the other. That's what's *supposed* to happen, if you listen to the so-called experts. But the truth is, there appears to be a sort of consciousness ceiling. Things level out after sixteen feeds or so and after that exposure doesn't make much difference.

Yes, I feel we've pretty much proven it as is. You can never have too much test data, though.

Exactly! You see, it's exactly like I was saying, there's so much we have to learn about these creatures, and instead we'd rather run around with this foolish notion that shabtis are—let me see— invested with their master's life essence, extensions of their master's, um, aura of darkness or whatever. So of course the longer the master feeds on them the more like him they become.

So Malik still has his famous ten-year shabti? Does he still go on about it the same way? Ten years! It doesn't make a blind bit of difference, you know. He could have sired it over twenty and it still wouldn't be able to think without moving its lips.

Anyway the point I'm making is, well, I couldn't possibly do all that feeding on my own. I do need shabtis for my later experiments, anyway, so . . . These humans over here, for example, are earmarked for a study on reiterative siring I'm running at the moment. You feed one of the humans to a shabti, wait for the body to rise, feed it a human, wait for that body to rise as a shabti, feed it a human and so on. So only the initial feeding needs to be carried out by myself. Actually Jack does most of the initial sirings these days.

Oh, the results were a little inconclusive to begin with. We had real problems getting any of the shabtis to feed without draining the next subject dry right there and then—we're not exactly talking about masters of delayed gratification, you know—so obviously, you end up with these one-feed shabtis which are little use to anyone. It's very hard to test for decline of mental faculties over successive generations when your starting point is a grunting imbecile that sits in the corner playing with itself.

Oh, yes, we've got the problems ironed out now, though. I mean, you'll never get a shabti to tear itself away from its meal once its started, no matter how much of a Hold you have over it. And they just chew through most types of harness or leash. We ended up coming up with a sort of case thing. Looks like one of those boxes the stage magician puts his assistant in before sawing her in half. Jack usually has a team of his helpers to hold the creature to the subject's neck while it feeds. Yes, it is something of a sight . . . quite droll, actually.

Oh, yes, the results. Clear deterioration. I mean, after five generations or so the shabti's incapable of basic motor functions, just lies there in a vegetative state, moaning.

Anyway, look at the state of them. I mean, look at this one. Would you want to eat that night after night? No, I keep my food supply quite separate from the lab specimens.

Yes, Jack does do a lot of the feeding himself. Insatiable appetite, that boy. I really don't know where he puts it all. No, I wouldn't touch these filthy things. Ugh. The thought of it.

Oh, really Thomas. That's disgusting. You're not serious. A bit of rough is one thing but you might as well be sucking on a wino in an alleyway. Honestly, I have some lovely imports just come in, much classier, well-fed and healthy . . . clean.

Well, OK, if you want him, you can have him. At least let me have him scrubbed up for you.

Oh, you have vile tastes, Thomas, vile. But . . . go ahead.

Yes, here, let me get the door for you. Do you want me to hold your coat?

No bother at all.

Ugh, really that is quite grotesque.

Well, each to his own.

I'll wait over here.

Yes, Jack, you know where they go. Just a second. You see Master Thomas with the human? After you've put them away, be a good boy and have one of the shabtis put the body in storage. Tag it for use in one of the garlic experiments.

OK.

Tum te tum.

Ugh.

Ah, Thomas. All done?

Don't be silly; no need to apologise. Would you like to—yes, of course—just down there. I'll tell you what. Jack! Jack, come here a minute. No, close the cage door first. Good boy. OK. Yes. Be a dear and show Master Thomas to my office.

Yes, you'll find a toilet in the back. You can wash up there.

Well, I have a couple of things to attend to here but if you just wait for me there, I'll be down in a couple of minutes. OK.

And You're Not Worried About His Loyalty?

. . . learned about the shabtis. It just goes to show what a little research can do.

That's the thing. I really have no idea. No. You'd think that, wouldn't you? But he was really just another test subject. Just a common-or-garden, run-of-the-mill eight-feed shabti. But it's not just the dancing . . . Jack, what's six times two?

Good. And what's twelve divided by three?

No, actually Jack it's four, but good try. Good try.

Did you see that? He actually tried to think about it. He can count pretty well. He can even recite the twelve times table. It's just division that stumps him. Doesn't seem to be able to do the same simple calculation backwards. I do find that fascinating. You know I'm so tempted to take him apart at times, just to see what makes him tick, but-

No, Jack. I do not wish to dissect you. You're more useful to me as you are, for the moment, thank you.

And would it matter if you *did* mind? Quite right.

Now that's what I find really remarkable. *Jack doesn't mind.* As if . . . as if it actually wanted to . . . reassure me. As I say, quite remarkable. Never known a shabti to be-

Yes, I suppose you're right. I wasn't thinking of it as *questioning* my decision. I'm sure it wasn't intended that way. But I suppose that's one way of putting it.

Well, yes, but I have other reasons, you see. Take a look around you. All these shabtis you see—they were all sired by Jack, directly or indirectly. Provides a failsafe, you see. It's inconceivable that anything could go wrong here, but just in case I *did* need to shut down the operation at short notice, well, Jack's my 'self-destruct button', so to speak. Kill him and they all die.

Loyalty?

Oh, come now. You don't think I've thought of that? No, I carried out some quite thorough experiments on precedence before I decided on-

Sorry? Well, actually I can give you a simple demonstration if you want.

Jack, we need you over here for a second. Oh, and you there. Here. Thank you, Jack. I believe this one has its sire around here somewhere, doesn't it. Can you point him out for us? Yes, good. Get him over here, will you?

You see, it did occur to me. We all know shabtis have a knee-jerk fawning reaction to any Chosen. We know they're loyal to their master and to their master's master. With shabtis sired by shabtis, for all intents and purposes, there should be no difference. These ones sired by Jack are utterly subservient to him and Jack is, of

course, utterly subservient to me. But what if there were a conflict of imperatives? Let's just suppose that Jack here decided that he wanted to be master of his own life. Better yet, let's just imagine that this shabti here, one of Jack's brood, decided that he wanted to take Jack's place at the top of the pecking order. Obviously, he's not actually capable of thinking like that, but let's just *imagine* that this shabti is some sort of threat to Jack.

Jack, I want you to tell the girl to kill her sire. Tell her to use this.

Watch. She'll kill her own sire because *his* sire tells her to . . . even though it means her own death. No question. Here we go.

Wonderful. Ah, Jack. Could you get someone to clear that up? Thank you.

So you see?

No, no, no. That's not the point at all, Thomas. No, you've completely missed the point of the whole exercise. She only killed her sire because Jack ordered her to, because her sire's sire told her to. I could have done it myself. I could have picked any one of these shabtis and ordered them to kill Jack. Why, I could have told them all to tear him limb from limb, and they'd have done it happily, even though they would have all ended up . . . well, like that. The point is these shabtis may have been sired by Jack but they're loyal to me, as Jack's sire. And before you say it, that's why I have old Reynard in a sound-proof vault, and that's why Jack is on express orders to never go down there, never under any circumstances. Or what will happen to you, Jack?

That's right.

But think about it, Thomas. It wouldn't have to be the old man. Anyone higher up in the bloodline could tell one of our shabtis to stake us in our sleep. Bear that in mind next time Malik drops in on you for a visit. If he *is* Reynard's sire, or grandsire for that matter, one word from him and your own shabtis would rip your head off, tear your heart out and stick it in a pickle-jar full of holy water while they had the rest of you hoisted on a cross in the midday sun.

That's the thing. They *do* know. At least, they seem to. I don't know how, but they seem to recognise it automatically. I've had Jack sire a whole brood that's never laid eyes on me, never heard my name mentioned; I walk into the room and, bang, they're grovelling on their knees in front of me before I can get a word out.

I don't know. Scent is all I can think of at the moment. Some sort of family scent. I don't understand it, but believe me, when I do you'll be the first to know. Because when I know how it works, I'll know how we can track down dear old Reynard's sire . . . and *his* sire, and *his*, and so on, all the way back to the First.

In the meantime, I'll just carry on with—what does Malik call it again?—my tinkering.

Tinkering, indeed. This way.

Oh, this is just one level of one wing. There's two more wings to the complex. Actually some of them are set up on an automated production-line model just to generate basic shabtis for the *real* experiments.

Ha ha. Army of darkness. I like that. No, no, nothing like that. I leave the darkness to the elders. It's the light of reason I'm interested in, Thomas. The light of reason.

You Don't Say

. . . what I call the Elizabeth Bathory Wing. Heh. I used to do most of the surgical work here on my own, but in recent years, I've had to expand. Most of this whole level's taken up with the experiments these days. I've had the place taken apart and put back together again. You'll see. Some of the equipment we've got here, you'd be amazed; I don't know how they got it down here at all.

Anyway, there's four key areas to investigate if you want to know what makes us all tick, four things that mark us out from the humans: one, preservation of youthful vitality; two, degeneration, slow or sudden, depending on what it results from; three, regeneration of severed limbs, removed organs . . . head excepted, obviously; and four, anaerobic sustenance –

Anaerobic? It means without respiration. Without breathing, Thomas.

Safe to say, I've been looking mainly at degeneration and preservation—what kills us and what keeps us alive—since those are rather more immediate. I'll show you some of the work I've done on cardiac penetration and decapitation in a minute, but, first—I don't suppose Malik passed on any of the data I sent him on garlic-toxicity and photosensitivity?

I might have known. Well, you know how all the elders go on? *Don't touch it. Garlic's bad for you. It'll kill you. Poison. Bad. Stay away.* As if they had to tell us not to eat something that smells like . . . well, garlic. Ugh.

The thing is . . . OK, have a look at these chaps strapped down over here. Yes, what I've been doing with these fellows is injecting them with various chemical compounds I've extracted from the raw root, or *combinations* of the various chemicals I've isolated. Anyway, they're injected with them—or made to ingest them, but that can be quite difficult.

Yes, they are quite noisy, aren't they? And—Stop that! Thank you.

And the thing is: for all the fuss they make, it doesn't do them the slightest bit of harm. Oh, some specific combinations of this chemical and that cause discomfort—well, you can see that, I suppose—but not disintegration. No it's not even comparable to, say, anaphylactic shock. More like a child throwing a tantrum because it doesn't like the cod liver oil it's been forced to swallow. No, there's no long-term damage to the creatures whatsoever.

Well, I'm not sure why it should cause such an adverse reaction, but it may be linked to this next experiment. Yes, over here. Through this door.

You see, I was curious about one particular human legend. It's quite obscure, but you may have heard of it. Supposedly one way to prevent the corpse of one of our poor pathetic victims from rising from the grave involves stuffing their mouth with garlic and sewing their lips shut. I believe they would usually cut the head off and drive a stake through the heart anyway, which would of course be quite sufficient—but still, when I heard this story I was curious. So . . .

We have three subjects. The first, here, is a shabti, mouth stuffed with garlic and sewn shut. As you can see, they do rather protest, but this one's been like this for a week now and, aside from the thrashing and wailing, there's no noticeable signs of any real negative effect. That's pretty much as you'd expect given . . . well how would *you* like it?

So. Next we have a human subject, again with his mouth stuffed with garlic bulbs, sewn shut. Yes. Hush now. It'll all be over soon. We feed these to the shabtis to see the effects.

No. The shabti has to be forced to eat; they're quite repelled by the smell. It is quite rank, isn't it. You can smell it easily, even over the urine and the-

It's an idea. Do you even get them in adult sizes?

You mean for incontinence, I take it, or . . .

Really? That's humans for you. They do think up some remarkable fetishes. Have you heard about the, ahem, 'vampires'. They have societies, you know?

Yes, that's what I thought.

No, anyway, you have to order the shabtis to eat and even then, some of them just—well—go mad. They can't disobey their master but they just can't bring themselves to bite the poisoned apple, so to speak. Sort of an irresistible force, immovable object thing, leads to total breakdown. The worst usually end up just driveling in the corner. It's actually put me in mind of an interesting experiment in its own right. I want to measure the influence of different imperatives, the natural repulsion of the noxious weed versus the absolute authority of his master's voice. I suspect there may be a strong correlation between mental development and the ability to override the repulsion. Jack managed to feed on one of them with his very first try. Of course, he was absolutely useless for three days— *Jack tummy hurt, Master . . . Jack no feel good, Master*—but . . . as I say, I have to do some more experiments on that.

So. Finally we have a normal human corpse, garlic-free until after desanguination. This one's a week old.

Well, yes I suppose it is obvious. As with the living specimens, we've stuffed the mouth with garlic and sewn it shut. And it seems to be quite effective. Normal rate of decomposition. The maggots are happily stripping it down. No sign of animation whatsoever. I've repeated this experiment a few times, by the way. Tried removing the garlic after different periods of time—hours, days, weeks. It varies but generally speaking the garlic has to be in there for a day or two to be successful. Any less and what you get is . . . well, it's not pleasant. Necrosis sets in quite quickly, you know. The things smell quite foul and, really, they're worse than fifth-generation shabtis.

Not so much risen from the grave as floundering in it like a fish out of water. They sort of . . . flop . . . and gasp a lot.

Anyway, at the moment, I'm trying to isolate whatever it is that interferes with the reanimation process. I'm working on the assumption that it's the same chemical or combination of chemicals that makes the stuff so damned noxious to us. These rooms over here, this is where I'm trialling the various concoctions. I've had some success with liquidised root, although injection into the bloodstream seems to be less successful than injecting into the spine at the base of the skull. Yes, same set-up. Shabti, pre-mortem human and post-mortem human. Base of the skull.

Well, no. I don't suppose they *do*.

I've tried various individual extracts in isolation and combination. No result so far, but I think I'm on the right track in looking for a cocktail.

Well, I'll get onto that. Thought you might like a little bit of a son-et-lumiere.

Over this way then.

Well, That Was ... Messy

Photosensitivity—one of the great banes of our lives. How many times have you felt that nostalgic longing to just sit and watch a sunset or a sunrise?

No, spontaneous combustion isn't my idea of a good time either. But, why, Thomas, why? Why do we react that way?

That's rather putting the cart before the horse—we're creatures of the night because sunlight kills us, not the other way round. More idiotic superstition. Here, these are what I call the light chambers.

Yes, same glass that was in the Rolls. Means you can actually watch what happens. Initially these were black box experiments, but once I'd developed the glass, I thought I may as well have a look at the fireworks displays. Quite spectacular.

Oh, it depends on the chamber. This one has a shaft that goes all the way up to the surface. All sorts of mirrors and gears inside it—really quite ingenious, if I do say so myself.

No, no, come in, come in. It's quite safe, locked tight at the moment; you can't open the shutter with the door open. You can see where I fit the various filters.

Yes, I've done experiments with standard sunlight, reflected sunlight, moonlight, starlight, diffuse sunlight, focused sunlight, focused moonlight, filtered sunlight, of all sorts -

Yes, moonlight. Well, it is just reflected sunlight, after all.

Oh, for crying out loud, Thomas. Where did you *think* the light came from?

Only over the long term, you'll be glad to know. I'll get to that.

Next door here is where I use artificial illuminants. It seemed a fair question. Could we simulate the effect of sunlight on a shabti? Tell you what—hold on a second. You. Yes, you. Come here. In you go. That's right.

Yes, completely artificial. This one's called D65; it's an industrial illuminant, closest thing you get to natural light, used all over the place these days—mostly for matching colours—by clothing manufacturers and suchlike.

Yes, these are the controls over here. Do you want to flick the switch or shall I?

No, I don't mind at all.

You see what I mean by *spectacular*? Messy, right enough. Yes, as you can see, it's not quite combustion so much as detonation. More extreme than staking, but it's the same thing, really—catastrophic integrity loss leading to complete tissue breakdown. It's a mix of light frequencies that causes it. I thought it might be a specific component . . . ultraviolet perhaps . . . but no, ultraviolet on its own is harmless, as are most other individual frequencies.

Yes, you have to have a critical level to cause degeneration. Low levels can be tolerated, although they do cause damage over time. If you have the level low enough, you can sort of melt a shabti. This one in this chamber here, for instance.

Yes, he's been in there for a couple of days.

Yes. The mental deterioration sets in fairly quickly; incoherent speech, stereotyped behaviour, alternating between manic and catatonic states. This one's well advanced. The tremors have started, so that means the motor control is starting to break down. This one over here's even further on. The convulsions are less frequent, less regular but more dramatic when they come. Oh, there's one now. Did you see the way his whole head just seemed to . . . *ripple*?

Jelly, yes. The liquefaction of the organism is usually complete after four days at this light level.

I'm not entirely sure but I do find the mental effects quite intriguing; it's almost as if the light is interfering with its thought patterns, breaking them up the way it disintegrates the body. Integrity of form . . . yes, integrity of form. Interference. That's got to be the key . . .

Sorry. Terribly sorry. My mind was quite away there for a second. What were you saying again?

Well, I tried exposing tissue samples to various levels and frequencies, and mixes of frequencies of electromagnetic radiation, looking for changes on the microscopic level. Other than D65, or natural sunlight, nothing really has any effect.

Mind you, it did prove quite revealing in other ways. Quite revealing.

Come through to the lab. I have some slides to show you.

A Stake, You Mean

. . . know the old ectoplasm story? Well, it's not so far from the truth. Oh, there's nothing spiritual about it. So the cellular structure of the body is replaced by a sort of granular plasma formed by ripping apart haemoglobin and putting it back together; it's really not the same thing as 'ethereal evil incarnate'.

Oh, tosh and nonsense. The only way you'd see one of the elders transform into a spectral mist is if you put them in a blender with a few litres of holy water. We're every bit as material as the humans.

Anyway, I call it ichor. Once introduced into the human vessel, the ichor replicates, you see, until it permeates and actually replaces all the biological organs.

No, not 'icky', Thomas, ichor. Blood of the gods. Greek mythology, Thomas. Honestly, I thought you went to public school.

Well, yes, after they've been in the light chamber, 'icky' is a somewhat more appropriate term.

It's only an hypothesis at the moment, I'm afraid, but I think the coherence of the organism is dependent on some sort of electromagnetic signal exchange between granules, something that's interfered with by light.

Well that's exactly what *I* thought, but, no, you can't trace lineage by it as far as I can see; it's not like human blood. As I say, no DNA, so there's no variation between subjects. But I did find one interesting thing . . .

Yes, those are all tissue samples.

Oh, Chosen as well as shabtis—proto-Chosen and proto-shabtis too, even a few human.

It is rather cramped; I'll have to get Jack to put another shelf up, I think. But one does need a range of specimens; all the pre-mortem and post-mortem stages have to be examined thoroughly.

What was I saying? Yes. Different patterns of infection. What I've found is that there's two quite different types of ichor.

Well, it's quite fascinating, really. The Chosen have active granules—agents, I call them—that replicate astoundingly quickly, replacing all the organs, as I say.

Astoundingly. Let's see. After your first taste of the old man's blood, how long was it with you before the hunger kicked in?

OK. I'll put it this way: by the time the hunger kicks in, every single part of your body would have already been replaced.

Yes, that quick.

But what I've found is that the majority of ichor is made up of these much smaller granules—drones—and while you and I do have these in abundance along with the agents, the shabtis *only* have these smaller granules, and they're rather . . . turgid. They replicate through the neural system, but they only really become fully active when the risen shabti begins feeding. You can actually watch the process, you know—take a sample of ichor from a new shabti before it feeds, add a drop of human blood; you can see the stuff just bursting into action.

That's the thing. We Chosen have the agents, and they replicate from day one.

It's obvious, surely. Don't you see? All those differences in mental abilities—it's all down to the ichor. In both shabtis and Chosen, infection results in neural transformation, but the drone ichor can only replicate basic autonomic functions; it kicks into action at the crisis point of the host's death and jumpstarts the host corpse with a single imperative, the urge to feed. The longer the shabti's been exposed, the more pervasive the drones are, so there's more of a chance of replicating slightly more complex neural behaviour, but the host corpse is essentially brain dead until it feeds.

Well, sometimes it does seem that way, but no, there is brain activity; it just depends on the level of necrosis. The less drones, the more decay sets in between desanguination and resanguination. There's certainly no personality left, though. With the Chosen, of course, there's no brain death, so we retain our personality.

Sort of. I think it's not so much that the shabti is dependent on its sire, as that the drones are dependent on the agents. It's like there's some sort of communication going on, between the Chosen's agents and the shabti's drones. You kill the shabti's sire and it doesn't just wander around aimlessly like a lost puppy because it doesn't have anyone to tell it what to do. It damn well—well, you've seen the results splattered over the floor upstairs.

OK, think of them as like humans—you know, no initiative, no individuality. They need their leaders to tell them what to do. Kill one little archduke, or a president, or a princess, and a whole nation of them becomes completely irrational. Wars, conspiracy theories, grown men crying like women. Utterly insane. What's the phrase? Headless chickens. That's it, yes. You cut off the head and the body, well, runs around for a bit, flapping its wings, but then it just falls over and dies. Destroy the sire, you see, and you destroy the agents. Destroy the agents and the drones just . . . fall apart. Literally.

Oh, I know, I know. We have our own agents, so theoretically we shouldn't be dependent on our sires. If only; dear old Reynard could have been put out of his misery a long time ago. Don't worry though; I'll get to the heart of it yet.

But I think of it as like the branches and leaves of a tree; the branches are the Chosen and the shabtis are the leaves. A branch may have other branches sprouting from it; both may have their own leaves. Either way, if you cut off the original branch, you kill all the branches and leaves that depend on it.

Think about it, Thomas. Our immortality is a somewhat precarious thing. All it would take is one woodsman with a large enough axe . . .

Oh, no, actually there's rather a large range of weaponry that can kill us.

Actually, that's the next stop on our little tour.

Well, You Certainly Have Some Neat Toys

So, what I've been doing mainly in this area is trying out different materials. You know: organic; inorganic; wood, obviously; bone; stone; metal; plastic. Even with wood alone, there's all the various types—hardwoods, softwoods. Does the material have to come into direct contact? I mean what if your staking implement has a wooden core but a thin coating of titanium-alloy steel, or just lacquer, or varnish for that matter? Imagine the look on that vampire-hunter's face when he pounds his prized stake into your heart only to find that he's varnished it one too many times.

Yes, it's a standard industrial drill, sort of thing you'd get in—I don't know—maybe an automobile factory. We have the shabti clamped in directly below it and, yes, it's adjustable, programmable so you can line the drill up with the heart. To be honest, it's a bit beyond me, all this—what's it called—CAD stuff. Jack, is this all set up?

Good.

Yes, you can put that in as part of the program. I think this one is set to just push straight through, but if you want to you can run a program to drop the drill at, say, a millimetre a minute, so you can measure quite precisely at what point degeneration occurs.

No, no wood. Well, wait and see. As I say, though, this one's just a straightforward skewering.

Oh no, I'm not expecting to learn anything from this. You need to have control experiments, though. Fundamental principle of science.

Yes, just push this red button here and . . .

The Boy Who Loved Death

Here it comes and . . .

Ooh. Spectacular, eh?

No, no wood at all. Diamond-tipped drill-bit. Graphite has the same effect. Actually there's a few things that are pretty damned lethal—basically anything with a sufficient concentration of carbon in it. And it took me—what?—a few months to find that out. The elders still think the worst they have to worry about is some mad Hun with a sharpened table-leg. Oh no. It wouldn't take some fearless vampire-hunter to bring down the great and powerful Malik. Any bloody idiot with a bunch of graphite ball-bearings loaded in a shotgun could do it. Believe me, Thomas, I've done the tests. You know the minimum thickness of carbon-rich material required to cause complete degeneration? Four millimetres. God, you could kill us with a sharpened chopstick, Thomas.

OK. What's next?

This? Well, this is actually my own design. I'm rather proud of it, actually. Based on the sort of thing they use to take core samples of ice or earth or whatnot. Well, I wanted to see what happens if you remove the heart completely, as part of a core.

Yes, I suppose it is sort of funny, being able to see right through the—yes, OK, Thomas, you can take your hand out of there now. Very droll.

No, no effect on him at all, unless, well, watch this. Yes, this is the thing's heart. It does look rather different doesn't it? I'm not at all sure what it does, but it's clearly serving some other purpose entirely now. Let's see . . . can you hand me that pencil, old boy. Thank you. And if I just . . .

And another one bites the dust, as they say.

Hand me that cloth, would you?

Thank you.

They're not toys, Thomas. They're scientific instruments.

Oh, yes. This is one of my favourites.

Well, this one's a bit more of a delicate operation, you might say. Scalpels, kitchen knives, anything steel is so much easier, but, you know, you do want to be thorough so I've had these sort of *saw* things manufactured out of the hardest wood available. It's still a little like trying to cut steak with a butter knife, but, as I say, one wants to cover all avenues of investigation. Thankfully, I've pretty much exhausted all the various types of incisions, penetrations, dissections and other assorted traumas you can impose on a subject with wood so I'm moving onto steel in some of the-

Well, there is carbon in steel, you know.

You didn't? You're joking?

Honestly? Sometimes you worry me, Thomas, really, you do.

Anyway, there's a sort of critical threshold of trauma. You can do a lot of damage to the heart before it completely fails but go just that little bit too deep and that's it. Immediate onset of degeneration.

Well, it takes a while to set up. I can show you this one in action if you want. Over here.

Yes. From a sawmill.

Indeed. I used to use this on whole subjects before I started removing the hearts. Very large, very messy, and it takes absolutely *ages* of slicing before you even get to the heart . . . if you start with the feet, anyway. No, I rather quickly realised it was more sensible to remove the entire lower body first and just work from, say, the solar plexus up. Or from the top of the skull down. Like this fellow here.

Well, I wanted to know exactly where the critical points are, you see. We all know what decapitation does, but what if you just slice off the top quarter of the brain matter, the top half, three quarters? Or, if you take the heart off in wafer thin slices?

Well, no the buzzsaw's too crude an instrument for that. As I say, I tend to remove the hearts now.

One of those meat slicers you get in a butcher's. You can do it really quite gradually. Again, there's a sort of critical threshold reached then—*bang*—immediate onset of degeneration.

He Doesn't Look Happy

. . . one's quite interesting because it does rather contradict some of the other results. As you've seen we can remove the heart intact and the subject doesn't degenerate. But you can't do the same with the head. I've tried—God knows I've tried—with all sorts of pure metals, alloys, whatever—no carbon at all. Doesn't matter whether it's organic or inorganic implements you use, wood, steel, or a bloody plastic fork; if you sever the connection between head and body, yes, you guessed it—immediate onset of degeneration. Anyway, as you can see here I've removed the soft tissue of the neck to expose the spine. As long as the spine is intact it seems, the subject retains integrity. What I've actually managed to do with these subjects is remove the vertebrae themselves, leave just the nerves.

Well, that's why his head's in the vice, obviously.

But, anyway, it seems that the degeneration happens when you sever too many of the nerves running down the spinal column. I don't know if it's this or that particular nerve, though, or if it's just down to numbers.

I can tell you this, though. You don't even need full decapitation.

Yes, I was doing an impalement, you see—full body, Vlad the impaler kind of thing.

Well, I wanted to look at angles of impalement. Anyway, this one shabti came down on the stave at quite the wrong angle, so I'm looking at him flopping there and I can see that it's missed his heart entirely; however I look closer and realise I can see the point of the stave coming out through his spinal column just at the base of the skull. That's where it exits the body. And as I'm watching him he wriggles a bit, I hear the vertebrae crack and suddenly he's just ooze running down the stick.

The point is, his head was not 'cleanly severed from his body with cold steel'.

Well, that's just it. If you take the heart out there's no neural link to the body. It's all really quite confusing. That's what's exciting about science, though, Thomas. These challenges.

Yes, overall, the results are conflicting, but look at what we now know. The shabti clearly cannot function without both its heart and its head at least largely intact. Neither organ appears to carry out any known anatomical function, but critical damage to either is utterly fatal. Common steel is quite capable of causing this damage, contrary to what the elders would have you believe, and even using non-carbon-based inorganic alloys of this metal or that, you can cause quite sufficient damage, if you so desire, as to render any of us unmistakeably and quite permanently dead. Put one of the

Chosen through a meat grinder and, believe me, what comes out the other end is not going to dissipate into mist and coalesce again with a mocking laugh. It is going to lie there on the floor in a lumpen puddle. Whether the ichor maintains integrity by biological connections or some sort of energy—and I'm yet to find any sign of an electromagnetic field or anything similar—this integrity can be suddenly and fatally interrupted by any number of pointy, edged, blunt, grinding or slicing, bullets, blades, spikes, saws or bloody cheese graters.

All such instruments have the rather unwelcome effect of turning us into sticky, icky, red goo, for want of a better term.

Needless to say, this is a matter of some concern to us. All it would take is for some senile old leech who happens to be our great-great-grandsire to meet with an unfortunate accident and you and I—along with countless others—would be history.

Yes, very droll. But this is serious. This is our survival.

I don't care if they take good care of themselves. All it takes is *one*. How long is the chain? How many Chosen are there who would take us with them if they died?

Well, no, I'm sure I'm not the only one to chain his old man up in the basement for safe-keeping. I don't think I'm the only one with a skeleton in the closet, so to speak. Who knows what some of the elders have in their vaults? The question is, do any of them have the First?

No, I haven't lost my senses. I know the First is a myth. A legend told to upstart broodlings to keep them in check. But think about it. Be logical. There has to be a First. You don't have branches without a trunk. And if he dies, we all die. No, I think one of the elders has the First tucked away safe and sound. They would find that rather amusing, don't you think? The broodling's bogeyman, the First of all Chosen, the Ancient prime vampire who sired a race, stuck in some nice padded cell where he can't come to any harm. Quite pathetic, really.

My *problem is* that, as far as I can see, every one of the elders is a geriatric cretin still stuck in the century they were sired, scared of television sets because they might have sunlight inside them, whining about how humans have too much garlic in their diet these days, afraid to go out in case it rains.

Grateful for their caution? Yes, but-

But how long do we have?

Well think about it. We can't go out in the rain, anymore. Can't drink the tap water. The rivers, the oceans, all polluted with two thousand years of holy water evaporated into the atmosphere. Oh, it's minimal amounts but it's enough to make us cower in our little airtight sanctums like . . . like some human with hayfever. The world isn't going to get any more comfortable. Every time a font is blessed. Every bottle sold at Lourdes. It's absurd. We're the masters of this world and we're all . . . housebound victims of a ridiculous allergy. Holy water. You know I've been measuring the increased levels over the last twenty years or so. Put a shabti or two out on the roof during a shower, measure their deterioration against the amount of rainfall. It's a slow climb but in a couple of centuries—maybe three or four— we'll probably need to live in bubbles. Haven't you noticed that blood doesn't taste quite as sweet as it used to?

That's right. It's contaminated. They bless the water, it evaporates, comes down as rain, gets into their water supply, they drink it and it ends up in their bloodstreams. It seems to be less toxic in blood, but, you understand, we're an endangered species. Four centuries and the rain will be like sulphuric acid to us. Five or six and their blood will be poison. We have to take action now. We have to understand these weaknesses so we can counteract them, safeguard ourselves, survive. The elders? They're too busy pining for the Dark Ages.

Six centuries is imminent doom if you think in terms of millennia. If we're going to be immortal, let's start thinking about the long-term.

I'll show you.

It Does Give Him An Interesting Aroma

Absolutely. We just blather on about "spiritual toxicity" with no idea what we're talking about, while the humans poison our world with their holy water.

No, not at all. There's no place for that in science.

Oh, Thomas. I point blank refuse to believe this Christian mumbo-jumbo.

Nonsense. I met someone who was in Jerusalem at the time—never heard of the man. Oh, there was no shortage of wandering prophets and madmen claiming to be the messiah. Zealots, sicarii, essenes. It's entirely possible that one of these upstart demagogues claimed to be the son of God and got himself crucified for it, but is there any *record* of these miracles? Resurrection, indeed. Not unless he was one of us, and the scriptures don't say anything about him travelling at night. No. Jumped-up cult leader—that's all he was. But some people will believe anything you tell them. Some people believe Elvis is still alive.

Crosses, yes. But it's not what you think.

See—right, come here—what I've done here is taken subjects from other cultures. We turn them, then expose them to all these various "spiritual toxins", holy water, crosses, and so on. Yes, this one's Muslim or something. They're in plentiful supply these days, as I was saying. Watch.

It's OK. I've got the rubber gloves.

Oh, don't be such a girl, Thomas. I won't get any on your face. Just watch.

Well, that's just it. The holy water has no effect whatsoever. Crucifixes are the same. But look at this.

Yes, it's Arabic. It means Allah, I believe. Doesn't mean a thing to you or I but you can see the way she's reacting. And if I just press it on her forehead here.

Now, now, dear. You've been told about the noise.

So as you can see—and smell—there's rather an adverse reaction to religious artefacts but it's entirely related to the subject's background. I'd find it rather amusing actually if it weren't so bloody inconvenient. As I say, the rain is not exactly a pleasant and refreshing experience these days. But it's all in the head.

I'm sure of it. We'd all be much better off without this God nonsense.

I don't know. Guilt? Angst? But, Thomas, we think of ourselves as supernatural, creatures of the night. We think God hates us, reviles us. So what if there *is* no God, there *is* no soul, there *is* no damnation. Perhaps we only believe in these nonsenses because they validate our absurd idea of what we are, damned souls, demons that walk the world. Think about it. Maybe we're not afraid of them because they burn us. Maybe they burn us because we're afraid of them.

Well, of course it's drastic, of course it's physical, but—look at the evidence—it has to be psychosomatic. Environmental conditioning, Thomas. Irrational reactions.

There are people with phobias about baked beans, Thomas, people who vomit at the sight of an unopened can.

That would be the eventual aim, yes. I mean, here's a subject I've raised in total isolation from religion. This Arabic thing has absolutely no effect on it. It would be the same with a Star of David or a crucifix. Absolutely no effect. You or I, though . . .

No, unfortunately I haven't really managed to get that far. It's most infuriating but . . . well, I was force-fed that clap-trap myself as a child and much as I understand the psychoanalytic theory, well, I've tried various forms of therapy but . . .

No, I can't quite overcome that feeling of dread, that crawling skin feeling of, ugh, just thinking about it makes me feel quite ill. And I must admit . . . well, this is rather shameful to admit but the shabtis seem to be better at it than us.

Really. I think it's because they're so . . . simple. You can just gradually increase their tolerance by exposing them for short periods at a time, build up their resistance until they eventually . . . forget to hiss and spit. They just don't bother. A cross becomes just another lump of metal, pretty much. Jack, he actually wears a crucifix around his neck. Under his shirt of course; God knows, I don't want to *see* one of those floating around in front of my face while I'm trying to eat.

Yes, that would have been his chest-hairs. You do get that charred pork, burning dog fur smell every so often, but he doesn't seem to notice. But shabtis are less aware, you see, so obviously they'll be less affected.

No, it's not perfect, but, don't you see how important this is now? The rain, the bloody rain is killing us, and it doesn't have to be that way.

Three or four centuries.

Well, yes you'd think a good analyst could cure any neurosis in that time, but these are the elders we're talking about. I think Freud himself would have his work cut out curing those demented pea-brains. With the shabtis it's just basic behaviourism. Conditioning. The Chosen are too bloody intelligent for their own good.

Um, well . . . yes. How else can-

But you can't just run these experiments on humans and shabtis, Thomas. Sooner or later you have to work with Chosen subjects.

I really don't care what Malik would think. Frankly, he'd be the first on the dissection slab if I had my way, with the rest of the Elders following close behind.

Obviously.

No, I wouldn't keep any of them up here; it's not secure enough. They're on the next level down. My high security section, so to speak. Follow me. The stairs are over here.

I Could Go Fetch Him For You

. . . from this fiery, willful human resisting the Hold, to the initiate of stage two drunk on their sire's blood. Clearly there's a superior will here. The spawn behaves quite differently to the slave. Far less servile, far more . . . defiant. Well we both remember what it's like don't we?

Anyway, I try not to leave them too long in stage three, wild with the Hunger; they're far too unpredictable during that period what with the blood lust. You have to give them enough time for the transformation to be complete but I try to fast-track them, as they say. So finally we end up with the stage fours, those who've tasted their first human blood, carried out their first kill. Fully-fledged Chosen.

Yes, this is the only way in or out, so it should be relatively safe. Wouldn't want any of these chaps getting loose and kicking up a stink.

Oh, they're all terminated eventually, one way or another.

Oh, hang the Law, Thomas. You and I both know that even the

elders only really pay lip-service to the Law. The only reason Chosen don't kill Chosen is that bloody chain of dependence. You think Malik hasn't killed the odd newblood here and there when they got too uppity? You think Reynard wouldn't have killed us both if he'd known what we were planning? Law! Law is for the humans, Thomas. If we want to advance our scientific knowledge, there's no room for this "dark brethren" nonsense. Answer me honestly, Thomas. Do you really care about anyone other than yourself? Do you really give a damn about Malik, or Reynard, or me for that matter? Do you have even the slightest hint of sympathy for these "dark brethren" of yours? I mean, look at them. Look at them in their chains and muzzles. Doesn't it just fill you with exactly the same contempt you feel about the shabtis, about the humans?

And I feel exactly the same way. We all do. It's our nature. None of us really, truly care.

I know. I know exactly what Malik would do if he found out that I was experimenting on Chosen. But that's never going to happen, is it, Thomas? There's only you and I that know about this part of my research, in the same way that there's only you and I who know what happened to Reynard, or what you did to Malik's beloved little Basquait.

Well now *that* wouldn't be very sensible. Oh, I know exactly where you're coming from. The look on his face would be delicious but . . . well, maybe someday you'll be able to tell him—you'd *have* to let me be there though, really you'd *have* to—if and when we find a way around the chain of dependence.

Talking of which . . .

Hang on a second. I want to get Jack down here to set something up.

A pager. He'll be down in a minute. Wait and see.

No need. He always finds me, no matter where I am. I think it's related to the recognition of other Chosen, the-

Well, I'm not entirely sure. Scent is just an hypothesis.

Hmm. I'm rather loathe to buy into the whole psychic connection thing. Smacks a little of the supernatural, don't you think?

Well, the Mongols drank blood too—OK, it was their horses', but still-

I think it's rather evident that we *can* be killed.

Mirrors. All in good time, Thomas. All in good time. Anyway, where was I?

Yes, the chain of dependence. Did you realise that the degree of independence doesn't relate directly to resistance to the Hold?

That's what we all thought. But it's quite wrong. It would be nice to think that you and I ganged up on old Reynard because we're both naturally stronger-willed than some of the simpering lackeys that the elders call their spawn. Sadly, no. There is a quite mechanical explanation for it, I'm afraid to say. The independence of the spawned newblood is inversely proportional to the quantity of the sire's blood consumed during the transformation. Feed them well and they're fundamentally loyal. Skimp on the portions and you end up . . . well, you're liable to end up in your own basement, in chains, with a gag around your mouth and a blindfold on your eyes.

Of course. I wasn't saying that. The physical dependence is quite another thing entirely.

Good question. Let me put it this way. We have a simple thesis: all Chosen are dependent on their sire, yes? You kill the sire and the spawn dies. This is pretty much the first thing a newblood learns. You are, like it or lump it, entirely dependent on the continuing existence of the Chosen whose blood runs in your veins.

Well here's a conjecture, a thought experiment. What would happen if one of us were to drink the blood of our *sire's* sire? If, for example, we were able to establish that old Malik was Reynard's sire, and we managed to steal a few sips of his substance, would we remain dependant on Reynard, dying if he dies, or would we, perhaps, cease to be dependent on him entirely, transferring our dependence to dear old Malik?

It is, isn't it? And I have the answer.

Ah, Jack. Perfect timing. Remember yesterday's experiment?

Yes, well, we're going to repeat it for Mr Thomas's education and entertainment. Be a good shabti and fetch me the gun.

Ooh! Can I Try?

So, yes. We begin with one that we've already sired. Call him A. Yes, this is A over here. And this one here—we'll call him B—is one of his brood. We then have a third Chosen, this female—C—sired from B. Simple, yes?

OK, so what we're going to do is feed C a little blood from A.

God, no. If we took the gag off she'd bring the house down, the little bitchbrood. And then there's always the chance, you know, if they weren't gagged . . . I mean Jack's the only shabti allowed down here and he's one hundred percent loyal. But even so, even the smartest shabti can be tricked. Some of these are spawned directly from my own blood, after all, and I'm not about to bleed myself dry for test subjects, so they're not exactly devoted disciples. No when I say "feed", I don't mean it literally. The syringe, Thomas. One of the wonders of modern technology. I've no time for all the mess and noise involved in-

Hang on a second, I'm just trying to find a vein.

Now, now. There's no point struggling, my friend. You'll only make me use you in one of the slower and more painful experiments. Aha. OK.

And voila. One syringe of Chosen blood which we take over here to Ms. C and—yes, you're about to be promoted, my dear. It's your lucky day.

Keen? Yes, one might say she's gagging for it.

Sorry. I know, I know. Right, just a moment.

OK, that's that. We just have to wait for a few minutes.

You'll see. Bring the gun over here, Jack.

Good boy, Jack.

Yes, this really *is* a toy, I must admit. Simple principle, D65 bulb, mirrors and lenses inside to focus the beam, more of a flashlight than a laser gun really, but it's bloody lethal all the same.

If you want. Here.

Be careful where you point it, will you?

Ha ha. Death by Duracell. I like that, Thomas. Very good.

Well, of course. It is rather fun to use. Just another minute.

Oh, nothing much. You know me. Work, work and more work.

Really? Sounds exciting.

With his *face*? Oh, Thomas, you are awful.

Oh. That should be time enough now. Just point it at B and—no, the middle one, the one in the middle. B, Thomas, B—yes. A, B, C. Were you even paying attention? Honestly-

OK. Well, just point it at B and pull the trigger.

Not the most eloquent comment, but, yes, it is, as you say "pretty fucking cool". But, do you notice anything strange here? Remember the purpose of this little experiment?

Exactly. Ms. C is still with us. Ms. C was sired by B. B is dead. She is *not*. What you're looking at, my boy, is probably the most important scientific discovery in the whole history of the Chosen. This could be revolutionary, Thomas. Literally. Ms. C has broken the chain of dependence, leapfrogged her own sire and bumped herself up to a position of much more security. Of course, she will still die if—can I see the gun for a second?—if we—you might want to stand back, Thomas—terminate A. But you can see how important this is, surely?

Exactly. Find out who has the First and we're free from those bloody elders forever. They're old and they're soft and complacent now, Thomas, and I know exactly how much damage you can inflict on one of the Chosen without killing them. Find the First and—just a few cc's of his blood and we're free of them.

Why would I do *that*? I can always use some fresh subjects, Thomas. There's a lot of work still to be done. Jack, put this somewhere safe, will you? So what do you say we stop by and pay a visit to the old man now? See his new accommodation. I know how much he enjoys your little visits.

Ha ha ha ha.

Oh!

Yes, it is something of a rabbit warren. A veritable labyrinth. Once you get to know your way around though . . .

Well, there are a couple of ways to get to the office but you can only get into the vault from the office itself, so I don't see what you're worried about.

Yes, it's basically a bank vault with some major high-tech add-ons, nuclear style decontamination unit in the airlock, climate control systems.

Oh, the sort of thing you get in zoos, museums, botanic gardens. Humidity, you see. I like to keep the humidity constant. This is us here.

Oh, but it's not normal water, Thomas. I keep old Reynard boxed up in an atmosphere that's absolutely rank with holy water. Actually, I have him on a drip of the stuff, with a few extracts of garlic thrown in for good measure. Nobody's going to be skipping the chain of dependence over me. So it's not just a matter of lock and key, old boy.

Clean suit. I keep a couple in a locker in the office that's coded to my thumbprint. And any shabti or Chosen walking into the vault without one, well let's just say they're not going to be doing much apart from writhing on the floor and squealing like a baby in an acid bath.

Yes, there is a bit of a smell. Sorry, I was in there yesterday and even with the airlock and the air conditioning—I think there's something wrong with the decontamination unit. Well the showers weren't really designed to spray blood and even with the dilutants and the anti-coagulants—I just don't think it's as effective as it should be. I've had Jack taking a look at it, but I'm going to have to get someone in, I think.

Well, no, the original architect is . . . unavailable now.

But, yes, there was something else I wanted to show you first.

Well you were asking about mirrors, about the good old lack of reflection.

Quite. It *was* a bit of a puzzler.

Yes. The Chosen have no souls so they have no reflections. That is the current wisdom on the topic, isn't it? Or perhaps it's that, as supernatural apparitions, we're not really there in a physical sense. Oh, we're there in a physical sense insofar as if you drive a wooden stake through our hearts we die. But we're not really there. In a physical sense. Except that we can stick our pointy little teeth into their soft, smooth necks and drink every last fluid ounce of blood out of them. But we're not really there. In a physical sense.

Oh, yes, that's a wonderfully rational view on the subject. Reminds me of those savages who think that cameras steal people's souls. The Chosen have no souls so they have no reflections. So why do *humans* have reflections? No, I think it's fairly easy to settle this one. You might find this rather surprising though.

Yes, just hang on a second . . . here we go.

My photograph album.

Let's see. Who do we have here? Well, that's me. And that's me, too. And that's Jack.

Yes, he does look rather like a trained chimp trying to smile. That's shabtis for you.

Well, yes I know it's common knowledge. I just wanted to . . . approach this logically. I mean, what are the obvious questions to ask here? Other than 'why'?

Yes, well, we know the answer to that one. Photographs, film, video tape. We show up on them all. It's just mirrors. What other obvious question is there?

Come on, Thomas.

No?

OK, I have a mirror over here. Over here. Look. What do you see?

That's right, nothing. You can't imagine how often I stood, well, right here, looking at this mirror and wondering why I couldn't see myself. I meant to ask, by the way, is that Armani? Yes, I thought so. You look good in it. Pity you can't see yourself in the mirror, eh?

I'm getting to it. Don't be impatient. Wait here a second.

Digital camera. Wonders of modern technology. No, quite cheap, actually. Just stay there a second. You don't mind, do you? Not worried that I'm going to steal your soul, are you? Ha ha. Please, humour me.

OK. Smile for the camera. Go on. Show me those teeth.

That's us. Now where was I? Oh, yes. Armani. Well, correct me if I'm wrong, but Armani haven't brought out a special line of Chosen-friendly non-reflected suits recently. No? And you don't find that a little curious? Or perhaps the suit doesn't show up in the mirror because it also happens to be a soulless, satanic creature of the night, damned for all eternity and blah blah blah.

Yes, that old chestnut. The touch of evil. Please. Touched in the head, more like.

Here we go. Have a look. Yes, you can see the picture in this little window.

Yes, you do, don't you. But that's not what I wanted to show you.

You don't see anything remarkable there? Take a closer look. What do you see in the background? Oh, for God's sake, Thomas, look at the bloody mirror. Look at the bloody mirror on the wall.

In the viewscreen, Thomas.

And the light dawns.

Yes. The reflection is there, Thomas. It's just that nobody sees it.

I have no idea. I presume it's something to do with our mesmeric abilities, an extension of the Hold. A particular side-effect. Quite useful, I should think—so much easier to sneak up behind some young virgin at her dresser if she can't see you in the mirror. I mean, think about it, Thomas. We've all heard these tales about the most powerful of the elders being able to change shape, to become a bat or a wolf, even a cloud of mist. Ludicrous, of course, but you listen to them wittering on about it, about the good old days, and you realise they actually believe it.

And they're *almost* right. An ability we have and we don't even know it. Not unnatural, at all, though. Not supernatural. No. It's so bloody natural, we do it without even thinking. And we're so good at this hypnosis trick, we even fool ourselves.

I have no idea. I suppose line of sight is too direct, too immediate, but as I say maybe some of us could become, for want of a better term, invisible, once upon a time . . . and maybe cameras are just, well, a mechanical thing we don't have the ability to deal with. Too removed, too distant. But I wouldn't like to speculate. I'm a man of science, Thomas. Empirical observation. Experimentation. Hypothesis, extrapolation, validation. I'm not interested in speculation, in fabricating some spurious rationale. I don't pluck theories out of the air, Thomas. That's how you end up with ideas like, let's see, the Chosen have no souls, so they have no reflections. Utter and complete bunkum.

Anyway, this is the door here. As you'll see the old man is quite safe. Where's the key? Ah, yes.

Ah. Well, no, that's not meant to be open, but-

Now, Thomas, there's no need for that language. So I forgot to lock the door. It's not as if the shabtis will come down here. They know what I'd do to them. No. Nothing gets in or out apart from me, nobody, not without my word, not even—

Jack?

Jack, I told you to put the gun somewhere safe.

Jack, what do you think you're-

Oh.

Actually, I've Been Doing Some Research of My Own

Aaah!

Aaah, Jesus, no.

No, I don't know where the First is. I don't.

Aaah! Not the—*aah*, Jesus Christ!

I don't know. I swear to God. I don't know.

Maybe Malik or one of the other elders, but you'll never get near them, Jack. Not without-

What?

Thomas? You—you wouldn't *dare*.

Are you *insane*? Do you have any idea what they'll do to you?

You're *both* insane. You can't touch them. For all you know, one of them is our own grandsire. It would be suicide.

But you don't know where the First is. You don't know who has him. You-

Oh.

You lying, conniving, scheming, little, faggot of a—*aaaaah!*

Thomas, for the love of God, man. You're going to throw your lot in with this—this animal? *Aaah!* No, I didn't mean that, Jack. I'm sorry. I'm sorry. You're not an animal. You're one of us now. You're Chosen. You're one of us. I don't know how, but-

Yes, I remember. But you only fought that first time. You submitted. You surrendered. You were mine. You *are* mine. You belong to me. My shabti, my—*aaah!*

The Boy Who Loved Death

What? When?

I can't remember my exact words. Something about fighting like a tiger.

That you kicked and punched and . . . scratched.

Ha ha ha ha ha. No? Ha ha ha ha ha. I don't believe it. Blood under the fingernails. My blood under your fingernails and you cowering in your cage and biting at them and . . . all this time?

Oh God. But wait, you're still bound to me. Kill me and-

Oh. Oh dear.

But wait, wait, don't you see? That's why you have to listen to me. You're just like us. I didn't know, Jack. I'm sorry for the way I treated you, but I didn't know. But think about it, Jack. You're one of us. Surely you should appreciate the work I'm doing. Surely— *aaaah!*

Please, Jack. Thomas, tell him. Please, I'm sorry. *Aaaah!*

Please. Don't kill me. I don't want to die. I don't want to die. *Thomas*, don't let him kill me. Tell him not to kill me. Tell him if he doesn't kill me, then you'll help him find the First. Then we can drink his blood and we'll all be safe—only one link in the chain. Only one. He's the only one that matters. If he dies we *all* die. If he's safe— that's what you want, isn't it? Then you can put him in a vault somewhere and keep him safe. That's what you . . .

That's not what you want. Oh, my God. That's not . . .

Thomas! Thomas, you bloody moron, don't trust him! For the love of God, he's mad. He doesn't care. He just wants to kill us a-

A Scruffian Christmas

1

Twas the night before Christmas, and all through the workhouse not a creature was stirring . . . on account of any stirring'd most likely lead to a sound thrashing and a night in the mortuary, like, if the master heard a peep of it. No, if there'd been a mouse in the workhouse even he'd have kept his squeaker shut for fear of a master crueller than any cat. Not that a mouse could've lived off the crumbs in that workhouse, mind, where the paupers were eating the peelings for the pigs, and sucking the bones as they were grinding for fertiliser.

No, not one little waif in the kiddies' dormitories give even a snottery sob into a scrap of sleeve. They all knowed what anyone *ascertained to be an agitant* was in for, yeah? A guinea for a gamin, the overseers'd say. You mind your manners and make your money, or you'll be sold for a Scruffian, you hear. They'll put the Stamp on yer, Fix yer forever, and all ye'll be is meat in the machine!

They didn't know 'xactly what Fixed meant, the littl'uns—not like us what's had it done, eh, scamps?—but they knowed it was bad.

No, the Waiftaker General, he were as strange a story to them as Father Christmas, and the Institute—yeah, that Bad Place where he put the thingy on yer chest and it hurt summat hellish, then he cut yer pinky off and it grew right back—the Institute were as far away as the North Pole to them. Indentured means enslaved, they knowed. But they didn't know how the Stamp makes yer Scruffian,

232

so's however yer starved or maimed by a master, well, ye'll always return to how yer Fixed. They just knowed enough to fear it.

Most of em.

See, there were one waif in the workhouse that Christmas Eve, and he were quiet as the rest of em—quieter even—but he were quiet in another way. Puckerscruff, you mind how Rake Jake Scallion looked as the stickmen carted him off to Newgate? All slyly smiling even in his chains, like it were all part of his plan? That were this unruffled lad as they led him to his bed and blanket. Oh, the soot that smeared every inch of him hid the look on his face a little, but them waifs saw the rebel in his eye.

A sweep's lad, so's his sad story went, when he turned up at the iron gates, bells ringing evenfall, night closing in, him shivering in the snow. A chimney-sweep's boy, only his master up and drinked himself to death, it being the season of celebrations. May the Good Lord punish this ungrateful wretch, sobs the urchin, but he'd *whip* me for saying my prayers, sir, even when I blessed him for his Christian charity. And now he's poisoned by gin, and I've nowhere to go, and . . . and . . .

Peter Black, he said his name was as they brung him in.

He's blessed, says they—leastways, there's a lot of blessings in their words—cause those iron gates was near locked for the night; a minute later and he would've been on a hiding to nothing. They don't hear him muttering how he's used to hiding and used to nothing; they's too busy ensuring his education in the *Christmas spirit* they're exemplifying, charitable Christians what they are, 'specially seeing as how it's well past supper and scrubbing-up time, with festive fun awaiting them as has families to be getting home to. Oh, they's most eloquent as regards his good fortune.

So now, here's this soot-covered sweep's lad, sat on a mouldy mattress, on a bed what stinks of the foundling as has recently vacated it, vacated the world in general, actually. Kicked into the room with a good-natured laugh and a gracious promise—breakfast and a good bath in the morning being, as they puts it, *the only gifts a filthy guttersnipe like you'll be getting, and be grateful even for that, wretch.* So here's he sits, this Peter Black, with all them other waifs laying in their beds, but awake, peering at his shadow in the dark.

2

When he stands up, they all starts to fret, like. When he walks to the window, they all sits up in their beds. When the floorboard under his foot gives a squeak, one of em's bold enough to hiss a shush at him, finger to his lips. There's panic in all of their eyes as the lad just smiles, his teeth so white in the pitch-black. Not one of em's brave enough to whisper him to stop though, as he fetches a match and a stub of candle from his ragged shirt, strikes the one and lights the other.

He moves the candle to the left, then to the right. He covers it with a hand, then he takes his hand away. Goes through this strange routine three times, so he does, before sauntering back to the middle of the room, cocky as can be, like as he'd have his paws in his pockets if his breeches only had em. Sets the candle down on the floor, yeah? Then sets himself down cross-pinned, with a glance of his glinting rebel eye around the room.

—Well, says he. I ain't never seen such timid tykes in all me natural.

—Hush! whispers one, his eyes as wide as a Whitechapel tart's snapper. The master'll hear yer and -

—It's Christmas Eve, says this saucy sweep's lad. Trust me, Tiny Timid, a Scruffian don't do nothing lest he's sure it's safe. Unless it's fun. Or he's got a good reason. Or leastways a reason. Well . . . never mind, in this here case, we's sent him a pressie—from the parishioners, so's he thinks. By now, the bugger should have polished off the port and be guggling out a glass of the finest brandy Lightfinger Larker ever half-inched. Laced with laudanum now, like.

Well, if there was ever a room of workhouse waifs as wonder-struck as them, I ain't never heard of it. Half of em was blowed over by the balls of this lad in speaking at all. Half of em was blowed over by that word what weren't *bleeder* or *blighter* or *blackguard*—and aimed at the workhouse master too, of all men! But half of em, all's they heard were the word Scruffian and that struck fear into their hearts. Why, if their ears weren't deceiving em, if they weren't bonkers to even believe in Scruffians, this were one.

—You're a Scruffian? whispers one.
   —What's ascruffying? hisses another.
   —Is it true? asks a third. Is it true they cuts yer soul out and they puts it in a box and then even fire can't burn yer and -
   —Nah, most of that's a load of bollocks, says the lad. But come cosy up round this here glim and I'll show yer what I am.
   And as he says this, he reaches his hand inside his shirt, stretching right round the back and down, as if to get summat tucked into his breeches. And out comes his hand holding a shiv.

The first waif comes tiptoeing timorously from his bed as our lad takes the edge of that shiv to the wrist of his left fam, cuts deep enough to spurt. The second and third come creeping, silent, as he puts that hand to his chest, starts rubbing at the soot there, *using* that squirting blood to wet and wipe the black. More of em come then, horrified by the gory muck, by the fact he's washing it crimson now. All of em's crowded round by the time's he wipes the blood off with his shirt, to show em the Stamp.

Even streaked with blood, now's the soot's gone it ain't hard to see the scars on him, criss-crossing this way and that, circling and spiraling, like the strangest script written in his skin. It's who he is, what's writ on him, says he, stamped into his flesh to Fix him forever. He was once a workhouse waif like them. He stops a second, gives a queer little smile, sorta sad. In a way, he *is* a workhouse waif like them, he says. Always will be.

—Still. It has its perks, says he.

3

As them waifs all sit in awe, he clambers to his pins, saunters to the door. He tells em to wait here for . . . half an hour or so, he reckons. Shouldn't take too long to sneak his way through the workhouse, do what has to be done. He don't say what that is, but his impish grin and the wink he tips em says it's all in the name of festive fun.

—Bless yer sweet souls, says he. It's a crime as waifs should want at Christmas.

Then off he slips, so softly, quiet as a thief in the night.

They waits then, the waifs. They waits for *minutes* and *minutes*. Ain't none of em as can imagine what might be in store, but every one of em is whipped up to whispers, and counting those minutes, the seconds, the beats of their hearts. Why, if it ain't a true Christmas Eve for em! All the anticipation they ain't never had before, on a night as only ever minded em of their motherless misery! One nipper peers out the window, pipes up that the gates is open now. Whatever could be happening?

—Come see, says the Scruffian at the door.

Now he leads em out the room. They're terrified at first, thinking what if the master catches em out, what if there's an overseer about, what if, what if! But our black-faced Scruffian seems so sure as he struts ahead that it ain't too long before their whispers become murmurs, and their murmurs become chatter, and their chatter becomes excited. And there's another Scruffian leading the girls from *their* dormitory. And they're all babbling chipper as chaffinches, like life'd never ground em down at all, as they piles into the refectory. And they hushes.

—Grub's up, says the Scruffian.

Now, us Scruffians learn to live with starving, Fixed with hunger in our bellies. It's a cruel thing, innit? Cause even when yer have a bang up feast—like what we had after yer liberation, mind, when Flashjack and Joey sprung yer from the Institute?—well it's barely over than yer tummy's torturing yer again. But it works both ways for us, that hunger Fixed so's it can't get worse. But think how's it is for them waifs what's *wasting*, wasting to the grave as the workhouse master gobbles up his roast goose. Maybes yer might even mind that misery.

Well, that's why, when them waifs walked into the refectory, well, most of em near wept for joy, cause what did they see but a score of Scruffians with pots of stew, and pies, and sausages—and was that rashers of bacon all piled up on a plate, and another with—could it be?—roast ham? Oh, the smell of that roast ham, it filled the very air! There weren't much in the way of veg, like, but bollocks to veg when there's meat on the table, eh? Meat, meat and more meat! They hadn't never seen such a thing!

I tell yer, there were a few of the Scruffians as didn't have dry eyes themselves, watching them tykes tuck in, smiling proudly whiles they nibbled on a sausage themselves or munched on a pie. It's a glorious feeling to give such a gift; that's why we does it, sore as it is on us. What's that, scamp? Every year. Different workhouse, natch. They tends to up the security afters, but they has to hush it up, cause they knows it's us. Can't exactly blab to the Bow Street Runners about them as they sold for Scruffian slaves. Not *officially*.

Oh, but the best is still to come. Yeah, stick that in the pot, scamp; good lad. No, Flashjack, not *that*. Scrape the meat off it for the sausage mince; don't want no bones in the stew. Where was I? Yeah, the best bit of the story! Cause that feast were only for Christmas *Eve*, to fill the bellies of them ravenous ragamuffins, give em a taste of happiness, so's they'd meet the morning with smiles on their faces. Grub as a gift's all fine and dandy, but bollocks to getting what yer *need* for Christmas. That's just shite, eh?

4

So, by some happy coincidence of timing—what might *seem* unlikely and invented, if one were a sour-faced sodding scofflaw as picks holes in stories, *Joey*—by some fluke of fate, as it happened, the last morsel of meat got its last munch in a waif's mouth, and was swallowed down on the very moment that, out in the cold, December night, Bow Bells began to chime.

    —Well, blow me! says that black-face Scruffian. Why, it's never . . .

And as all the waifs look round at him, he grins.

    —It ain't never *midnight*, is it? That means . . .

    —MERRY CHRISTMAS!

And fuck me up the cracker with a stickman's cosh if the voice that bellows out that Yuletide blessing don't belong to none other than Bold Nick Scantilaw. The oldest Rake what ever lived, and the most Scruffian of em all, for all his size and shape, a true Scruffian in his heart. Bold Nick Scantilaw, Fixed in his infirmity, fatter than Falstaff and fine with that. Oh, he's a jolly old soul, with his beard and belly, his robes as red as the robin's breast. When the stickmen's bloodstains are fresh, that is. Mostly they're sorta reddish-brown, like.

MERRY CHRISTMAS! says he. Why, the night I've had, bashing in the brains of blackguards who'd sell waifs into slavery, ripping out the hearts of the rich and ruthless who'd buy em, lopping off limbs of factory-owners who'd throw scamps and scrags into the grinding gears. Oh, the stickmen are trembling in their beds tonight, my foundlings and furies! Bold Nick's hellion crew's abroad, and the Waiftaker General himself wouldn't dare show his face on my streets. You can call me a fool, but I'm king for the night! This night is mine, and I call it MERRY CHRISTMAS!

And out he swaggers among the wide-eyed waifs, hauling presents from the sack unslung from his shoulder. Here's a locket as once belonged to your mother, says he to one. And this wipe was swiped across your father's brow, he says to another. This fob watch was your Uncle Jake's, says he to a third. You didn't *know* you had an Uncle Jake? he says. Ho ho *ho*! My boy, you *did*, and he *so* wanted you to have this. Why, Bold Nick Scantilaw has gifts for all—better still, presents as could only *truly* be precious to them.

You should've seen the smiles on those waifs' faces, scamps. A beauty to behold, it were. Well, ye'll see it tonight. He always has pressies for the Scruffians too, you know, maybes a tarnished trinket, maybes the gaudiest gold, but always summat as only *you* would truly cherish. Where do he get them? He's Bold Nick Scantilaw! He takes em back, from them powerful privileged fuckers as prised em from their rightful place. What? *Of course* they really belonged to them waifs' folks. Give me this very ticker last year, what I played with on me grandad's knee. God's truth!

Well, there ain't much more to tell than that, really. Bold Nick Scantilaw, he gives out them pressies, but he has to be offsky after, sharpish like, cause it's Christmas and that ain't the only workhouse in the world, eh? And the Scruffians, they has to be offsky before the stickmen or the traps come. And the waifs? Well, we offers em to come with us if they wants, but ain't more'n a handful of em ever does. Ain't like it's that much safer being an *escaped* slave, on the streets. No, most're happy with just having had . . . a Christmas.

See, it's the *giving* as matters, scamps. Course, ain't much yer can give when ye've got fuck all yerselves; really, all's we've got to give em *is* ourselves. But us Scruffians can give plenty of that, right? Yeah, I know it hurts, but it'll grow back. See? The stumps already sprouting. And don't the stew taste scrummy? Now, you trot offsky, go get yer shivs from Flashjack.

Psst, Joey. How's that Scantilaw costume coming along? Yes, you have to. Yer the only one as can do the voice. And you loves it anyways. Besides, it wouldn't be Christmas without Scantilaw.

‘

About the Author

Hal Duncan is the award-winning author of *VELLUM* and *INK*, along with numerous short stories, poems, essays, and even a few musicals. Homophobic hatemail once dubbed him "THE . . . Sodomite Hal Duncan!!" (sic), a monicker he wears proudly onstage during his spoken word shenanigans, and you can find him online at www.halduncan.com, revelling in that role.

Boiled Americans by Matthew Allen Rose

Boiled Americans is a puzzle box in book form, inspired by the violence of living in urban America and exploding the tendency to forget or ignore.

Great American Slasher by David C. Hayes

Baseball, apple pie . . . and murder.

The Bohemian Guide to Monogamy
by Andrew Armacost

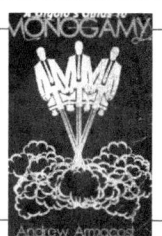

Here, a strange labyrinth of interlinked short fiction assembles itself into a darkly moving novella that deftly explores the bottomless pain and pleasure of love and commitment, the hinterland between youth and adulthood.

Surreal Worlds edited by Sean Leonard

An anthology of surrealistic compositions created by some of the finest names in genre fiction. A showcase of international talent undaunted by the conventions of language and common narrative structures. Here is timelessness. Here is Surreal Worlds

How to Succesfully Kidnap Strangers by Max Booth III

Do not respond to bad reviews. If you must respond to bad reviews, please do not kidnap the reviewer.

ADHD Vampire by Matthew Vaughn

He came, he conquered, he was distracted a lot

Notes from the Guts of a Hippo
by Grant Wamack

A rugged journalist travels to Brazil in search of a missing hippo researcher and the notes left behind lead to something earth shatteringly revelatory.

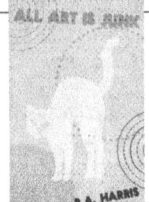

All Art is Junk by R. A. Harris

Lana Rivers, a girl with paintbrush hair, is missing and it's up to Lancelot, her cyborg knight, and his bionic conjoined twin, Cilia, to find her before her evil father, a disrespected artist turned mad-scientist, performs a terrible experiment on her.

Cherub by David C. Hayes

Cherub wasn't like the other boys—too slow, too rough—but he didn't deserve what that hospital did to him, and now he will make them pay.

Skinners by Adam Millard

Los Angeles, the City of Angels. At least, that's what the brochure says. What it fails to mention is the earthquakes. Oh, and the flesh-eating creatures lying dormant beneath the concrete, waiting for the chance to surface once again. Their wait is over . . .

The After-Life Story of Pork Knuckles Malone by MP Johnson

What's a farm boy to do when his pet pig becomes an evil, decaying hunk of ham with slime-spewing psychic powers?

A Lightbulb's Lament by Grant Wamack

A gentleman with a lightbulb for head wakes up in a world full of darkness, hooks up with a beautiful ex-prostitute, and an old man who can heal people; he travels down south to find the mysterious Creator.

The Horror Show by Vincenzo Bilof

A poetry novel—a narcoleptic, amnesiac Nobel Prize-winning poet becomes the subject of an experiment to cure madness.

Beyond by Jordan Krall

From Jerusalem to Mars, psychiatry and the unraveling of the universe

Gravity Comics Massacre
by Vincenzo Bilof

An absolutely shitty novella involving comic books, aliens, a serial killer, teenagers in an abandoned town, horror-trope dream sequences, and an ending you're going to hate.

Glue by Scott Lange

Sticky bowels and sticky situations.

Ascent by Matthew Bialer

Is the 8 foot tall creature haunting a small town in Iowa in the fall of the year 1903 the product of a hoax and collective imagination or was it one of the first documented paranormal event in America? This epic poem grapples with these questions.

Fecal Terror by David Bernstein

A killer turd is on the loose!

The Fairy Princess of Trains
by Christopher Boyle

Danny's mediocre life turns upside-down when his couch starts whispering to him. Then he's charged with a supernatural mission: Rescue the Fairy Princess of Trains.

Terence, Mephisto & Viscera Eyes
by Chris Kelso

9 new science fiction stories from Chris Kelso

Industrial Carpet Drag by Bruce Taylor

Chemicals make you do great things!

Bizarro Bizarro: An Anthology

The finest bizarro short stories from 2013.

Necrosaurus Rex by Nicolas Day

Necrosaurus Rex tells the tale of Martin, a simple janitor, who takes an unfortunate trip through time, becomes a violent mutant, and the father of us all. There's 14 billion years crushed inside these pages, and most of them are pretty nasty.

Day of the Milkman by S. T. Cartledge

In a world dominated by the milk industry, only one milkman survives after a terrible storm sinks all the ships and throws the Great White Sea out of balance.

Moosejaw Frontier by Chris Kelso

An unapologetic disaster of metafiction

The Boy Who Loved Death by Hal Duncan

From blackest humour to bleakest horror, with twisted relish, Hal Duncan's eighteen tales dig into death—and the life that goes with it.

www.ingramcontent.com/pod-product-compliance
Lightning Source LLC
Chambersburg PA
CBHW060424180626
46817CB00007B/2656